Engines of Desire

Engines of Desire

tales of love & other horrors

Livia Llewellyn

introduction by Laird Barron

LETHE PRESS, MAPLE SHADE, NJ

Published in 2011 by LETHE PRESS, INC.
118 Heritage Avenue ◆ Maple Shade, NJ 08052-3018
www.lethepressbooks.com ◆ lethepress@aol.com
ISBN: 1-59021-324-6
ISBN-13: 978-1-59021-324-7

Credits for previous publication appear on page 198.

This is a work of fiction. Names, characters, places, and incidents are products of the author's imagination or are used fictitiously.

Set in Jenson, Platthand, and Truesdell.
Cover art: "Schattengefluester" by Katharina Fösel.
Cover and interior design: Alex Jeffers.

LIBRARY OF CONGRESS CATALOGING-IN-PUBLICATION DATA
Llewellyn, Livia.
  Engines of desire : tales of love & other horrors / Livia Llewellyn ; introduction by Laird Barron.
    p. cm.
  ISBN 978-1-59021-324-7 (pbk. : alk. paper)
  1. Fantasy fiction, American. 2. Horror tales, American. 3. Erotic stories, American. I. Title.
  PS3612.L495E54 2011
  813'.6--dc22
                    2010050875

Acknowledgements

Thanks to a wonderful group of writers, and editors, friends, and family, and wee beasties, who often had more faith in me than I did: Pirate Jenny, Brenda Ihssen, Will Ludwigsen, Aimee Payne, Sarah Castle, Peggy Alexander, Debra Englander, Joy Marchand, Hannah Wolf Bowen, Nickolaus Kaufmann, Lee Thomas, Nathan Ballingrud, Ellen Datlow, Cherie Priest, John Langan, Paul Tremblay, Kelly Link, Holly Black, John Skipp, Brett Alexander Savory, Matt Kressel, Cecelia Tan, Jason Eric Lundberg, Vince Liaguno, William Schafer, Peter Crowther, and Nick Gevers. Special thanks to my parents, Paul and Mary Llewellyn, who let me read any book I wanted in their library, including and especially the dark and disturbing ones.

Thanks also to Lethe Press publisher Steve Berman, and to Daulton Nombroth and Alex Jeffers for all their hard work in creating such a beautiful book. And thanks to Katharina Fösel, for her stupendous photograph.

Special thanks to Laird Barron, who's been a champion of my work ever since I nervously sent him a story to read, many years ago.

This book is dedicated to my best friend, my confidant, my rock:
ROBERT LEVY

Table of Contents

Love, Sex, and the Heat Death of the Universe

BY LAIRD BARRON

The thing you need to know, to be braced for, is that Livia Llewellyn doesn't screw around. There are images you can't un-see because they're scorched on your brain. Steel yourself.

Engines of Desire is that rare kind of encounter with art I can only liken to unexpectedly coming face to face with a dangerous animal in the wild, or leaping into a body of water that proves colder and deeper than anticipated, or the raw spurt of euphoria that rushes through one's system upon feeling thin ice crack beneath one's feet. Her writing is simply fearsome – it possesses all the madness of Sylvia Plath and the ornate and mythic flourishes of Angela Carter, yet synthesized and refined into an alloy that is uniquely Llewellyn. The old saw about opening a vein holds true, except if you hold still for a moment and permit her prose to fasten tight, and it will, then you'll find you're the one doing the bleeding. What she's got to show you isn't pretty, and that which glitters isn't gold; it's ground glass or the business end of a blade, the jagged tooth of a predator, the bloody gleaming bones of its prey.

My initial experience with Llewellyn's fiction was "At the Edge of Ellensburg," a murderously erotic tale that fuses elements of Lovecraft's ultra-pessimism with the sexual explicitness of Jackie Collins or Harold Robbins or the blue letters between James Joyce and Nora Barnacle, twisted and deformed into a glimpse of the pathological landscape of a Bundy, Dahmer, or Gacy. "At the Edge of Ellensburg" is representative of the Llewellyn aesthetic, the mother shell of a Russian nesting

doll. Here is a tale shot through with scenes of sexual and emotional violence, depravity and murder, betrayal and self-annihilation. It examines the reduction of self, through emotional and physical abuse, to a static, supercharged core. A reduction to a particle perhaps analogous to the ultra-heavy element that exploded in the Beginning and vomited forth the cosmos. Indeed, in a thread that slithers through much of her work, the piece suggests this pattern of decay and degradation, then transformation, if not transmogrification of the fragile mortal vessel and its mercurial contents, is reflective of the life cycle of the universe – its approaching heat death, inertness, then ultimate resurrection. Paradoxically, despite the recurring themes of brutality and violence , that resurrection counters the ghastliness and the pitch-dark fates of Llewellyn's protagonists, the immediacy of their travails. We are left to stew: is that glimmer of light at the end of the tunnel indicative of redemption and spiritual succor? Or is it the baleful headlight of Satan's Express? The ambiguity cuts like razor wire – the dividing line between ecstasy and agony, of heaven and hell, is all too thin.

The tales that comprise *Engines of Desire* grapple with the tragicomedies of human existence, its ephemeral nature, built like a sand castle so perilously upon the cosmic tide line. Death and sex, love and mutually assured destruction, these are the songs. Apocalyptic wastelands without and within the human heart, supernatural incursions, serial killers, demons that feast upon blood, lovers scorned, clone armies harvested lottery-fashion from the wombs of teenage girls to perpetuate forever wars, eaters of souls, the machinery of darkness … these too are the songs. Baudelaire read his love's fortune in the fly-blown entrails of a horse carcass in an anonymous ditch. His song echoes to us down through the decades. Llewellyn's dark poetics are similarly affecting in that she speaks so frankly to the intimacies of the flesh, its fragility and weakness, its hunger matched only by the insatiability of the void. Like some modern day anthropomancer, she revels in the fecundity and baseness of the human animal, seeking auguries in the guts and the gore, flaying bare the primal urges so glibly sublimated by the suit- and dress-wearing masses. Llewellyn casts the runes and shows us that after the fires of apocalypse, all circles the drain back to the mud and the womb, then darkness. And then, and then….

Active for only a few years, but already establishing a reputation as a formidable stylist, I sense big things are in store for this author. If there is any justice in the world Livia Llewellyn is on her way to ever greater recognition and acclaim. I'm hopeful this collection serves as the clarion call that alerts many new readers and critics alike to the presence of a powerful and original force on the literary scene. The field is experiencing one hell of a renaissance with the appearance of writers such as Paul Tremblay, John Langan, Stephen Graham

Jones, Sarah Langan, and Allyson Bird; and the continued efforts of Jeff Ford, Norm Partridge, Caitlin Kiernan, and Michael Shea, among so many others. When writers, editors, and publishers at the dark end of the lit spectrum talk about strong new writers, one hears time and again of Don Tumasonis, Richard Gavin, Simon Strantzas, Barbara Roden, Glen Hirshberg, and Sarah Pinborough – well, add Llewellyn to the list. She is as deserving as any of the aforementioned and her star is surely ascendant.

As I said at the top: steel yourself. Scant difference exists between exquisite pleasure and pain. There's a kind of beauty so sharp and cruel that it leaves a mark on the beholder; and here it comes now.

LAIRD BARRON, author of *Occultation*
December 1, 2010,
Olympia Wa

Horses

THUNDER
CONQUEST
WHITE

...clouds drift overhead, faint strands against the cobalt blue of night. Missile Facilities Technician Angela Kingston presses her nose to the cool glass. Cirrostratus. They'll burn off before morning, she's sure of that. If anything, Kingston knows the rising eastern sun, knows the searing heat that coats the dead-brown scab lands of Washington. In ten hours, deep orange will bleed from the horizon, as day rips itself once more from a star-studded womb.

Kingston turns away from the window. Across the room, her face floats in the mirror under a cap of dark brown hair, pixie-neat against her skull. She looks like a teenager, not a woman pushing forty. Below the mirror, a rectangle of plastic balances upright on her dresser, revealing a pink line bisecting a circle of white. The alchemical wedding of urine and litmus have combined to create the line—the closest thing to marriage she'll ever know. It's proof that two missed periods are more than the product of stress from the looming war, the constant fear that the next twin turn of the launch keys won't be a test, but—like that faint pink line—the real thing.

The watch at her wrist beeps. With absolute economy of movement, sculpted by a year-old routine, Kingston inspects the apartment. She couldn't bear to leave it for good, knowing it was a mess. In the bathroom, she slips a small plastic vial into her pants pocket, next to the

stick. It contains a powerful abortive drug, military issue. In the next twenty-four hours, she'll take the pill, or a bullet. Which one it will be, she cannot say.

Outside, gravel crunches under tires—her ride to silo 7-4 is here. Kingston hoists a duffel bag over her shoulder, and grabs a photo before locking the front door behind her. It's part of her routine, so much so that she doesn't notice pausing to caress its scalloped sepia edges. The photo is of a young man in uniform, a grim-faced cavalry officer astride a large pale horse. The rider's a distant relative, whose name on the back, scribbled in fading brown ink, is "Ensley." That's all she knows of him. Why he rides, what it is he and his horse race toward, is lost.

"Keep me safe, Ensley," she mutters as she starts down the stairs. "Just one more day."

Sanders, the Deputy Crew Commander, drives Kingston's crew of four to the silo without speaking. He keeps the radio in his hummer tuned to the news station. Border skirmishes, food shortages, riots and martial law—it's their country newscasters speak of. Public figures scramble, civilians protest and pray for a second chance at peace, but Kingston and her crew know it's too late. The only negotiations going on now are over the best hour to begin the war.

Beside Kingston, Ballistic Missile Analyst Cabrera slumps in light sleep. Up in the front next to Sanders, Major Hewitt talks into his phone—his wife calls every morning. All the men on the team are married, and they all have children. Kingston stares out the window at the flat farmlands. She thinks about the apartment, how the sun will soon shine into rooms that look like no one ever lived there. She wanted to be an astronaut when she was little. She wanted to fly to the moon, or maybe Mars. Instead, she's headed to a Titan-class missile silo, where her crew will stand on alert for twenty-four hours, waiting for the order to push a button. She's proud of what she's doing to defend her country, proud of eighteen years served. Sometimes, though, at night, she cradles a phantom weight as she slips into uneasy dreams....

Hewitt whispers "I love you" into the phone. Kingston closes her eyes, concentrates on the news.

Their shift passes in half-hours of systems checks and double-checks. Wing Command Post calls every hour with the same message: launch in one hour. Each hour passes with no launch. In the short calm between false alarms, Kingston stares at Sanders' neck, his shoulders hunched over cold coffee and clipboards, jotting words down—a letter to his wife, his last farewell? "Useless," Kingston mutters. Sanders looks up. Kingston reaches for a report, her face like stone.

At 03:29, Kingston glances at the clock's second hand. The latest message was for 03:30 launch. Her hands press against her pants, fingering the pregnancy stick and plastic vial. They feel heavier than her sidearm. Is this continual, low-grade fear imprinting on the fetus? Maybe the lack of fear is worse, the low-grade irritation that they haven't yet released Black Beauty from her shackles. 03:29:30. Kingston wishes she had some gum, or a Lifesaver, anything to get the aftertaste of the MRI out of her mouth. Maybe she should take the capsule now. Her fetus and the missile, shooting out of the gate on the very same day. Thoughts like that don't shock her. They never did.

03:29:55. Kingston mouths the seconds down to 03:30.

Silence.

03:30:01.

"Goddamnit, here we go again," Cabrera says. His lips form the words, but Kingston can't hear his voice: the alarm is wailing. Kingston feels her heart stop, and all emotions bleed away. Black Beauty is a go.

Kingston and Sanders scan their equipment panels while Hewitt and Cabrera verify the authenticity of the SAC message coming through. No more nerves or baby thoughts or boredom, only buttons and switches at her fingertips—she's the missile now. She always has been. Above ground, rotating beacons will be flashing red warnings as sirens howl. Hewitt is asking if they're ready to launch, and Kingston's voice gives a distant affirmative. All throughout the complex, systems shut down as they rout electricity and power to Black Beauty. Kingston licks her lips. The taste in her mouth has mutated into an unnamed desire.

By 03:41, Hewitt has verified target selection. It's one of two possibilities, neither of which has been revealed to the team. Kingston will never know where Black Beauty and her multiple warheads are headed, and she doesn't care. Trans-Pacific fallout will ensure that the winds bring it all right back to America. Sanders and Hewitt have their keys out. They break the seals off the launch commit covers. It sounds like the snapping of spines.

"...three, two, one, mark."

Both keys turn. The LAUNCH ENABLE light glows. They have nothing left to do but sit, and wait.

Out in the dark earth, the Titan powers up, gathering every single bit of energy into herself, readying for birth. Kingston's hands creep over her belly. The man was Nez Perce, like her grandpa's family on her mother's side. He told her his name, but she doesn't remember it. She didn't care. His skin was dark, hot. Black beauty.

The SILO SOFT lights wink on. Above, the great doors are sliding open, spreading apart like a woman's willing legs.

FIRE IN THE ENGINE.

Lights in the control room fade. They hunch in the dark, waiting for release. The tick of the fans, the thump of her heart, the race horse rasp of her breath: she's at the starting gate, straining against metal bars. Kingston snaps open the leather casing holding her side arm. This is how it must be. They have a new type of ICBM across the ocean, a hydra-headed destroyer of nations. This whole planet is fucked. And she deserves life least of all, because she had the audacity to conceive it. That taste in her mouth: she knows what it is. She aches for the taste of the gun.

Klaxons wail out one shrill warning after another. Kingston slides her weapon out, cocks the trigger. But it remains on her thigh, pointed away. *Lift it. Lift it up, you spineless cunt.* Her whole body shakes, but she can't tell if it's nerves or the colossal springs under the cement hollow of the control center, keeping them from cracking apart. *"WE HAVE LIFTOFF,"* Hewitt shouts over the last of the klaxons, and a low, long rush of air thunders through the complex as Black Beauty's engines reach full speed: she lifts. Kingston clutches her stomach, bites her tongue. The heartbeat of some ancient god of war drills into them like jackhammers, wave after quaking wave setting their bones to ring like funeral bells…

…and now it fades: a reprieve back to silence, as Black Beauty arcs into cold skies. Panel lights wink on and off, but Kingston ignores them. Hewitt is on the phone, confirming what they already suspect: other launches, from every silo in the nation. And in two hours time, another missile will slam back into the complex, filling the void. A constellation is soaring across the ocean, right back into their arms.

"Officer. Hand over your weapon." Hewitt's voice is calm. He's staring at the drawn weapon pressed at her thigh.

"No, sir, I cannot," Kingston says. "I'm getting out." She raises her arm, moving the barrel to her head.

"Well," Cabrera says as he pulls his weapon, "good-fucking-bye to you, too."

From all directions, bullets fly. Guess they're all getting out of the silo, one way or another. Kingston turns the barrel and blindly fires out as she drops to the floor, tucking herself into the space between her console and the wall. Cabrera slams against his chair, leaving behind a black slick as he falls to the floor. Kingston sets her sights and shoots, nailing Hewitt in the chest. Blood pumps from his shirt, staining the floor around him in an uneven circle.

"Kingston, drop your weapon!" Sanders, somewhere in the dark.

Kingston checks her clip, touches her belly. Suddenly, surprisingly, she wants to stay alive. Down in the empty silo, smoke and flame is roiling—the afterbirth of the engines. They'd put it out, if it had been a test. Now they can let it burn.

Kingston stands up, weapon pointed.

"I was going to kill myself, you stupid motherfucker. You should have left me alone." From across the room, Sanders mimics her stance, even with his shot-up arm. Overhead, clocks tick away the seconds they have left.

"It doesn't have to be like this," Sanders finally speaks. "I know a place—an underground shelter. I can take you there."

Kingston keeps calm.

"A bomb shelter?"

"No, a real habitat—a place to live, not just survive."

What does he care if she lives or dies? "You're lying," Kingston says. "You need me to let you go."

"I swear on my fucking life I'm telling the truth." Sanders lowers his weapon a touch. "We've been planning it for years."

"We?"

"People—military, civilian. People who knew this was coming. My wife and son are already there." He's babbling. "It's got everything, we can live there for years."

"And they'll let you bring some stranger in? An extra mouth eating your food, stealing your air?"

"Jesus Christ, Kingston, why are we arguing? We're out of time!"

Kingston looks down. Hewitt stares at the ceiling as he bleeds out. He might still be alive in two hours, when the warhead hits. He was a good commander.

Kingston puts a bullet in his head.

"Let's go," she says. Her lips taste like blood, and she licks them clean. Yeah, she's going to hell.

Damned if she'll go there alone.

FIRE

WAR

RED

...footprints trail behind them as Kingston and Sanders drag several large duffel bags back through the blast doors, up smoky stairs to the surface. Together they'd stripped Hewitt and Cabrera of their weapons, then proceeded to take anything else that might be of use. Sanders insisted on taking their dog tags, with the launch keys threaded onto the chains. "We owe it to them," he

said as he lowered Hewitt's tags over her head. It's a sentimental gesture, one that repels Kingston. She'll take them off later, when there's time.

The sky is black, blazing with stars. The guards have disappeared—no one stops them as they cram the bags into the already packed hummer.

"You're driving," Sanders says, holding out the keys.

"I don't know where the shelter is. Wouldn't it be easier for you to drive?"

Sanders nods at his wounds. "I can't shift, and I'll barely be able to grip the wheel. I need you to drive."

"This is why you're taking me, isn't it?"

Sanders says nothing, but she sees the affirmation in his eyes. She's dead to him. Once she drives him to safety, it won't be hard for him to finish the job.

She takes the keys.

Driving the huge machine gives her focus. She rolls down the window, letting the night air rush in as 904 slips past in a ribbon of slick blacktop. Several campers and trucks loaded with boxes and luggage barrel past her in both directions. This is military country—they know. An ancient Volkswagen camper draws up, and for a moment they race side by side down the empty stretch, each bathed in the other's lights. In the passenger seat, a woman with a tear-streaked face shoots her a baleful glare. Kingston realizes that the woman sees her uniform. The woman leans toward the glass, and lips spit out two angry words.

FUCK YOU.

Kingston presses down on the gas. She shoots ahead, away from the woman's accusing face. "We did it for you, you fucking bitch," Kingston mutters. "You paid us to."

"What?" Sanders' head lolls up. "Problem?"

"No."

"What time is it?"

"04:47. Sunrise should start around 05:15. We'll be past the town by then."

Sanders falls silent again. Kingston takes the exit, navigates the quiet streets. Small ramblers and faded Victorians sit under trees, crowned by telephone wires and stars. Everyone asleep, unaware that everything in their lives has changed, and they're alone. The town dribbles down into isolated trailers, abandoned shacks. Overhead, the sky grows light blue, with bands of pink and purple pushing up from the horizon. Cloudless, so far. Kingston keeps her eyes fixed on the low brown hills ahead.

"Time to get off the road," Sanders says. "You're going to get off to the left— there's no road, but it's drivable. Just past the bend." As Kingston steers the hummer over the blacktop and into the brush, Sanders flips the radio on. Static fills the space. Kingston waits for a recognizable sound. Nothing. Sanders flicks the radio off.

Sunrise comes early in this flat part of the world, yet on the western side the sky is still speckled with stars. Kingston steers in sweeping curves between night and day, through the rough and gaping wounds of the scab lands, reminders of the glaciers and floods that once scoured the land. Every hill and shallow looks the same, but Sanders never falters in his directions. At 05:40, he leads her up one of the larger mounds, and she cuts the engine. After close to two hours of driving, the silence is shocking.

"How's the arm."

"It's fine. Get out."

Is this it? Kingston's mouth dries up as she walks to the front of the hummer.

"Where's the shelter?" She might as well ask, though she knows there won't be an answer.

"The large barrow over there." Sanders gestures southwest. In the morning haze, Kingston makes out a stretch of barrow-like hills at the horizon, dark green with scrub and brush. A couple hundred miles away, but a straight shot through flat land. Easy to get to with just one arm at the wheel.

"Which larger one? They all look the same from here."

No answer.

"We need to keep moving. Let's go." Kingston turns, but Sanders only points at the far horizon, in the direction they came from. To the north and east, dappled patterns of farmlands and towns all lie in peaceful quiet, and birds circle overhead in lazy loops. Another beautiful morning has begun.

Kingston's heart slows. She knows what he's looking for. She looks for it, too.

They wait.

The horizon erupts in brilliant white light: this is what they wanted, needed to see. Too many to count, in too many places to see—voluptuous jets of lightning-shot ziggurats unfurling past the cloud line. A metropolis of death, created in an instant. Deep, low booms wash over them, like the thunder of incoming storms. Kingston presses her hand against her chest. They're safe here. This place is too desolate to destroy.

The clouds columns keep pluming, faster and higher than any she's ever seen. "Tsars, maybe—fifty megatons, at least," Sanders speculates. "Multiple warheads. We did the right thing. They would have done it anyway."

Sanders hand creeps down to his holster.

"We need to go," Kingston says, turning away.

She turns again.

Two shots ring out. Hawks wheel and scatter away.

Sanders' weapon hits his foot with a thud. Blood blossoms in the center of his chest. He looks at her, confused. Behind him, the distant clouds spread higher, drift apart. "Bitch." Blood drivels out of his mouth. "I would have let you go—"

Another shot rips the air, echoing over the scabby hills.

"No," she says. "You couldn't."

Grimacing, she holsters her weapon. He clipped her right thigh, a nice deep slice that'll keep her limping for weeks. There's no time for the pain, though. Not today. She puts his tags around her neck with the rest. They smell of hot metal and desperation. As she steers the hummer off the hill, Kingston doesn't look back at his body. He's dead, she tells herself. Things won't get any worse.

An hour later, when the engine sputters to a halt, Kingston remembers her words. Her cracked lips form a parody of a smile, and bits of dried blood flake down her chin and neck. Did Sanders lie about the shelter, too? She pulls everything out of the back, looking for any clue of where it might be. Not one fucking map or drawing. There's bottled water and MRI's, but the rest is weapons and medicine. And a small stuffed bear—for his kid? Kingston runs her fingers over the bear's soft head. Maybe this is proof enough. He was a cautious man, a planner. He wouldn't forget to store extra gas. Maybe she ran out when she did, because this is where she's supposed to be. It's just a hunch, and a shitty one at that, but it's all she has left to go on.

Kingston loads two duffel bags, tucking the bear next to the boxes of ammo. She takes the keys, but leaves the windows open. The winds will come, then the rains. Radiation will eat the rest.

Two hours walking puts her in a small shallow leading to the hills Sanders had pointed to—massive mounds, sitting like beached leviathans, petrified and lost to time. It's there that she sees a glint of metal halfway up the longer mound—an air intake valve, or exhaust vent. Thick clouds roll overhead, and the winds have picked up speed. Kingston stops, and fishes out a small plastic bottle of KI tablets. She swallows two with a gulp of water, then tosses the bottle back in the bag. As she zips it up, she remembers: and pats at the ripped fabric of her pants, where the bullet tore its path. Her fingers feel the pregnancy stick, wedged in what's left of the pocket, but the abortion pill is gone. No matter. There are other, older methods. No fucking way is she bringing a child into this world. Not now. Not ever.

Kingston hoists the bags up again, and limps forward, her face contorted with the weight and pain, with the heat pressing down from above. Big fucking deal, she tells herself. She's walked down this road of pain before, in other years, for lesser reasons. She can make this one. Never mind the bile burning a trail up your throat, the piss trickling down your legs, the blisters and battered bones. Never mind the dark presence riding up behind you, the whip of fear spurring you on. Take one more step, bitch. No one's going to help you. You're alone. Take another.

Take another.

Take…

…

Kingston stands, legs trembling, on the concrete lip of the bunker entrance. "What," she says, realizing she's repeating herself. Dark spots dance in her eyes, and she blinks. How much time did she lose?

"A man," an older woman says. "We were expecting a man." Her face is worn and leathery, but her eyes are bright blue—intelligent, wary. *Farmer, or rancher,* Kingston thinks. *A survivor.* Can she be like this woman? Her hand slides into her pocket, a cautious movement under the gaze of the woman and her rifle. Kingston pulls out the pregnancy stick and holds it up. Why not make that unborn bit of flesh work for her survival, just like everyone else.

"Help me," she says. "Help *us.*"

The woman shakes her head. "We corresponded with a military man—"

"Sanders. He knew me."

"I don't know you from jack shit."

"But his wife and son should be here." Kingston peers past the woman—all she can see is an industrial-sized conveyor belt leading down into darkness. "Ask her, she'll know my name."

"Really."

"We were crew members at Fairchild. He died on the way here." Kingston points to the duffel bags. "His ID and papers are in there. And I brought weapons, medicine."

"We already have weapons and medicine. We weren't expecting a pregnant woman. This isn't a hospital or a spa."

Kingston bristles. "I'm a technician—a mechanic. I can work with anything you have down there—generators, water, air, electrical systems. You need me."

"She can fix things." A man behind the woman moves forward, speaking up for the first time. "We can use her."

"We don't need a baby." The woman is emphatic.

Above their heads, dark clouds roll in an unbroken wave, blotting out the sun. This is her last chance. Kingston keeps her voice devoid of emotion, even

Engines of Desire

10

though she's swimming in despair. She thought she couldn't go lower, deeper, but she can. She always will.

"Neither do I."

The woman doesn't blink. She's harder than the ground.

"All right," Kingston says. "But you know you can't just let me walk away. Take me in or fucking shoot me. It's what I'd do."

Kingston and the woman stare at each other. Wind rattles against the entrance, rolling bits of gravel down the ramp. Particles of radiation already float around them, nestling into cells, blooming like flowers in their bones. How surprised they'll be when they reach her heart, and find it's already gone.

The man moves forward, whispers something in the woman's ear. She sniffs and pulls a frown. "Give him all your weapons," she says, "then get inside. Hurry."

Kingston disarms, handing the four weapons and both duffel bags over to a young Hispanic man. The older man pats her down. Kingston's breath catches in her throat as the man finds the photo. He steps aside, his dirt-creased fingers still caressing its worn edges. She walks into the corridor, turning to watch as they push the thick door shut. Slowly day fades, reduces to a single line of hot white light, the wind to a thin scream.

"Why's he running," the man says.

"What?"

The man holds out the photo. "What was coming after him? He's riding for his motherfucking life."

Kingston takes the photo. And she sees.

"Oh god," Kingston says over the screech of metal slamming tight, to the sun, the wind, the world. At her fingertips, the officer rides his pale horse into the unknown.

DESOLATION
FAMINE
BLACK

...bugs flutter in loops around the ceiling light. They dip and dive away, return and dance again. Kingston watches them from her cot, amazed to see proof that beyond the concrete walls and press of earth, there's still life in the world. What lies sleeping beside her is too horrible a joke to be proof enough.

As if reading her thoughts, one tiny hand uncurls and reaches out. Kingston recoils, then tucks the arm back under the blanket—an unkind gesture. The stale air is stifling hot. But Kingston can't stand to be touched. Especially by the child.

"Knock, knock." It's Ephraim, behind the curtain. There aren't any doors down here, except on cages and lockers that hold medicine, weapons, and electrical equipment. The rest is all open corridors and rooms, constructed from fifty gutted school buses that were lowered into a hole and covered with concrete. This is the shelter Sanders had spoken of with hope: half-finished, filled with faulty plumbing and wiring, and silence. Sometimes it's so quiet, Kingston hears the land shift about the ceilings. She hears the far-off boom of thunder storms, the sifting of metal as it rusts and flakes away. She hears herself grow old.

And that thing they cut out of her womb, that creature, grows old with her.

"Come in," Kingston whispers as she sits up. Loud noises and swift movements horrify the girl, send her into fits that last for hours. Not that Kingston has the strength to yell or move quickly, nowadays. Neither of them do. They're on strict rations, semi-starvation amounts, with most of it going to the girl, at Ephraim's insistence.

Kingston watches Ephraim slip his satchel off a bone-thin frame. His hands shake more than usual as he pulls out a carton of soy milk. It's the one thing they had in abundance—cloying, vanilla soy. Despite her howling stomach, the thought of that taste in her mouth makes Kingston's gorge rise. She stopped drinking it months ago. Just as well. There's almost none left.

"Alice, Uncle Ephraim's going to stay with you for a while, while Mommy goes for a walk."

"Stop calling her that. Stop calling me 'Mommy.'"

"Sorry, I forgot. Alice, your monster is going for a walk."

"Whatever."

Their voices are flat, monotonous. Is this the first or fiftieth time they've had this fight? It doesn't matter. It always ends the same.

"And I told you, she doesn't have a name."

"She's your daughter, she's almost three. She needs a name."

"She came out of me. That doesn't make her my daughter."

"That's exactly why she's your daughter: she came out of *you*." Ephraim's voice catches. "She *is* you."

"Shit comes out of me, too."

Ephraim turns away.

Kingston watches the girl rub her eyes and yawn. Does she understand a word? Her face, as always, is a luminous cipher, her mind a mystery. She made a beautiful baby, that's for sure, her and that Nez Perce. And all fucked up inside, just like her mom.

"Something funny?" Ephraim glares at her.

"No." Kingston turns away, biting her tongue. He doesn't know she lied to him. She did give the child a name, one she's never said out loud. It's what she sees every time she looks at the child, what she wants to draw over her, a sign for the world to remove its mistake. She calls her Ex.

"Get her off the bed. I need my jacket." She doesn't like to touch Ex, if she can help it.

"Fine." Despite his diminished strength, Ephraim lifts Ex easily, handing her the teddy bear. As always, Kingston feels a momentary imbalance whenever she watch Ephraim hold Ex, as if some vital part of her has fallen away, never to be found again. She doesn't know what that feeling is, and it frightens her.

"Which areas did you check?" Kingston asks as she slips her jacket on, willing the feeling away.

"Most of the middle section. I gave up after the toilet. I just don't—" Ephraim breaks off. He's young enough to be her son, and he's wrinkled and aged, with sunken eyes. "I'm tired," he finishes. He sounds just like the woman sounded, after her husband died. Whatever's eating away at them gnaws at Ephraim more quickly than Kingston. Radiation poisoning, no doubt, although the defective dosimeters can't confirm it. She knew they couldn't escape it, even down here.

"We're all tired." Kingston pulls her satchel strap over her shoulders, and a wave of dizzy nausea hits her—low grade, nothing new, she can take it. "Take a nap. You don't look so good."

"You're no beauty queen."

"Never was." She smiles—a tight-lipped grin that hides the holes left by those loose teeth of long ago. No matter. It's been months since she's felt sorrow or self-pity. Years.

Ephraim sings a Spanish lullaby as Kingston limps into the corridor. Almost immediately, a weight drops from her thin shoulders. Looking in the girl's face is like looking in a mirror held by a cruel god. After the woman hacked Ex out of Kingston, silent and swollen, Kingston had hobbled out of the room without so much as a glance back, dragging placenta and bloody strands behind her. It wasn't her fault. Four months in, she knew it was wrong, but the man wouldn't let her abort it. He'd kept her under close watch, him and the teenage Ephraim, who they'd found wandering the scab lands on their way to the shelter. Maybe it'd have been different, if Sanders' wife and child had showed up. The man wouldn't have fixated on that lump in her stomach, "our future" as he put it once. Then again, maybe they did show up. Kingston heard knocking, once, maybe….

But maybe that was just a machine—in all the years they've been down here, no one's broken through those steel doors. Now, in every hour of this endless night, Kingston prays that someone will. Because no matter what she's tried, she can't break out. The keys are missing, secreted away by that old country bitch in a fit of grief after her husband died. Maybe she figured if her man could never leave the shelter, none of them would. Whatever her reasoning, she damned them all.

Kingston walks into the library—a few crates of books stacked next to a moldering upholstered chair. Kingston points her flashlight at the first crate, and pulls out a large photo album. Has she checked this before? The pages crackle with age as she opens them. The album is old, but some of the photos are recent—picnics and holidays, births and weddings. Kingston sighs. Tables laden with Kodachrome-colored meals. Children, radiant and laughing in sunny rooms. Thick-furred dogs, plump cattle, glossy mares—

The album slips from her hands. Quick, before the thought races from her head like a horse slipping its reins. She lopes into the hallway, heading to the farthest end of the shelter, where the storage rooms sit. Several times she pauses, hands trembling against crumbling walls. She took a journey like this, once before. All she's ever done is race down empty highways, with no destination in sight.

In the last room, next to a half-dug exit tunnel, the man lies on a cot, dead almost two years now from the cancer that ate him down to nubs. The last time Kingston was down here, the woman's weapon had just fallen from her mouth. She'd refused food and water for days, just sat there in silence after he'd died. Kingston had left her alone, figured she'd stop mourning eventually. She couldn't. A bullet did it for her.

Kingston's fingers feel for the light switch, click it back and forth several times. The bulb must have burned out long ago. Kingston gives her flashlight several shakes to reactivate the cells. A circle of faint blue pops onto an empty chair.

"Shit." Kingston falls back against the door. "No fucking way." Steadying her hand, she points the beam over the man's desiccated body, then moves it down. The light hits a pair of withered feet.

A shaky laugh erupts from her mouth. The body slid off the chair onto the floor, that's all. No ghosts or ghouls here. Kingston pushes the chair aside, then kicks the body with her boot. It rolls back, revealing a wizened face, empty eye sockets, and a broken nose to compliment the teeth.

"I hope you're in hell." Kingston kicks the body again as she turns to the man—skeletal and crippled, with a face locked in pain. She and Ephraim had listened to his screaming for days. Oddly, the sounds hadn't upset Ex at all.

She'd been the most well-behaved she'd ever been. Kingston should have recorded his death howls, to play them back for her as lullabies.

Kingston pats him down. "Please let it be here," she says, as she pushes his body over and rips the stiff fabric from his flesh. The old photo of her relative—Kingston had hidden it away in her room, but it vanished not long after. She told herself he'd stolen it, an easy lie to live with. Easier than thinking she'd lost the one thing that meant more to her than anything else in the world.

"No." It wasn't anywhere on him. And this was the only place she hadn't searched. Kingston sits on the edge of the bed, her shoulders slumping as she runs the light over the woman. She stares at the weapon. The woman's finger still laces through the trigger—one brown digit has separated from the hand, pointing to the woman's head like a twiggy arrow. Kingston reaches down, and the flashlight catches the glint of the barrel, a silver filling, and—

No, not a filling. A beaded chain—two, created for one purpose: to hold something.

Like keys.

"You swallowed them. You shot them into yourself."

Kingston tugs at the chains. They run deep into her head, where the bullet rammed them. She hears the faint clink of metal, and a strange rasp—she'd swear the woman was choking even now. Well, fuck her. Kingston pulls, hard. The woman's head lifts, and inside, cartilage and tendons crack. It sounds like the saltwater taffy pulls her mother used to buy for her at the fair, the ones that broke in sharp pieces if you whacked them just the right way. Kingston lets go of the chains. All that hot metal and blood and brains have fused into a single stubborn mass.

Not a problem.

Kingston brings her boot down, hard. A satisfying crunch fills the room as bones and tissue grind beneath her heel. "Someone walking on your grave, bitch?" She raises her foot, and stomps on the head again. A loud crack: the entire jaw breaks off, and the rest of the face caves inward. Kingston smiles.

Her boot comes down again. The head is pulp now, a sticky-dry mash of brain and bone slivers. The woman's hair lies on the floor like silver-threaded silk, beaded with ivory teeth. Kingston admires it as she reaches down.

This time, the chains lift freely, clusters of keys swinging from looped ends. Most will open electrical lockers, weapon and drug caches—keys Ephraim and Kingston already have duplicates of. But six of them should unlock the entrance door. Kingston runs a ragged fingertip over serrated edges. She thinks of the town she and Sanders drove through, the sleepy houses and the soft sound of leaves rustling in the cool night air.

Maybe it's not too late.

Kingston's halfway back to her room when she stops. Flakes of concrete crinkle onto her face as she listens. At the end of the hall, Ephraim sits behind the curtain, holding that thing she birthed. She hear snatches of words and phrases, and an occasional squeal or grunt as Ex replies as best she can.

Kingston's fingers steal up to the tangle of dog tags and launch keys resting between her flat breasts. They've rubbed the skin down to red cuts and rashes, thumping at her chest every time she breathes or moves. A vision of the girl as she might have been hovers next to them, staining her soul. She's always there, inescapable.

Unless....

Before she has a chance to ask herself *could I?*, her feet are backtracking away from Ephraim, away from— Away. Kingston glides in quiet steps past the de-contamination rooms, past a reception area that's never received anything other than dust, and up the conveyer belt ramp to the thick metal door. After so many years, this is it. She's free.

The locks are dusty, but undamaged. Kingston picks out the cleanest key, try-ing to work it into the lower lock. It doesn't fit the first keyhole, or any of the others. She moves to the next key, slightly bent but intact. It fits the fourth lock. Kingston turns the key and the sound of the tumblers clicking fills her with such joy that she almost passes out. One down, five to go.

And then the rest of the keys, and then—

She doesn't know how long she's been leaning against the door, sweat drib-bling into her boots. She only knows that at some point, the only keys left are the mangled lumps of metal that the bullet destroyed. If she could rip the bones from the woman's body and whittle them into the two missing keys she needs—but, it's no use. They're here now till they die, and long after.

Kingston slides to the floor. The thought of walking back into that maze, back to that child, of spending her final days trapped in the earth—she can't do it. Kingston wraps the chains tight around her fingers until they turn blue. She stares at them, blinking hard.

"Two door keys on each chain. Two chains."

She pauses, the headache dissolving.

"There should be three chains, each with two keys. One for the man. One for the woman. And—"

Kingston stands.

"And one."

Decay
Death
Pale

…skin floats up through the dark, as if a swimmer is breaking the surface of the ocean. Kingston tightens her grip on her weapon. Hold onto that, she thinks, don't go away again. There's nothing for her in that mindless black.

Ephraim stands before her, stripped bare, skeletal. Black and purple bruises smudge his decaying skin. He's at the end.

"Satisfied?" Tears trickle down his face, but his voice is calm. At his feet, Ex clings to her bear. "I told you, the keys aren't on me. Or in me."

"But you have them."

"I had them."

"If you had them, what the fuck where you pretending to look for all this time?"

"It doesn't matter. There's nothing for us out there."

"That's not the point."

"Then what is the point? All we'll do out there is die."

"But we'll die *outside*, under the sky—we'll be free!"

"We stopped being free the day a bunch of assholes in uniform dropped the bomb."

Kingston's finger jumps against the trigger.

"Fine. You and that—" she points to Ex "—can stay here as long as you like. Give me the keys."

A peaceful look steals over Ephraim's face, giving him an almost sculptural beauty. He's preparing himself. She can tell.

"No."

"You tell me where those motherfucking keys are or I'll kill you, you fucking fag piece of shit!"

The girl begins crying, howls that make Kingston cringe. Something hot and hard burns in Kingston. Columns of smoke and flame, pluming up—

"No."

"Tell me!"

"No."

It's like he's already gone, and she's still stuck inside the rotting cunt of the world. Kingston points the weapon up, and fires. Sparks shower over them like fireworks. Ex convulses against Ephraim's leg.

"*TELL ME!*"

Silence, then:

"All right."

Kingston feels a cold finger press against her soul.

"I'll tell you on one condition." Ephraim touches Ex's head.

"Give your daughter a name."

Kingston opens her mouth.

"Give your daughter a name, and I'll give you the keys."

Nothing comes out.

"You won't," Ephraim says. "But you don't need them anyway. You're already dead, Angela. You've always been dead."

Ephraim leans in, smiling.

"*Pale rider.*"

Kingston slams the weapon handle into Ephraim's head, and he hits the floor with a wet crack. A crimson crown surrounds his head, expanding like the corona of the summer sun. Kingston drops onto his chest, crouched like an animal. His eyes are open, but she knows what they see is not in this room or world.

"Where are the keys? Where are they, you bastard!" She slaps his face, but only the faint traces of a last breath slip from his lips, then nothing more. He's gone.

"Get up, you son of a bitch. Get up, don't leave me here alone!" Ex begins to cry again, and Kingston whips around. "Shut up, just shut the fuck up and let me think for one goddamn second!"

The girl's mouth opens wider. That noise, that fucking noise—

Kingston grabs Ex hard, fingers clenching down on flesh and bone. "SHUT UP YOU FUCKING PIECE OF SHIT I NEVER WANTED YOU I NEVER WANTED YOU—"

Ex's eyes roll back, body going hard. Her face is a bright cherry of broken blood vessels and puffed flesh. And she doesn't stop howling—

Kingston screams. Again and again, colossal screams lurch out of her like the limbs of some primeval monster unfurling from the dead void inside. She sits before Ex, hands reaching out, grasping for something incomprehensible, something beyond the sorrow, beyond the pain. Ex raises her hands as she rages in reply, but Kingston's fingers stretch past her, only holding empty air like reins.

But this fire can't rage forever, can't feed itself. Kingston feels it wilting, falling away. She can't say what is happening—she's never had the words for things like this. She's always avoided things like this. Ex chokes, gasping. Half-fallen against Ephraim's body, glossy ringlets of black hair soaked with sweat, her head barely rises from his grey flesh. Kingston stares, the sounds fading in her throat. In Ex's sorrowful face, she sees the faint memory of summer, the sounds

of leafy night sifting through the screens. Her mother smelled like fresh bread, and it lingered on Kingston's skin long after she'd left the room. Kingston would drift to sleep with her nose in her palms, safe in the dark. The feeling was in that smell.

Exhausted. She can't go on like this anymore. Kingston wraps her hands around the girl's trembling body and pulls her close. The girl's shit herself, it runs down her legs in stinking clumps. Kingston ignores it. Still howling, almost singing the sobs in one mournful note, Ex shivers, but doesn't draw away. Kingston buries her face in Ex's wet hair, breathing deep. Sweat, shit and soy, traces of hard soap and metallic water, and—

And.

Tears gush from Kingston's swollen eyes: it's there, soft and delicate, the scent that tells her that, no matter how hard she denies it, how far she tries to run, this child has always been, will always be, her daughter.

"Ensley," Kingston whispers into her hair, letting the word wash over the girl. "Your name is Ensley."

Kingston sits in the shower stall, stripping her daughter's clothes off her tiny body. When she pulls the shift over her head, revealing a braided yarn necklace holding a soft felt pouch, Kingston doesn't need to open it to know what's inside. If she'd held her daughter just once all these years, she would have known. Ephraim's final gift, perhaps, his faith that she would do one right thing, someday. Kingston runs bits of yellow soap over Ensley's limbs, careful not to get it in her eyes. Ensley sleeps most of the time, but sometimes her eyes flutter open, and she stares into Kingston's face with a look of dazed wonder. Each time, Kingston steels herself, waits for Ensley to realize that she isn't Ephraim, to recoil in fear from the monster. Instead, she only curls back into her mother's arms, as if she'd been doing this all her short life.

Long after the last of the water runs out, Kingston sits in the stall, listening to the slow beat of her daughter's heart. They can't go on like this. She can't go on. There's no place for them, below or above. Even after all that's happened in this small pocket of time, she'll never be a good mother. A monster cannot change what she was born to be.

It is too late, after all.

Kingston carries Ensley back to the room. She leaves the two keys behind. Ephraim's body lies under a blanket—he'd want to stay close to them, right up to the end. She dresses Ensley in a t-shirt for a nightgown, smoothing it past her naked rear. Diaper—she's never put one on a child in her entire life. How did Ephraim do it? Where did he get them? It doesn't matter. In a few hours, nothing will.

The lock to the medicine room is broken, and there's not much left inside. Kingston inspects each bottle label, searching for the right combination to toss in the box she cradles, empty except for a carton of vanilla soy. She thinks about the pill that Sanders shot away, as the skies erupted around them. She should have dropped to her knees, scoured the earth for it. Well, she'll make do. It's the most compassionate she can be for the both of them. Then again, if it doesn't work—she stops in the weapons room on the way back to reload her side arm. She can be both quick and dead, if she has to.

As she places the side arm back in its holster, a thin screech rolls down the corridor like a sigh, followed by a massive crash—metal being bent and torn apart. Every hair on the back of Kingston's neck prickles. She pulls out her weapon, and takes another from the cabinet. Maybe it's a machine breaking down, the generators are long past falling apart. She glides down the hallway, knowing it's not that at all.

At the junction where the conveyor belts lead to the loading ramp, Kingston stops. Goosebumps erupt on her arms. She takes a deep breath.

Night air.

The door is open.

Kingston creeps up the hall, hugging the conveyor belt as she rounds the corner, raises her weapon and fires a warning shot into the florescent tube overhead. Ahead, several figures halt in the doorway, their silhouettes outlined by the cobalt of an early morning sky.

The sky.

"Hey!" A man's voice calls out. "We're unarmed, don't shoot!"

Kingston points her weapons out, starts up the ramp. "I *am* armed, so don't move—one step closer and you're dead."

"Sure, fine—we just—"

"Who are you and what do you want?"

One of the men drops a massive pry bar to the ground with a clang as he steps forward. She sees a hard, thin face, desperate eyes. Is that what she looks like to him?

"We've been traveling; we need a place to stay. We didn't think anyone lived here."

"The door was bolted and locked."

"We didn't see any signs of life. Listen, we just need shelter, a little food and water." He points at the men behind him. All men, no women. "Hard times, right?"

"There's nothing here. You have to leave."

The man takes another step down the ramp, his hands raised as if in peace. He smiles, a yellow-fanged Stonehenge rising up from scab lands of skin. "Well, maybe we can just rest a while, away from the sun. Gonna be another scorcher today."

Kingston doesn't move. "Look at me," she snarls, "does it look like I have anything? Come back in a week when I'm dead."

His smile fades. "Put down the guns, honey. Ten of us, one of you. No need to die. Not just yet, that is."

Overhead, stars wink. She sees them now, clear and high, calling to her like beacons in a storm.

"Is it—how is it, out there?" She has to ask. "Did we win? The radiation, did it kill everything? Is this still America?"

Silence: and then, something she hasn't heard in years. Laughter. Loud mocking laughter as the men repeat her questions, *jesus christ did we win is this still America*, wiping tears from their eyes. As they bend over in hysterics, Kingston spies someone at the far end of the loading ramp, a small figure in rags peering down at her in the gloom. A girl. She fingers a large chain running between small breasts, attached to a thick collar at her neck. Kingston starts, and the girl does the same, eyes widening under shanks of greasy hair before slinking away from the ramp.

Two weapons, twenty-nine bullets—against ten men, all of them armed. She's weak, she's tired. But she's angry. And she was always the best.

"Keep sleeping, Ensley," she whispers, as she opens fire. "I won't leave you alo—"

She doesn't know how many she kills: the first bullet back gets her right in the gut, and two more clip her as she slams against the wall and crashes onto the ground. The weapons fall from her hands, spinning down the ramp.

And, so, that's it. This is the end.

It's so banal.

The men say nothing as they walk down the ramp, dragging their dead as they pass. Kingston lies with her legs pointing to the surface, and her head in the dark, neither outside in the world or within it. A herd of scuffed boots pushes past, and then three pairs of brown, delicate feet shuffle after the men. They're heavily chained and scarred, stained with dried shit and blood.

Tears bead down her face. They'll find Ensley. The things they'll do to her, and she won't understand. Or worse, she will, and she'll never have the words for her pain.

For the first time in her life, Kingston truly weeps.

...

...sun beats down on her face, searing her pale skin. Noon. Kingston gasps, forces a swollen tongue over lips split and bleeding. The shots to her arms, they're painful, but nothing compared to the one in her stomach. Slow death, those gut shots. Yeah, like she deserved better. Always quick to kill and walk away. It felt good. It was clean. But shouldn't she have called her sister to say goodbye? Her name.... Kingston cries again, a feeble whine. She can't remember her sister's name....

...

...found her, they found her, and the men so large and rough, so desperate, and Ensley the angel of the underground, all soft black curls and pale skin. She's screaming. Kingston tries to rise, and can't. Her right hand presses against her stomach, as more blood and bile dribble out. Pages and papers, little notes roll up the ramp, float away. They're trashing everything. Laughter, deep voices, footsteps, all fading. Ensley's screams sink into the pitch black void, where Kingston cannot follow. Only her blood makes the effort, snaking in thin streams down the ramp, reaching out one last time before succumbing, before giving in....

...

...shadows flicker against the walls. The sun is setting. Kingston drifts, each dip into the dark a bit longer than before. Somewhere deep, wherever her daughter now lies, wind whistles through thin cracks, and the mournful song filters back through the tunnels. Kingston's heart thumps painfully as little threads of electricity fire in her head before winking out forever: evergreens tossing in blue skies and high winds over a little yellow house, a woman in a flowered dress throwing a red plastic ball up up up, the scent of cut grass and daffodils. A summer scene from her childhood? Her mother? Or maybe a dream of what might have been, in a peaceful world. No matter. There will never be a summer like that again....

...

...and now there is only wind, the rattle of gravel down the ramp, the flapping edge of a photo as the currents dance it closer to her. Fear bolts through Kingston, and her body jerks. Blood spurts from her lips, and some hidden warhead of pain finally explodes as she grasps the scalloped edges. She sees, oh god she sees....

...it's the image of a young man, a pale-faced rider astride a paler horse, lunging into a future yet unknown. Kingston sees that future now. It's behind the photo, the gaping maw of darkness that creeps closer as the sun gallops across the sky. Galloping like the rider, galloping like the arrhythmic apocalypse trav-

eling through her bones, throwing her body into painful curves, her mouth snarling open in a soundless cry. Her fingers spasm, and the photo flies up and away, the pale rider thunders into the dark....

...and she is the pale rider, grasping the neck of the lunging beast as they begin the final ride through eternal night.

And for one sliver of a moment, Kingston remembers a name that rends her soul. There is someone she must look for here in this wasteland, someone she must find. But the horse does not slow, and the night does not end, and her memories sink into the land with the western sun. There is no one else beside her, behind her or ahead. Five billion people, five billion pale thundering horses, all looking for lovers, daughters, sons. All of them, each of them, alone....

There is only Kingston.

There is only the pale rider, hurtling into the void.

There is only the void.

At the Edge of Ellensburg

CORDILLERAN

"Yes."

Jeff lay before me on the back seat of his Chevy Duster, cock in hand. The trapped summer air, thick with breath and sweat, clung to our skin like matted fur. I wiped my face with the back of my hand, and felt water trickle down my breast.

"No. It's too hot. I feel sick. Next time, I promise."

"You say that every time." Jeff moved his hand up and down, pushing the dark skin through the funnel of his fingers. I licked my lips.

"I don't swallow for just any man."

"You don't swallow for any man."

"It's not about the swallowing. It's about submitting. I don't like submission. It means I'm defeated."

"Or victorious." Jeff smiled and leaned forward. His skin tore away from the seat with a slow crackle.

My white foot pressed against the hot glass of the car. Above me, Jeff grunted and bore down, pushing me deeper into the sticky leather as he thrust into me. Adjusting beneath his weight, my foot shifted and dropped to the metal handle, leaving behind the outline of my skin in a corona of fading sweat and steam. Beyond the ephemeral smears, the gold-brown hills of the land rose and fell away, baking in the summer sun. I watched my ghost-foot fade as Jeff shuddered and cried out,

drops of his sweat splashing on my face before the rest of him crashed over me, spent in the heat.

Later, we sat on the edges of the back seat, doors open to the empty road, half-dressed and drinking lukewarm beer. We didn't touch each other—after we came, there was no need. Besides, it was too hot.

"Radio?"

"Sure," I said. Jeff leaned across the seat and fiddled with the dial, channeling faint guitar chords through the static. No wires or signals this far out of Ellensburg, far beyond the town and the orchards, the cattle farms and layers of earth carved by ancient glacial retreat. Here, with hills behind us, we stared out onto a flat expanse of low scrub and rock that ran straight to the horizon. The low sun puddled at its edges, and together they caught fire in a line of gold that stretched as far as I could see. The dirt road ran before us into that line, but we'd never gone further than the edges of the hills. It seemed safer with the land at our backs.

I leaned my head out the door, hoping for a stray breeze to lift the sticky shanks of hair off my neck. Jeff muttered something about finals—back in the real world, the end of the semester and all the fury of last-minute cramming awaited us. Neither of us were good students. We did the minimum and squeaked by with B's, just like everyone else. Jeff's finals were serious—his first in his new life as a psychology grad student. Mine? Well, let's just say I could have graduated in the spring, but chose to polish my knowledge a few semesters more. Truth be told, I didn't want to leave the confines and culture of the dorms, the dusty classrooms and late-night strolls around campus, talking about nothing and staring at the sky. I didn't want the oppression of the real world. I loved my lazy daydreaming life, and didn't want to leave it.

"We better get back, it's getting late." Jeff stood up and stretched, his tan body reaching for the cloudless sky as he heaved his empty bottle in a high arc. It caught the light of the sun and sparkled furiously as it disappeared with the road into the earth's molten edge.

"Why did you do that?"

Jeff shrugged and slipped into the front seat.

"You have to get that."

"Why?"

"Hello, did you see the NO TRESPASSING sign back there? If someone finds out, we'll never get back in." It was true: kids from college had the reputation for breaking and entering all the surrounding farmlands and orchards. All those empty spaces were irresistible—but the remnants of our parties had made landowners crack down, and the results were barbed wire, shotguns, and

dogs. This silent place had been accessible through an unlocked gate of rotting wood, and I wanted to keep it that way at least to the end of summer.

"No one's gonna dust it for fingerprints. I'm not getting it, it's too hot."

"Fine, I'll get it." I grabbed my shirt.

"Knock yourself out."

"Don't leave without me," I said. Jeff grabbed the steering wheel in a display of mock abandonment. I smiled. I couldn't help myself. He was corn-fed handsome, all muscle and blond hair and soft blue eyes. How a skinny, redheaded bitch like me ended up with him, I had no idea. Did I love him? No. But I wanted to keep him, same as the land. All for myself, at least to the end of summer. So I smiled.

"I'm not running," I said as I loped down the road. Rocks and dirt crunched under my sandals, but I didn't leave a wake of dust behind. Nothing rose in the oppressive heat except shimmers of light, rolling up into the air as we all baked together. The sun hitched, slipped lower, and above me deep purple stained the skies.

"It landed to the right of the road!" Jeff's voice floated to me, barely cutting a path through the silence. No insects, no rustle of wind in the bushes, no creep of animal. Nothing but me, looking for a sliver of glass in the wilderness. I stepped off the road, just two parallel grooves of pressed earth, and wandered to the right, hoping the white paper label would catch my eye.

"Too fucking hot for this," I mumbled to myself. I ran my fingers over my arms—by next morning, the white of my skin would glow bright red. It never took long for the poisonous heat to kiss its way into my cells and blossom. Everywhere I looked, there was nothing: just low shrubs and jagged rocks. "Where the fuck are you. Asshole."

A faint crinkle of breaking glass caught my attention, and I turned back. The hills were a dirty smear against the horizon—had I really wandered that far away? Stunned, I shielded my eyes with my hands and squinted hard, looking for a sign of the Duster. Nothing. I turned back, looked directly into the sun.

A piece of it fell off.

I stood and stared in the press and roar of heat as it floated to the ground, flaring white in the liquid gold of the sky. It disappeared at the earth's edge, then, after several seconds, from behind the low line of bushes a faint but steady glitter beckoned me.

It took another five minutes to reach the spot. My lips had long given up the fight, and my tongue continually ran its tip over their stiff cracks. Dirt mixed with sweat, and caked up between my toes and under my heels. I couldn't see very well—everything blurred as my eyes teared up from a permanent squint. I

was walking to the edge of the earth, it seemed, with only the occasional spark to guide me. At some point, I didn't even remember if I was in Ellensburg anymore. My desire to see what had fallen had taken me over the limit, beyond the edge of the earth, and I traveled on the cusp of the sun.

"There." The word fell out of me like a stone. Just yards away, a steady gleam in the dirt. I stumbled over a thick root, and half-danced, half-fell the rest of the way. It seemed appropriate, landing on my knees. I saw my hand, didn't feel it, reach out. White fingers plucked at the spark, lifted it from the earth back into the air. A gold disk—as small as my fingernail, thin, smooth as glass, and shot through with an enchanting blue iridescence. A small hole had been bored into the top. I turned it over and the tips of my fingers prickled with pain.

"A scale."

A low growl of a car engine drifted across the plain as the wind picked up, and even in the heat, I shivered. Something cold swept over my skin as I watched a thin line of dust kick up at the edge of the horizon, as if some great being had descended from that great space beyond, touched land, and was now racing toward me. Something relentless and all-devouring.

I turned and ran back toward the hills, forgetting about the bottle, ignoring the burn of thirst at my throat and the hammering of my heart. I didn't stop running until I reached the Duster, falling into Jeff's arms like a child and begging him to drive.

If I had only known, I would have kept running.

INVISIBLE SUN

Eastern Washington is nothing but space. No matter where you are, you can find a hill, walk to the top, and turn around in a circle: all you will see is land and sky. Long seas of apple orchards stretch to the horizon, herds of Black Angus thunder over miles of brown grass, miles of barbed wire hold back the bleak beauty of the scab lands. High red cliffs split into gorges and wide lakes; and always in the distance low mountains hover and shift in the heavy air. Civilization doesn't take here, it can't put down roots. It perches on the crust of a billion years of geology, tentative and wary. Under the thick crops and brick buildings, the earth crouches, ready to fling us off at a moments notice. We are only visitors here. We are nothing but lies.

The college campus is no different than any other part of Ellensburg, except that it is neater—more manicured and pristine. I stood at the top of the central walkway in the early morning sun, feeling the hard plastic of my bike seat grow

hot between my legs. To the right of me, the massive brick library loomed over a field of clipped grass split in two by a small stream—named The Ganges by the students in my mother's graduating class, thirty years ago. To my left, more brick and mortar—human silos of a sort, for learning and studying, for fucking and fighting and sleeping. Activities that, like the buildings, seemed ephemeral wisps of nothing before the vastness of the land and sky.

And that's why he stood out among all the students streaming back and forth—because he had the quality nothing else here but the land itself had. He was new here, but he was no visitor. I saw him at the other end of the walkway, standing in the center of the concrete slabs as if he'd always been there—a thick pole of bone and tanned flesh, capped with dirty-blond hair. Glaciers had come and gone, waters risen and receded, and yet— My fingers crept up, touching the scale that hung on a silver chain around my neck. As if on cue, the man turned and slipped behind the education buildings to the left.

My toes pulled at the concrete, and the bike began rolling down the walkway. I wove in and out of the light foot traffic, taking my time. Three weeks had passed since I'd passed out from heat stroke in the scab lands. In the ensuing weeks, summer school had ended, and autumn weather had crept in, taking the edge off the heat, both in the world and in myself. I'd dumped Jeff and moved into my own apartment in Student Village, kept mostly to myself. But I felt something of the old summer burn as I turned the bike around the corner, stopping to chain the bike to the rack. I looked around while fumbling with the lock—he had disappeared, but I knew he was somewhere near. Where he'd walked between the buildings, the air shimmered slightly, as if he'd left a jet stream of heat in his wake.

Between the two larger buildings stood a small octagonal building surrounded by a moat of water and a lush garden. It seemed a complete anomaly in a campus filled with neo-Gothic buildings and ugly dorms—a wild and tangled mess of life in the middle of so much landscaping. I shivered in the cooler air, shivered as branches and low ferns brushed my skin, shivered as my hand brushed across the railing of the short bridge. The building was a meeting room of sorts, almost completely glass, and I saw he wasn't inside. I walked around the concrete balcony surrounding the building, my breath unnaturally loud amidst the rustle of water and leaves. As I rounded the corner, a whiff of cigarette smoke hit my nostrils. I breathed it in deeply, and the burn of it raced through my lungs and settled with my blood in all the little folds of flesh between my legs.

The man stood at the railing, leaning back slightly as if he'd expected me. He looked like a lion, with his messy straw hair, pale sky-blue eyes, and a true Ro-

man nose that jutted from a face covered in light stubble. He was handsome in a feral way, not like the complacent and beefy undergrads I was used to—this was a man, not a boy. He'd taken off his t-shirt and it hung over the railing beside him. His body was lean and muscular, without a trace of fat. Small scars covered his ropey arms, and soft hair covered his chest, tapering down to just below his flat stomach, where it flared out again into a lush matt of dark pubic hair. The top of his jeans was unbuttoned and partially unzipped. He'd probably been pissing into the moat—I didn't know a single guy who hadn't. The water was irresistible.

"Sorry," I said. "I didn't know anyone was here." The tip of the cigarette glowed like a firefly, and his mouth tightened into a sardonic smile. I felt stupid—obviously I'd followed him here. I'd always been a terrible liar.

"Are you a student?" His lips moved around the cigarette, and the glowing tip bobbed up and down in the air.

"Yeah."

"I thought school was out." He took one last drag, and flicked the butt into the water. Smoke shot from his nostrils and mouth—he looked more dragon-like now, less leonine. I shivered again. We were all alone here. No one could see us. He could do anything.

Then again, so could I.

"It'll start up in a couple of weeks. I was here for summer school. You're not a student, are you?"

"Nah." He smiled, a real smile this time, soft and wide. "I'm visiting friends. I've been traveling up the coast, from San Francisco. I'll be here a few months."

"Oh." I shifted on my feet, and touched the scale at my throat. It was becoming something of a nervous affectation. "This must be quite a change from California."

He looked around, and his hand absently moved across his stomach. I felt myself staring at the curls of hair, and my eyes slipped down to the half-open zipper, and the long curve of flesh straining the fabric to the left and below.

"Not really," he finally spoke. "A lot of things are the same." He extended his hand. "My name's Brett."

I slipped my hand into his. His skin was dry and warm, the fingers strong. "I'm Tesla. Nice to meet you." I felt like an idiot, and started to slip my hand away, but his grasp tightened. I didn't fight him.

"So." His fingers moved slightly, caressing the back of my hand in small circles. I felt that burn again, like the burn of the summer sun, eating up my blood as it raced through my arm and across my breasts. My legs shifted and opened, as

the heat dropped into my pussy, and the rush of liquid and blood pooled in the folds of flesh. "Do you have a boyfriend, Tesla?"

I was going to say no, but it didn't seem right. There was a better answer, a more honest one.

"Does it matter?"

Brett pulled me forward, the arms in his muscle flexing slightly as he parted his legs and firmly pressed me into him. His hands wrapped around my ass, and I ground my pelvis against his, feeling his cock shift back and forth under the fabric. His stubble burned my face, and his lips and mouth tasted of tobacco. Hot and wet, with a smoky tang—our tongues locked and danced, darted in and out as I ran one hand through his hair. The skin at the back of his neck was so warm and soft, so unlike the rest of him. I moaned, and it settled on his tongue like his own sighs.

With one fluid motion, Brett hooked the straps of my backpack and slid it off my shoulders, then caught the edges of my shirt and ripped it over my head and off. His hands covered my breasts, squeezing and kneading the flesh until I thought they'd burst between his fingers. I slid my hands under his jeans and grabbed his ass, pushing him harder against me while his mouth tugged on my nipples. I felt my movements slow, and my head dropped back as Brett moved between each hard dot of red flesh, making soft suckling noises with his mouth. His breath was hot and wet, and my pussy throbbed with each beat of my heart. I clenched down, felt the muscles contract and expand, and a flood of wetness soaked my panties.

It was too much to bear—I pushed his face away, and dropped down to my knees as my hands tugged at his waistband. His cock sprang free as his jeans slid down his thighs. It jutted from his body almost grotesquely—long and muscular like he was, only harder and darker. In this neat veneer of campus and town around us, it ignored the niceties of civilization and leered at me with an angry red stare. I wrapped my hands around it, and it shivered as a thick drop of liquid welled up at the tip. My fingers rubbed the soft skin, marveling at how such softness could contain such a hard and relentless core at its center. I held history in my hand, geology and time, and all the violent life of the land. The tip of my tongue ran up the soft groove of flesh and rested in the hollow, letting the liquid pool and run into my mouth.

Above me, Brett breathed deep, his stomach contracted, and his hands grabbed my hair, pulling the mass of red curls around me as if binding my face to his cock. As I squatted before him, moving the soft flesh of his tip back and forth past my lips, I fingered the folds of my cunt, working the juice out of the tangle of coarse hair and flesh. When my clit ached so hard the tears came to

my eyes, I raised my soaking hand and cupped his balls, rubbing my scent into his skin. Marking my territory, even though I knew it wouldn't take.

"Fuck me," I murmured, letting my lips form the words around his hard shaft, as if writing them onto his skin. "Fuck me now."

He pulled me up by my hair, not gently, and bent me over his t-shirt on the metal railing. My breasts slammed into the bars below, and my hair fell forward, forming a curtain around my face. I felt his hands ripping my shorts off me, then parting my ass, thick fingers grabbing the flesh and pulling the lips wide. I spread my legs apart in a rigid *V*. For a second, he stood behind me, holding my aching flesh open to the world. Cool air rushed over my exposed ass and pussy, and I let out a slow gasp as a wave of fear swept through me. I was vulnerable, a target, and he was in control—that's what he was teaching me. I could have moved, but I didn't. I waited.

I felt his thighs press inward, heavy and sure. It took only a single thrust—a deep guttural grunt pushed out of me as my body plunged forward. His cock moved in and out in quick, hard thrusts, and with each push forward, with each fresh wave of pain, my body moved further over the railing. The edges of my hair trailed in the weed-choked water, and I watched the watery reflection of my face, watched the O of my mouth as each cry slid out, watched my tits pound back and forth in frenzy of motion. My raw clit rubbed against the t-shirt, soaked with our sweat and juices, and I felt that wave build between my thighs, the foamy heaviness that coalesced into a dark explosion of pleasure. I cried out, and my reflection below broke into a thousands silver waves—together we watched the brush fire of the afterglow as it ate through our energy, leaving a dulled and shining ache in the landscape of our bodies. Behind me, a shuddering moan broke free from Brett, and he bent over with a final thrust, almost impaling me against the metal rail as his semen shot deep inside. He grew still, and I felt all the little twitchings of his body as he draped over my back and rested. For one peaceful moment, there was only the sound of our breath, and the bright ache of flesh cooling in the aftermath, like the sun slipping below the desert's edge.

Without warning, he pushed away, and I felt his cock slide out of me. A slick of semen ran down my legs, followed by the always melancholy ache of my muscles, as the sudden hollow of my pussy mourned the loss of flesh within flesh. "Help me up." I groaned slightly as Brett grabbed my hair and lifted me back from the railing with as much gentility as if he were lifting a bag of dead leaves.

"Not bad for our first time." His voice sounded distant and cool. Brett grabbed his t-shirt and passed it over his stomach and cock. It swung heavily between

his legs, and I noticed for the first time the thick sack of flesh it rested against, and the mass of brown pubic hair.

"Not bad?" My legs trembled violently, and my stomach and thighs felt as if someone had punched them over and over again. I crumbled to the pavement, unable to stand. Red marks criss-crossed my torso, and when I passed my hand between my legs and drew it back, a thin film of pink stained the skin. I was bleeding. I lay back against the concrete, not caring that the pebbly surface grazed my spine. Every other part of me hurt, so it didn't seem to matter.

"We can do better." He draped his t-shirt over his shoulder and slipped his jeans back up, then drew a pack of cigarettes out of the back pocket. "Next time, maybe. You've got a nice mouth—are you any good at sucking cock?"

"Yeah," I said, staring up at his smirking face. "I'm great. But I don't swallow for any man."

His smile wavered behind the flare of smoke and light, only for a second. All the same, I saw it, and his answer struck my heart like a spark against anthracite.

"I'm not any man."

JHARIA FIRE

Days and nights moved across the unchanging face of the earth, nothing more than cogs in the clock of the universe. And we moved with them, scurrying back and forth between buildings, wrapping our fall semester around our hearts as if it would save us from the same fate as the fall of the stars each morning, the fall of the sun at the end of each day. I threw myself into the routine much as I had any other year, and looked forward to early morning coffee and the crunch of dying leaves underfoot as I walked to class. I spent two afternoons a week in the small anthropology museum, cleaning the displays for credit; and weekends found me in the library, with the whisper of pages and crack of heads against wood as students fought sleep, and lost.

The fifth floor of the library held the art books, and its cathedral ceilings and high windows turned studying into an almost religious pleasure. I pored over books, wrote notes, watched the skies turn blue to grey to pearly white. I slipped to the end of the stacks, where all the brick walls curved into a small space that almost seemed a part of the sky itself. I placed my back against the glass, pressed my soles hard into the carpet, and bit down hard on my lip as my fingers passed back and forth over my wet clit, faster and faster, until I thought the intensity of the orgasm would send me crashing through the window, down

to the green lawns in a shower of glass-shot bone and blood. I couldn't think of anything else but him. He filled every moment I was awake, haunted my dreams at night. He filled every part of my heart and soul. And he knew it: which was why he'd never answered my calls.

"Him again. He never stops, does he?"

Richard pointed from our balcony out across the cement courtyard of Student Village. At the northernmost edge of the campus, a series of ugly brick and wood apartment buildings squatted in giant circle of cement—the place I, and several hundred upperclassmen, called home. Richard and I shared a small apartment on the third floor, with a view of the entire courtyard, and spent most of our free afternoons sitting on the balcony steps, drinking beer and gossiping about our neighbors as they came and went.

"Oh. Him." I took a long pull at my beer. Richard watched as, across the courtyard, Brett held court with a group of freshmen. I'd found out several weeks after we met that he'd come up from San Francisco with a stunningly large stash of drugs, which he dispensed from his friend's apartment—the friend who happened to live across the way. I'd never told Richard about the encounter—I'd been too embarrassed at having been so easily used and forgotten. But this time it was too much, and as I watched Brett flirt with the two girls who lived next door to him, my ugly frown gave me away.

"Do you know him? You know him."

"In a way." I didn't want to, but I smiled.

"Oh my god. You fucked him!" Richard laughed and punched me in the arm.

"Once. He seems to have forgotten about me. It was nothing."

"Was he good? He's hot." Richard shaded his eyes and peered across the courtyard, pursing his heavily-glossed mouth. "I bet he has a big cock. He walks like he does."

"Yeah, he's hot." Once again, my fingers wrapped around the scale at my throat. "He's fucking hot. And he's got a cock like a piston. Happy?" I punched Richard back, and suddenly the weight of my obsession lifted as our laughter echoed across the wide space. I grabbed another beer, noting as I turned my head that Brett was staring across the way, the two sloe-eyed girls momentarily silenced. Suddenly every movement was one of victory, every toss of my hair a crack of the cape in front of the bull.

"So, why haven't you seen him again?"

"He gave me his number. I called. He never answered. I'm not dealing with that shit." The last word shot out of my mouth, harsh and wet. "Fuck him."

"Was it good? Did you enjoy fucking him?"

"Yeah. It was the best sex I've ever had in my life." I pretended to examine the cracked polish on my toes, until his silence forced me to look at his face. I knew what was coming.

"So?" Richard stared at me, that "I challenge you" look I hated so much. "What's your problem? Go over there. Fuck him again."

"But he won't answer my ca—"

"Oh shut up! He's right across the fucking courtyard! You don't want to marry the guy, just go over there and have a good time. If you don't, he'll just give it to someone else."

I watched the two girls. They hung on him like glittering strands of Christmas lights, all pretty colors and tanned skin and straight blonde hair. Bitches.

"What if he says no?"

"Well, then…do you think he'd fuck me?" Richard raised his eyebrows, hope flooding his face. I laughed harder.

"Uh, I don't think so. Although, he did have me bent like a schoolboy over the rail. You know, the rail behind the—"

"Please. I've worn a groove in that rail, bitch. Welcome to the club." We clinked our bottles and drank. As my head raised up, my eyes slid across the courtyard again.

"Hey, faggot!" From below, a beefy face peered up between the stair slats. "I'm trying to study! Shut up or I'll shove that bottle up your fucking ass!" Our downstairs neighbor, a hulking blob of a boy who spent most of his afternoons sleeping off hangovers—but he usually wasn't this vocal when we woke him up. The balcony rocked slightly as he slammed his door, and we sat in amazed silence, then started snickering. Richard rolled his eyes as he stood up, grabbing both six-packs with his long-nailed hands.

"I think it's time to move the party." He started down the stairs, then turned. "Well?"

I stood up. "I—" My mouth grew dry, and a strange hammering started up in my chest.

"No, no, no. None of that serious shit. It's all fun. We're just friendly neighbors looking for a little party. And we have booze. Who can resist us?"

"I'm sorry. I can't." It was true—I couldn't move my feet.

"I thought you liked this guy."

"I do."

"Then what's wrong with you? What's the problem?"

The gold scale slid between my fingertips, burning the flesh. "The problem is—I like this guy. I can't stop thinking about him. At all."

Richard clomped down the stairs, and disappeared. "Whatever. You know what to do!" His voice floated back up, taunting me. I picked up my empty bottles, and walked inside the dark of our apartment. I threw the bottles into the trash and turned the lights on in the bathroom. My reflection swam up from the surface of the mirror—pale freckled skin surrounded by a corona of unruly red hair. I stared until my eyes blurred, until it looked like I was melting into the dark, consumed from the inside by my own dreams and desires. When I finally blinked and tore myself away, twenty minutes had passed.

"Something's wrong with me," I muttered as I sped to my bedroom, throwing clothes onto the floor as I wriggled out of them. I slipped on a sundress, something light and loose—easy to pull up, or down. After a second of hesitation, I slipped my underwear off as well, then sped back to the bathroom, passing a wet washcloth between my legs and ending my grooming with a few well-placed spritzes of perfume. I looked at myself in the mirror one last time: I wasn't as pretty as the blondes, but I wasn't ugly. The color in my cheeks was high, and my lips were dark and full. I smiled. My face didn't matter, anyway. I knew what to do with it. That's what counted.

Students gathered at the edges of the courtyard, clustered around benches as they unwound from the long day. Overhead, stars sparked in the cobalt sky, as the cool of evening pushed day over the edge of Ellensburg and into the great beyond. Young men and women stood on the balcony, draped over the thick posts of wood, talking and smoking and drinking. I navigated across the space under Brett's gaze, under the glare of the girls and the bemused and silent smile of Richard. Other people had joined them, all of them flushed from the booze, or dreamy from the drugs. Acid—that's what I'd heard Brett sold, in neat sheets like stamps. One Hello Kitty under the tongue, and everything flowed.

"I was looking for you!" I called out to Richard. "I thought we were going to go to the library." He placed a hand on his chest, his mouth open in surprise.

"What? I'm so sorry, I completely forgot! Well, fuck that. Come on up and have a beer!" He motioned vigorously, and I demurely walked up the stairs, stepping neatly around empty bottles and full ashtrays. Who was I to ignore the request of my beloved roommate?

Music poured from the open door of the apartment, and the lights of the television flickered like a strobe. In the muted light, bongs littered the floor, and smoke rose in thick waves like the smoldering fire in a coal mine. I counted five couples making out. Not even dark outside, and already this party was going to be epic. I could tell—there was a vibe in the air, a sense of recklessness. To throw caution to the wind so early in the quarter, and in the middle of the week,

no less, was something that rarely happened. When it did, it was the stuff of legends.

"Hey." Richard gave me a quick kiss on the cheek as he handed me a cold bottle—half-full, as he knew I'd want. "You owe me," he mouthed as he steered me toward Brett. He held court in a lounge chair, his long legs splayed wide, and the usual cigarette decorating his lips. A girl sat on his lap—one of the girls I'd seen earlier. I knew her from a couple years ago, when she worked at a Lerner store in the mall in Yakima. She was a slut and an idiot—two qualities that made her prized among college women. I had my work cut out for me.

"Tesla, this is Brett. Brett, Tesla." Richard smiled innocently as he pushed me forward. The slut scowled, but Brett smiled.

"Yeah, well." Smoke coiled around his face like gray dragons. "How've you been."

"I've been fine."

"Haven't seen you around."

"Haven't answered your calls."

"I'm not a dog. I don't come when I'm called." The slut giggled and wriggled her ass against Brett's thigh.

I smiled and threw my neck back in a long white arch. The beer bottle slid past my lips, and as I opened the back of my throat, the entire neck disappeared into my mouth. The beer disappeared in a single rush of gold. I didn't slide the bottle out until it was empty. As I wiped my lips and smiled, the slut made a loud scoffing sound.

"Well." I stepped back and placed the empty on the deck. "You're busy, so…. See you around." I walked into the apartment, rubbing my stomach. The urge to puke it all up would pass in a minute. The image of me deep-throating the bottle, however—that would last a lifetime.

"The goddess with the golden throat strikes again," Richard said as he caught up to me. "The bathroom's just past the kitchen."

"I'll be fine. It was the perfect amount. Are there any chips? I haven't had dinner."

"Look in the kitchen. I think there's some pizza, but I wouldn't touch it. I don't think that meat is pepperoni."

Michael, the guy who rented the apartment, was seated at the counter, shoveling slices of pizza into his mouth. I'd seen him on campus before, and we gave each other a friendly smile. He was an ok guy, not much into studying, but friendlier than our homophobic neighbor downstairs.

"You're that girl Brett hooked up with, the redhead," he said between mouthfuls of pizza. A slice of mushroom hung off his beard, and he flicked it away into a corner.

"He told you about me?" I wasn't embarrassed—I'd fucked too many guys to care about who talked about me. But I was curious—his words made me hopeful, and I wasn't sure I wanted it, after resigning myself to its loss.

"I didn't think he remembered. He's hooked up with a lot of girls here." I didn't know if it was true, but I wanted to find out. Michael shrugged and reached for his bottle to wash down the food.

"He keeps to himself a lot. I don't know. I think he fucked those girls next door."

"Oh. I didn't know he was seeing them."

"No, I don't think he's seeing anyone." Michael stared down at his dirty fingers. "You know, Brett's not really into the relationship thing. I think he's leaving after Thanksgiving. Heading back East to visit family."

Michael had seen through my transparent questions, but I was grateful that he wasn't being an asshole about it. Still. I reached for a slice of pizza, and crammed it into my mouth. Anything to keep the scream of frustration from leaving my throat. Richard saw, but said nothing.

"You were right about the pizza." I had to keep the small talk going—it was that, or grab a knife and go after those sluts. "Wow. Got anything to get rid of this taste in my mouth?"

"I got something!" Michael grabbed his dick through his pants, leaving a smear of marinara sauce next to the zipper. Richard turned away, smiling.

"Hmm. Tempting, but I think my mouth should be a meat-free zone the rest of the evening." Michael didn't look unhappy about it—he always liked to tease me, and I think he preferred pizza to redheads. I can't say I blamed him.

"Here." Someone tapped me on the shoulder, and I turned. Brett stood in front of me, holding a well-rolled joint. My heart skipped a beat, but I kept my face bland and calm. "Okanogan Gold," he said as he offered it to me.

"I don't smoke much."

Brett glared. Even I felt myself shrink under the flat, ugly light of his eyes, my nipples hardened as they rubbed against the cotton dress. "You don't smoke," he said in a low voice. "You don't swallow."

I licked my lips and shifted my legs, then reached out for the joint. "Like I said—not for any man. Maybe for the right man."

Something in Brett's face softened. "Good girl."

Behind him, another explosion of disgust erupted from the slut, as she stumbled into the kitchen. She started to wrap her arms around him, but Brett

turned and gave her the same stony look: she was dismissed. She froze, then slowly backed out of the kitchen, disappearing in the tangle of people. I felt a little sorry for her. I knew what she'd seen in his face.

I took the roach from his fingers, carefully placing it to my lips. It was a peace offering, I'd realized, a second chance. I really didn't like to smoke, but I didn't have a choice. I took a long drag, held the thick smoke in as I handed it back to Brett. Our fingertips brushed against each other, and a tingle of electricity passed between our dry skin.

"She's going to cough, it happens every time." I shook my head at Richard, my eyes getting wider as I fought the impulse to choke. He began to laugh, and Brett joined him as my body convulsed slightly, tears leaking out of the corners of my eyes. I suddenly caught the reflection of myself in the back window by the kitchen, shaking like a boneless Raggedy Ann doll, and I burst out laughing, gagging as the smoke rolled from my mouth and nostrils. Brett handed me his beer, rubbing my back as I drank.

"Told you," I finally choked out.

"You'll be fine." Brett's fingers moved gently down the ridges of my spine to the base of my back. I leaned back against his palm as it came to rest just above the curve of my ass. He didn't pull away.

I lifted my hand, and Brett put the roach back between my fingers. "Now I'm really going to be hungry," I said as I sucked the smoke in again. Richard smiled and tipped his bottle in salute as he withdrew to the living room. I followed his body as it wound around the dancing couples, the young men passing white sheets of stamps back and forth, groups of girls preening and shrieking as they arched their thin bodies and thrust their breasts high into the air. The music grew louder, the bass deeper, and outside, constellations crowned the black evening sky. Brett leaned over me, pressing his mouth against mine, sucking the smoke out of my lungs. I coughed again, and felt him smile as he moved his face down to my neck, nuzzling the curve just below my ear. I signed and leaned in, running my hands up and down his back as I pressed against him.

"Here." Brett broke away, grabbing my hand as he led me through the kitchen to a small bathroom. He pushed me in, closing and locking the door behind us, then immediately turned and leaned against it, pushing down his jeans. I grabbed his balls, rolling the heavy flesh around in my fingers as I nuzzled them with my nose. He smelled like the earth, musky and ancient. I bit gently into the flesh, his thick hair tickling my cheeks as it caught in my teeth, then pulled his cock up, and pressed my lips at its base, running my tongue in small wet circles around and around as it hardened in my hands. He moaned and thrust

his pelvis forward as his hands circled my head. I resisted his subtle tuggings at my hair—I'd do this my way. He'd have to wait for it.

My lips parted as they moved up the shaft of his cock, pushing the silky soft flesh against the hard inner core. As my tongue grew closer to the tip, I moved my other hand, wet from my pussy, and grabbed him, working the juices into his skin as I began pumping him in slow and steady strokes. His hands pressed harder around me, grabbing my hair and roughly trying to direct my mouth over the head of his cock. Again, I resisted, and he loosened his grip. As my hand slide back and forth on the lower half of his cock, I slowly moved my mouth just around the edges of the head, sliding the tongue under the groove of flesh and onto the small wet hole—my tongue was long with a very pointed tip, a lucky gift. I worked the tip into the hole of his cock, fucking him in gentle thrusts. Brett bucked, but I kept my distance. I knew he was watching me, watching my hand running up and down the angry red shaft, watching my tongue as it extended from my red lips, working the wetness out of him, watching my fingers as they ran over his balls, squeezing the soft flesh and damp curls of hair. I knew he was excited, and I knew he was angry.

My tongue curled back inside, licking my lips in a quick spiral motion, and I stopped stroking him. I now kneeled before his cock, my mouth slightly open, hot breath streaming from parted teeth over his sticky flesh. Brett was motionless this time, waiting. My lips barely touched the tip. I could feel the heat rising in waves from his body. He shivered, and slowed his breath. We didn't move. Everything else faded: there was only my hand grasping the pillar of my world, my wet lips burning before the dark red shaft of the sun.

I moved only when he sighed—a quiet and tremulous sound, almost like a sob of pain. My tongue slid over the tip of his head, and my lips followed—first in a soft, lingering kiss, then parting as I slowly slid his cock into my mouth. I stopped at the base of the head, letting my saliva wash over his skin as my tongue wound around and around. I clamped down, suckling at him as my fingers began rippling up and down again, pressing his flesh forward to my mouth and away. Brett sighed again, louder, and I echoed him, letting the vibrations of my moans ripple through his flesh. With each movement of my head, his cock thrust deeper into my mouth—I let him guide the movements now, and his hand stole around my head again, winding his fingers through the hair at the base of my head. Saliva poured out of my mouth, slicking up the shaft as he pounded against me. My fingers squeezed, gripped, and my mouth convulsed, and the movement spread from my tongue through his cock and all up and down his body. I felt the jets of hot liquid gush against my mouth before he cried out, before his body shivered and back bowed forward as he came.

But I was quicker than his cum. As I pulled his shivering cock out of my mouth, I pushed the semen out. It dribbled out of my mouth—a bit of it had slid down the back of my throat, but that was always the way of it, and it didn't count. I kneeled before him, my head raised up and lips open wide, with thick trails of pearl white forming small rivulets down my chin and neck. Brett stared down at me, cock in hand, trembling and breathing hard. I wiped the semen off my face with the back of my hand, and rubbed it across the front of my dress.

Brett closed his eyes, and ran a hand through his hair. He grabbed his jeans and pulled them up, shoving his cock and balls out of sight. "We'd better get back to the party." He looked in the mirror, then turned on the water, splashing it up toward his face in a wide spray.

I rose to my feet, grabbing the edge of the counter for support. My knees were red, and ached from the hard tile floor. I lifted my right foot onto the toilet, raising my dress up past my thighs to my waist.

"What about me?" My fingers played with the folds of my labia—one longer than the other, red and dripping wet, as if my pussy had a tongue of its own.

"What?" He flashed me a sweet smile, as if unable to comprehend my need, as if it didn't exist. I pressed my hands into the soft flesh just above the mound of hair, as if that could stem the ache that was almost crippling me. I wanted him, I wanted his lips on my pussy, his fingers thrusting into my cunt, I wanted to come in his mouth, to grind around his cock like a fish trapped on a hook. And all I could do was stare back at him, the throb of blood in my clit keeping time with each beat of my heart.

"What about me?" I lifted my fingers, watching the tendrils of thick juice strand between them like spiders webs. I sucked the juice off, my eyes never leaving his face. Brett stepped forward, placed one hand on my knee and running it up to the top of my dress, where he fingered the edge of fabric. I hesitated—had I gone too far?

"Come on." He opened the door, and I wiggled my dress back down over my ass as I followed him into the kitchen, my heart pounding with joy.

"Go upstairs. I'll be up in a minute." Brett pointed to the small set of steps leading to loft above. "Go to the right, to the bed in the small alcove. Wait for me." He kissed me, and our tongues touched lightly. I felt his hand hover briefly over my breast, then he was pushing me toward the stairs with a small pat on my ass. I started up the steps, and turned back to smile at him. He'd already disappeared into the living room. I smiled at no one.

After a second's hesitation, I crept back downstairs and grabbed a beer, then headed up to the alcove. I held the bottle tight as I sat down on the small bed,

my knuckles hard and white as I nursed the liquid, nursed my smile, nursed the heavy wet ache between my legs and the terrible fire in my heart.

Below me, the party thundered on, pulling the night past the midnight hour.

I knew he was going to make me wait a long time.

I knew he wouldn't come back.

I waited all the same.

BLACK DAYS

The routine became as relentless as the spread of cold weather through the land. Autumn days bloomed in full, with high color and bright skies; but October nights always belonged to winter. I dutifully attended classes, but did no homework. One by one my grades began to slip, but it didn't bother me. If one thing fell by the wayside, it made it that much easier for everything else to fall as well. Myself included.

Richard stopped pressing me to see Brett again, and I didn't bring up his name. We went to concerts and games, we spent early mornings walking through old neighborhoods and studied late nights in the library. The midnight walks up the campus to our apartment were beautiful, with crisp air and star-studded skies. I always walked on his left, so that when I spoke to him, I couldn't see Michael's apartment as we entered the courtyard. Sometimes, we stopped and kissed—despite Richard's preference for boys, he still played with girls, and his lips were irresistible. For those few warm minutes of necking in the light of the walkways, it was a pleasure to forget about Brett, to forget my fury at knowing there was one man in the world who didn't want me as much as I wanted him.

But in the pitch-black cold of night, long after Richard had gone to sleep, I crept into the living room, to the large window looking out over the courtyard. I positioned myself on the floor in the far corner, and cautiously raised the curtain, letting it drape over me like a shroud. With the dark of the room behind me, and the night spread thick across the campus, I could see all the way across the courtyard to Michael's apartment. I could see everything. And I spent night after night watching Brett as he went about his business dealing drugs, and fucking all the girls in Student Village, one by one.

I couldn't stop myself. It infuriated me that he wanted nothing to do with me, that he didn't seem to be affected by me at all. As I predicted, he never came back after sending me to his little sleeping alcove. I spent half the night there, stewing in my thwarted desire and rage. Long after most of the party had dissipated, I'd crept downstairs to find Michael passed out on the couch next

to a girl I'd never seen before. Brett wasn't there. He wasn't on the balcony, he wasn't in the courtyard. I'd stormed to my apartment, careful not to let Richard hear me as I let myself in, and walked over to the living room window to close the curtains before I fell into bed. I told myself it was innocent. I didn't want to look across the courtyard. But I did. And I never went to bed. Brett had appeared shortly before dawn, walking calmly out of the apartment two doors down, gray smoke trailing in his wake. He never glanced over at my apartment as he closed the door behind him. I don't know if he'd expected to find me in his bed, dutifully waiting. But I could well imagine the look in his eyes as he found his empty bed. Now he knew I didn't swallow, and he knew I wouldn't wait.

I blinked, tearing myself away from the memory of his bed, and the long, humiliating hours by myself. A thin stream of light flashed, then grew wide as Brett appeared in his open doorway. I cringed, resisting the temptation to duck. I didn't dare move, despite the fact that he couldn't see me—my apartment was completely dark, and there were no outdoor lights near our windows. I knew—I'd snuck over a dozen times to make sure the curtains couldn't be seen. Brett closed the door. I waited.

After a few minutes, a small red glow flared up. He was smoking. He was probably sitting on the chair, staring out at the courtyard. He did that some-times, after fucking his latest conquest. If his routine held, he'd stay on the balcony through two cigarettes. By the time he started his third, the slut of the hour would appear at the door, usually half naked and stoned out of her mind. There would be words, and gestures—from her, not from Brett. By the time the third cigarette was finished, the girl would be gone. At least I had that to console me. A month since I'd gotten on my knees, but no girl had lasted any longer with him than me.

The red light flared again as Brett took another drag from his cigarette. It was a lifeline, that small bit of flame, it sustained and nourished my soul and all the festering clumps of love that clung to it. It nourished my insanity and jealousy as well, but I didn't care. It was a small price to pay.

"Why don't you admit you want me?" My breath fogged the glass slightly as I whispered, the words sounding as hollow as I felt. I wound my hands through the folds of my bathrobe, and began fingering the curls of hair between my legs. I imagined the pads of my fingers to be his, the gentle tugging of flesh to be his touch. "Why don't you need me? I hate you."

"If you hate him so much, why do you do this to yourself?"

My body jerked in fear as Richard's voice sounded from behind the curtain. "Fuck, you scared the shit out of me," I said, trying to keep the embarrassed tone out of my voice. "Just leave me alone, ok?"

"Get away from that window. I need to talk to you."

"I said leave me alone."

"You know, I could have turned on the light. I still can, if you don't mind being seen."

My hand crept out of my bathrobe, and I carefully moved my body away from the window, trying not to disturb the folds of fabric. "This isn't any of your fucking business," I said as I scooted away from the window, then rose to my feet and walked to the kitchen. I turned on the small light over the oven, and looked back. Richard sat on the couch, naked, with his arms around his drawn-up legs. Strands of long black hair fell over his shoulders in silky tangles. With his pale skin and long limbs, he looked less like a human and more like some strange, fey demon child—a look he loved to cultivate for his conquests in the goth circles he ran in.

"How long were you there?" I sat opposite him, mimicking his guarded position. For once I felt unnerved by him—I felt betrayed. "I can't believe you were spying on me. You had no right!"

"I can't believe you spend every fucking night staring out that window."

"I don't spend every night staring at—out the window."

"Yeah. Sometimes you follow him." I felt my heart shrivel up in my chest. It was true, sometimes I wandered Ellensburg, trailing his movements as he roamed from conquest to conquest. It never occurred to me that Richard had known. "I know—I've followed you. You're stalking him, Tesla. It has to stop."

"And you're stalking me!"

"No, I'm not—there's a difference! I'm trying to look out for you!"

"You're pathetic—"

"And you're psychotic! It's disgusting. You have to stop this." He moved suddenly, pounding the couch with his fists. I shrank back, and felt the tears start to form in my eyes. God, I hated myself.

"You don't love him," Richard continued, his voice rising with anger, "you think you love him but you're just pissed because he fucked you and left you. Well, welcome to the world, little girl. Men fuck women and they leave them, because it doesn't mean anything. It doesn't have to mean something every goddamn time. But hey: women do the same thing! You're angry because you can't control him, but you can't even control yourself! Just fucking forget him, ok? What do you want, an orgasm to validate your existence? If he gets you off and tells you he loves you, is that 'permission' to start taking care of yourself again?"

"That's bullshit and you know it! You don't understand—!" I started to rise up, but, quick as a shot, Richard was over me, one long arm pinning each of my shoulders against the chair.

"No, I don't understand! I don't know what this has to do with anything, I don't know why you're freaking out over this complete asshole and loser, but you need to get your fucking shit together and move on, because I am not going to pick up the pieces when you fall apart. I've done that with too many friends, and I am *not* about to start that shit with you. That man is not important enough for either of us to fuck up our lives over!"

"You're blowing this way out of proportion!"

"Tesla, he's a *drug dealer*. He played with you and let you go—you should be glad he didn't do anything worse."

"You don't have any idea what he's like!"

"Neither do you!" He shook me, then stopped. He'd never treated me like this before, never touched me so violently. My hands were over my mouth—I didn't want him to see the ugly pull of my lips as I started to cry. But he saw. It didn't matter, anyway. The next thing I knew, I was sobbing in his arms, my hot tears running down his chest. He held me like a child, for how long I don't know, kissing the top of my head and stroking my hair till it tangled with his into strands of black and red.

When there was nothing left in me to cry over, I rested in his arms, feeling the warmth of his chest, the steady beat of his heart. My tears had dampened the soft strands of hair on his chest, and I stroked his skin, feeling his nipples harden as my palm brushed against them. Richard sighed, and his chest rose and fell as his arms shifted, pulling me tighter against him. We'd been standing for a while, but only now did I realize his entire body pressed against mine, his legs and feet entwined with mine. My bathrobe had opened, and his cock twitched and hardened slightly as it rubbed against my mound. He released me, but only for a second as his hands slipped past my bathrobe, pulling it down as he held me again. We swayed back and forth, luxuriating in the feel of skin against skin, in the swell of his cock as it rolled over my stomach, in the warmth of his chest against my breasts.

Finally he pushed slightly away from me, but only to slip his hands over my breasts. I shifted my legs, opening them slightly—my pussy was slick with juice, throbbing dully as I shifted onto my toes and began rubbing it against his cock, wetting his shaft and hair. Richard bent over, grabbing and lifting my breasts so that my nipples stuck out in two red points between his fingers. Back and forth his mouth moved, sucking and biting, his mouth making soft noises as he moved his lips around the hard dots of flesh. I grabbed his ass and humped him in slow, steady movements, feeling his cock grow harder with each pass between my legs.

Richard stopped suddenly, and laughed. "I'm about to fall over," he said, as we began to pitch forward in a tangle of flesh. He spun me back to the couch, and I landed on my back, legs spread wide apart. Richard placed one of my legs at the top of the cushions, and the other on the coffee table, as he positioned himself between them. His black hair formed a curtain around our faces, as he lowered himself and began kissing me. I held his jaw in my hands, feeling the movements of his face as he fed off me in slow, deep thrusts of his tongue. His face was soft, smooth, and he tasted like cloves. I kept my hands on his head, caressing his black hair, as he lowered his mouth to the hollow at my throat, then once more to my nipples. This time his touch was gentler, and my back arched under the caress of his silky tongue. I held the back of his head, feeling the heat flood off him as his mouth moved between my breasts down to the hollow of my stomach, then just above the thick mound of red hair. Richard took his time, nuzzling it, breathing in its damp scent, winding clumps of curls around the tip of his tongue. Just below, hot liquid gushed around the thick folds of flesh, anticipating his touch. I resisted pushing his head lower, only keeping my fingers lightly entwined in his hair as I enjoyed the motion of his head hovering over me.

One of Richard's hands disappeared from my nipples, and a second later, his body began to move in that familiar motion as he masturbated. I looked between the tangle of limbs, watching the white of his hand run quickly up and down the dark red flesh. A low moan rose up in my mouth, as I realized all that joyful pumping of flesh was for me, was because he wanted me. Richard heard me—as his hand moved faster, his lips slipped down through the hair, finding the groove that led to the small button of flesh secreted away in all the softer folds. I moaned again, full-throated now, as his hot mouth surrounded my clit, and his tongue passed over the tiny nub, coaxing the vibrations of pleasure deeper and deeper through my body. A flair of pain spiked in my nipples as the nerves caught fire, and I bucked against him. Richard pressed me down, forcing me flat as his lips and tongue moved faster, then his hand slid from my stomach to my cunt. Two long fingers slid inside, hooking up hard against the soaking flesh, then pumping back and forth in time with his hand against his cock. I pressed down, clenching my muscles around his hand, feeling every joint as it shuddered back and forth inside me.

It was too much to bear—I cried out as I came, as my pussy exploded under the press of his lips, as the flames of desire shot through my body in a network of electric connections. My cunt, my nipples, my mouth, and all the spaces in between filled up with hot needles, heavy and warm. Richard's mouth and fingers slowed, and he pulled himself away, but quickly arched over me, his face

dark with blood. With a few hard strokes of his hand he came, and thick jets of white spurted over me as he gasped and shuddered in relief. Richard fingered the plump tip of his cock deftly, directing wet droplets across my stomach and breasts as his other hand rubbed the semen into my skin. "Marking my territory," he said between sighs, as his hand moved gently up and down my body. For a moment we lay in peaceful silence as his semen dried on my skin, while his cock rested against my stomach, fragile and trembling under my cupped hand.

But his movements slowed as his fingers came to the deep hollow between my breasts. I looked up at him, and he saw my face. The orgasm was fading, and that familiar obsession crept back into my eyes, dulling the glow. Richard had marked my body, but he both knew he hadn't marked my heart.

"Richard—" He rose with out a word, and walked into his bedroom, closing the door behind him. I lay on the couch, panting, running my hands over my body before I raised then to my nose. The faint smell of his sweat and cum clung to my skin. It reminded me of when I was a child, and my parents took me to the ocean. I remembered that same salty, musky dampness in the woods and sands, in the spray of white foam as it hit my naked skin. It was a comforting smell—but already it was fading, burning away as images of Brett filled my mind once more. I pulled the bathrobe around me, turned off the kitchen light, and crept to the window once more, like an abandoned dog returning to its master's grave.

SAMHAIN

Richard and I fell into an uneasy routine after that night, but after a while, it simply became a part of all my other uneasy routines. We found a way to avoid each other in the morning and evenings, and if he stood in the shadows of the hallway at night, watching me watch Brett, he never gave himself away and I never looked for him. Days and nights bled together into one dark mass of rotting leaves and swollen skies. Pumpkins leered out at me from the courtyard corners, and bones hung from kitchen windows, clattering like chimes. The comings and goings at Michael's apartment reached fever pitch: Halloween descended, and everyone wanted a little bit of Brett's paper under the tongue, to make the decadence of the season that much more real.

Last year I'd gone to one of the off-campus parties with Richard—the art and theatre crowd threw huge bashes in their lofts, and though we left with different people, we always arrived together. Not this year. When the thirty-first

rolled around, I dawdled in the library, purposely wasting time, and came home late enough to miss him. Once again, I dimmed the lights and took my place at the window. This time however, there was something else to look forward to other than a night of masturbating at the sight of an empty doorway.

Sure enough, Brett and Michael slipped out before midnight—I almost didn't catch them, as they'd turned out all the lights behind them. I'd managed to worm out of friends that the two planned on showing up at a party off-campus, where Brett would have more of a free hand to do business and indulge himself. Campus police tended to patrol a bit more vigilantly on Halloween, and as I suspected, Brett had no intention of letting the night go to waste. As soon as they hit the courtyard, I was at my front door, watching them through the crack. When they disappeared, I waited several minutes, then slipped down the stairs. I was in no rush—I knew where they were going. But it wasn't where I was going.

I stood in the shadow of the stairwell, watching the ebb and flow of students. I couldn't believe what I was about to do. It was one thing to stalk someone. If they didn't know about it, what harm did it do to them? But it wasn't enough for me. It was too passive, and it meant Brett didn't have to think about me. The whole point was that I wanted him to think about me, always.

I walked across the courtyard in the direction of the lower campus, passing a few drunken students along the way. No one paid any attention to me—I wore black jeans and a black leather jacket, and a small mask over my face. It was lame, but no one cared. Everyone was looking for booze and sex, they weren't looking at me. Behind me, laughter and music drifted, doors slammed and girls screamed in glee. I emerged from the cluster of buildings, but instead of following the path across the road, I took a hard right, hugging the edges of the buildings as I crept around them to their silent backs. Here the music was faint, and the low grass field I waded through rustled in the lazy night wind. I'd plotted my way before, many times. It took five minutes total to get to the far side of Michael's apartment, where I stared up at the dark rectangle of the porch door, and the small balcony it opened onto.

I can't believe I'm doing this, I thought as I pushed the mask up off my face and climbed onto the table on the porch just below the balcony. It gave me just enough height to sling my way up and over the railing, although my arms trembled a bit as my feet hit the wood deck. I'd forgotten how hard it was the first time I'd done it. I didn't need to check if the door would open—I grabbed the handle and slid it aside, walking into the empty room without a problem. I'd broken the small lock at the bottom of the door a few days ago, knowing that Michael was too lazy to bother to fix it. Breaking and entering—I'd resorted to

this, and why? How would this get me any closer to Brett? What did I expect to find?

I removed the small flashlight from my inside jacket pocket, and switched it on as I climbed the stairs, careful to keep the beam away from the windows. I rounded the wall at the top of the stairs, and stood in the small alcove where Brett's bed was. There wasn't much else—a tiny desk and chair, and a small dresser with a suitcase on top. Right at the top of the stairs, a small closet held a few coats, but nothing that looked like it belonged to Brett.

I shone the light from one thing to the next, my heart hammering away in my chest. Would the key to his heart be in one of those dresser drawers? I found change, a small bracelet of beads, underwear that I balled up and pressed against my face. I found faded jeans, dirty t-shirts, and a thick plastic bag filled with dope. I found cigarettes and sheets of stamps. But no papers. No passport or ID, no letters or notes. Nothing to tell me who he really was, where he really came from. I thought of the spark falling from the sun, and once again I felt the scale at my throat. It was as if he'd been born of flame and fire, a avatar of the sun, to torture me until I burned like the summer land.

I sidled up to the desk, which was crammed in the corner at the foot of the bed. Five large cream photo albums were stacked on the top shelf, next to several stacks of photo envelopes from the drugstore. Jackpot. I reached for the nearest envelope, but as I started to peel open the top, I stopped: the front door was opening to the sound of two girls squealing, followed by a low voice. Brett.

Panicking, I fumbled to seal the envelope and put it back in the pile, then switched off the flashlight. The girls stood in the kitchen now, chattering in slurred, drunken voices about which beer to swipe from the fridge—the sluts next door, I realized as I recognized the nasal patter. "Go upstairs. I'll be up in a minute," Brett called out. I almost vomited in terror—the girls were already on the steps, falling over each other as they shrieked with laughter. Quickly I opened the closet door, closing it behind me. The hose of a vacuum cleaner tangled around my legs, and a wire hanger poked my cheek, but there was nothing to do about it. Light poured over the tops of my sneakers, as one of the girls flipped the switch on the weak desk lamp.

"Fuck me, that's bright!"

"Fuck you! How's my lipstick look?"

"Why do you care? It's gonna be all over his cock in five minutes." Both girls cackled, and there was a crash, followed the by sound of a beer bottle rolling across the floor. The light muted suddenly—I snickered, in spite of myself. What girl hadn't thrown some scarf or piece of clothing over the lamp by the bed to make it more "romantic"? I prayed they wouldn't burn the place down.

"Breeeett! Oh Breeeeett!" Heavy footsteps up the stairs—I sucked in my breath, willing my blood to stop pounding in my ears.

"Shut the fuck up, both of you." Brett growled the words, and the girls grew quiet. There was rustling, the sounds of kissing, and a few giggles that faded to nothing. I could hear him slip their costumes off, hear the tinkle of bracelets and earrings hitting the floor, and soft moans as lips pressed against breasts. I slipped my hand under my jacket, pulling aside the black halter top to fondle my hardening nipples. I couldn't help myself.

Footsteps, as Brett stepped back, and I heard the familiar sound of denim slipping down his thighs. "Yeah, that's it," he murmured, and his words of encouragement continued, as I heard the creak of the bedsprings, followed by the girls pressing their mouths and tongues against each other's bodies. Slurping and suckling noises, and little mutterings of pleasure seeped in through the door, and I moved closer to the crack, my own hands moving faster. One of the girls cried out, and Brett grunted: I knew he was masturbating as he watched each girl eat the other's pussy.

I slid my hands down to my jeans, carefully unzipping them, then working a finger past my hair over my wet clit. Despite the fact that I hated those sluts, despite my despair and rage that Brett was with them, and not me, I couldn't stop thinking about that angry red pole between his legs, or his rough skin and the burn of his stubble against my tits. The girls cried out again, and I rubbed my clit harder. Despite all my pain, and because of it, I wanted him even more.

"Get off her." Movement, bedsprings squeaking, and the crash of his body against the mattress. In that second, I pushed at the door, and it sprang open, slightly. Just enough that no one could see, but enough that I could. I leaned against the door frame, careful that my body wouldn't slip and push the door open wider, and switched my hand in my pants to my left. As I sucked the thick juice from under my nail, I resumed rubbing my clit, and watched as the two girls began sucking Brett's cock, their mouths and tongues running up and down his shaft while their hands pulled at his balls.

After a few minutes, my hand slowed, as I tried to stem the rising tide of laughter in my throat—it had to be the worst blowjob I'd ever seen in my life. The sluts were drunk, and they kept missing his slick cock, and hitting each other in the face with the swollen tip. Brett's hands directed their heads, but even his sure grip on their blonde hair couldn't keep their mouths on his shaft. He was getting frustrated, I could tell. Gradually his hands crept down, replacing their mouths as he began to pump up and down.

"You, get on it." The girl he was pointing to shot him an indignant grimace, and tossed her hair.

"I'm tired. Why can't she get on it?" Quick as a cobra, Brett rose up, his hand lashing across her face in a hard crack. The girl gasped, and grew still, her hand against her cheek. The other girl said nothing, only looking down at his cock in respectful silence. Brett wasn't even staring at them—the flat and dulled look on his face was directed into the dark, and for a horrifying second I thought he stared right at me. I resisted moving, but finally closed my eyes, as if that would make him go away. When I opened them a second later, he was lying back on the bed, looking calm and composed.

"Fine," he said. "Get off the bed." The girl complied with a huff, but as she bent down to scoop up her clothes, Brett rolled, his hand sweeping under the bed, then against her arms. In one fluid motion, he handcuffed her wrist, then pulled her to the desk, handcuffing her to the small leg under the bottom of the drawers. The girl shrieked, and jerked: but the desk was bolted to the floor and wall—a preventive measure against sticky-fingered students. I wondered when he'd realized the desk was bolted, and how many times he'd used those cuffs before.

"I'm not going to hurt you, bitch, so shut up." He slapped her again, and she shrank back, clutching her clothes with her free hand. "I just want to make sure you get a chance to see what you're missing. You, come here."

The other girl, who'd been cowering at the edge of the mattress, crawled next to him. He grabbed her tan ass, directing her to turn around and straddle his head. I let my breath out in a long, muffled sigh as the girl's cunt rested against his mouth. She arched her neck back and moaned, her hair falling back over her shoulders as Brett began working his tongue back and forth over her clit, then sliding his tongue in and out of her pussy. Unlike me, she had almost no pubic hair at all, only a small strip of straw thinning out where the groove of her cunt began. I could see every movement of Brett's lips and tongue, every gentle roll of his mouth over the dark folds of her flesh. I jammed my fingers into my pussy, and the zipper teeth bit against my knuckles, drawing blood. I didn't care. I saw the way Brett touched that girl, saw how gentle he was with her. Why couldn't he be that way with me?

The slurping sounds grew louder, and the girl writhed and groaned. Brett's chin shone with her juices, and he slid his hands up and down the insides of her thighs. She leaned forward suddenly, landing on her hands, and he moved his fingers to her tits, tugging at them as if milking the soft flesh. The girl cried out, and beside the bed, the girl on the floor writhed. I couldn't see her face, but I could tell by the way her toes curled that she felt the same way I did.

"Get on your back," Brett's spoke, his voice harsh and thick with desire. The girl complied, spreading her legs wide in the air. Brett turned her body roughly,

so that she lay across the width of the bed, and a low flush of fear pinched my cheeks. He knew I was in the closet. He must have seen me open the door, because he was positioning the girl so I could see her. Through the slit of the open door, her pussy shone wet in the dim light, the dark red folds of flesh like a wound between her long brown legs. He held one leg high, and bent down slightly, pressing the tip of his cock back and forth against her labia and clit until it was shining with her juices. My pussy clenched around my fingers, and I bore down on them, pretending they were his cock ramming into me.

Fuck her, I mouthed.

As if he could hear me, Brett rammed into her, sliding in and out in hard, sure thrusts. Both he and the girl grunted with every thrust, and his shaft grew slick and wide. A small moan escaped my lips, as I worked all four of my fingers into my pussy, violently jerking my arm back and forth. The girl on the floor was doing the same, fucking herself with her fingers, her legs spread wide on the cold floor. I grabbed my breast with my free hand and pinched my nipple hard, and I came as Brett cried out, pushing the girl's head into the wall with a final thrust as he came. I rested my head against the door frame, panting as I drew my sticky hand from my pussy. It felt like someone had fucked me with a brick, and I could barely move my swollen fingers. Brett pushed the girl away from him, and stood up, staring at his cock as it curved down against his balls. He smiled, and so did I.

"Did you cum?" The girl on the bed smiled at his question, a simpering and self-satisfied grin.

"Of course. You were so good, I—"

"Get out."

"What?" The girl on the bed rubbed her head as she clumsily stood up. Brett uncuffed the other girl from the desk, pulling her to her feet, and handing her a pile of clothes.

"Go on. Get out. Both of you."

"You motherfucker! You can't just treat us like this and tell us to get out!" The girl with the bruised head was screaming as she scrambled to put on her underwear. "I want my fucking drugs! You promised us drugs!" I almost laughed out loud—how old was this girl, twelve? Didn't they see the look in his eyes?

They didn't—Brett grabbed the girl's hair and pushed her around the wall, and down the stairs. She didn't fall, but I heard her stumble, and her drunken shouting turned to tears. I stopped laughing. Suddenly I realized what Richard had been trying to tell me, that this man was dangerous, that I didn't know anything about him. No one knew where I was. If I disappeared tonight, no one would ever find the body.

The other girl ran down the stairs, and I heard the rest of their clothes hitting the stairs—Brett must have thrown them. Sobbing and incoherent ranting rose and fell as the girls made their way through the dark apartment; then the front door slammed shut, and I was alone with him.

I stood in the dark of the closet, my fingers drying together, my pubic hair sticking out of my unzipped jeans, one tit hanging from my halter. I didn't dare move. I heard footsteps, and the door swung open, letting in the light. Brett stood before me, naked and slick with sweat, heat radiating from him in waves. The look on his face was indecipherable. I gave him a crooked smile—I didn't know what else to do.

"Trick or treat?"

Brett began to laugh, the dry, rippling sound of a rattlesnake rolling out of his mouth. "Get out of there. Cover yourself up." He turned away, reaching for his cigarettes as I hurriedly adjusted my clothes. "I could call the police. This is breaking and entering, you know. Invasion of privacy." He sat down in the small chair, his legs spread wide. He was still smiling, but he was serious, and I realized once again how dangerous a situation I'd put myself in.

"I was—I only meant—it was a surprise. I thought you might like—" I made a feeble gesture at the bed, as if I'd planned on surprising him with a vigorous bout of Halloween sexing. Neither of us believed me.

"What do you want from me?" He stood up, and I took a step back. He was even more threatening without clothes, an animal, completely feral and uncontrolled. "I owe you nothing. I never promised you anything, never lied. And you have no fucking respect for that!" He took the cigarette out of his mouth, smashing it into the ashtray on the desk, then turned to me. The gold hair on his body caught the smoky light, making him look like some kind of werewolf. I caught myself cringing in his glare.

"I do respect you," I began to babble. "I respect you so much, I care for you so much—"

"You don't know me, how can you care about me? I don't want that! I don't need that shit from you!"

"But you don't understand, we had something—back when we met, there was a connection!" I moved toward him, even as I realized he was recoiling in disgust. "There's something between us, you can't deny that! And you said that you weren't just any man—I know that! You aren't just any man, and I want to prove it to you, I want to show you how much I care for you. Just let me do that." I lowered my voice, trying to keep calm. "Just give me one more chance. I'll do anything you want, I just want to be with you one more time. And then I'll leave you alone."

He leaned back, a smirk on his face. "You love me, but you'll be with me one more time, then leave me forever?"

"I didn't say I love you." My words cracked slightly. God, I disgusted myself, but the words and the ugly, naked need for him just kept vomiting out of me. "I just—we had a good time, and I want that again. No strings. I swear to god, we'll just have one last time together, and I'll leave you alone forever. I promise. I swear." I put my hand over my heart, blinking hard. "Promise."

Brett looked down, shaking his head as he rubbed his hand over his face. He sighed, low and long, then looked up. I said nothing, tried to keep my face calm. If he just said yes, if he let me do all the things I knew I could do, he'd fall in love. I knew it.

He looked up at the photo albums, then took the top packet off the shelf, noting the torn edges. My cheeks burned.

"Yeah." Brett didn't look at me, but fingered the paper as he slowly nodded his head. "Yeah. We could have one more time together. You were right, we were good together. One last time, something good. Something to erase all the shit." He flung the packet onto the shelf, then came over to me, taking my face in his hands. I thought I was going to faint. His bright blue eyes stared down at me, blue like high summer skies.

"One last time," he said, and kissed my forehead. "Go home, I'll call you tomorrow. We'll plan something wonderful."

"All right. Thank you. Thank you." Brett released me, and I stepped back, staggering slightly as I turned and skipped down the stairs. I wanted to believe him, I wanted so badly to believe that everything would be fine.

The moon was full and high as I crossed the courtyard, and pumpkins glittered like orange stars from all the windows and doors. I touched the scale at my throat, and when I drew my fingers back in a sharp gasp, red dripped from the fingertips. I sucked at the blood, ignoring the warning pain.

TOMANOWOS

Yellow dragons bisecting the black, the flash of highway lamps as they swayed and shimmied, and red smears of floating cars in the early evening glow—and I was a deep-sea creature, something luminous and sparkling, pushing through æons of mud into light waters and life.

"Give me another." Brett pointed to the glove compartment, and I pawed through the detritus of his travels, finding the slip of an envelope. I sighed heavily as I placed another miniscule slip of paper on the tip of my tongue.

Hello Kitty dissolved as I closed my mouth, and the highway once again became the serpent, flying us into the cold jaws of the north.

He'd done it, despite my skepticism. Brett had kept his promise, and we were winding up Highway 2, toward the high hills surrounding Leavenworth. The town itself was a popular tourist spot—small Bavarian-style gingerbread buildings in neat rows along the streets, so ridiculously out-of-place in the ancient forests and gorges that people couldn't help but flock to them. But that's not where we were going. Beyond the small town, beyond the frilly bed-and-breakfast houses and rough campgrounds, the Wenatchee River snaked through beds of gravel, rough and rapid, and utterly untamed.

"Just like you," I murmured as I chewed on the straw in my drink.

"Huh?"

"Nothing." I shook my head, embarrassed to think my thoughts were so close to the surface. I'd never taken acid before, and I found that it punctured the thin membrane between the inner world and the outer. I couldn't tell if I was thinking something or saying it, imagining something or seeing it.

It also bothered me that, after spending the past three months doing everything in my power to spend time alone with Brett, I found I had nothing to say to him. *I love you, I want you, I need you* didn't make for much of a conversation, and my attempts to find out more about his past were deftly derailed by Brett. I found myself talking about my childhood, how I'd met Richard, what it had been like to live in London. He smiled and nodded his head as I happily chattered away, oblivious to his indifference until long after we'd steered off the main highway and onto a smaller road. I calculated the numbers on the signs—forty miles of babbling about nothing. I squirmed in my seat, looking back to see if I could find the dark squiggles of letters floating in the air, cursive markers leading the way back to Richard, and home.

"Changed your mind?"

"No." I turned back and began fishing for ice at the bottom of the cup. "It's getting dark."

"There's still a couple hours of daylight." Brett peered up at the sky above the trees. "It's just darker here under the trees. It'll lighten up by the river. Don't worry. We'll be able to see everything."

I opened my mouth to say something important, but the impulse faded with the thought. It was difficult to keep my mind in order. The smoke from Brett's cigarettes wafted through the car, small dragons forming in the white curls. I watched them coil around my hands, delighted and distracted. I knew it was the acid, but it wasn't. The veil that hung over the world had been pushed aside, and I could see things as they really were. Dragons sailed through the smoky

air, traffic lights winked at me, and evergreens thundered and cracked overhead, sending signals to the river: *they are arriving.*

She is here.

"Wake up." Soft lips brushed against mine, and I sat up, spilling the remains of my drink over the seat. "What? Are we here?"

"You conked out. Yeah. This is it." Brett got out of the car while I rubbed my eyes, trying to get back my equilibrium. I'd been watching the trees talk to each other as we sped by on the road, and now I was looking out over a low gravel bank, a thick curve of low white rapids chattering over jagged rocks and rushing past small clumps of trees mid-stream. I got out of the car and stretched, luxuriating in the tangle of wild beauty. Beyond the stream, low mountains crowded the horizon—the first foreboding tendrils of the Cascades—and ancient woods rolled over them in a blanket of dark green. They looked desolate, yet inconsolably perfect. They did not need me. I shuddered, and turned away.

We ate on the gravel banks of the Wenatchee, on a wool blanket Brett spread out over the warm rocks. I was stunned by his thoughtfulness—he'd brought wine and cheese, long loaves of bread and small ceramic pots of foie gras and raspberry jam, cold chicken breasts, bars of expensive chocolate, and crisp grapes on the vine. The acid made me listless and lethargic, I didn't want to eat, I wanted to lie on the blanket and stare at the shape-shifting clouds. But several sharp remarks from Brett made me shovel it into my mouth. I didn't want to displease him, especially today of all days—although some dark oily thought squirmed in the back of my mind, telling me something was obscenely wrong. But what could be wrong? Wasn't this everything I wanted?

Other than insisting that I eat, Brett said little. He stared at me much of the time, and I blushed much of the time. Perhaps he was coming around, after all. I wasn't like those sluts he banged every other day. Every day. I was better than that, I had more to offer him. And it had taken some thought to make up the picnic basket—if he'd just wanted to bang me outside somewhere, he wouldn't have gone to all this expense and trouble. I ate his food and drank his wine, and he brushed away the crumbs with a gentle brush of his hand, and kissed the droplets of wine from my mouth. I stuck out my long tongue for more squares of white paper, which Brett balanced on its tip with great delicacy and care. I lost count of how many hits I took, or how many joints I smoked. It didn't matter—I was safe. I could do anything I wanted, and Brett would take care of me.

After, he set the food aside, and stripped me bare. I barely noticed—each movement of our bodies stretched out as far as the mountains, and I was too busy watching the waters of the river. Silver serpents cascaded over the rocks,

rising with short bursts of stunted wings into the air, then crashing back down into the freezing waters.

"Hey." Brett stood over me, naked. With the giant evergreens framing his body, and the sun catching his long dirty hair, he looked more like a part of the land than I'd ever seen. If I'd been here thirteen thousand years ago to see the glacier recede, he would have been here, rising up from the dirty waters and shifting land, as unyielding as the boulders left behind. Or maybe—maybe—

"You're high as a kite." He was laughing at me as he lowered himself onto the blanket, stretching his lean body beside me. We lay there together, not touching but staring into each other's faces. I stared at his clear blue eyes, the fine lines radiating down his face, the golden blur of stubble on his skin, and I realized then that I could love this man forever, that I would love him forever, and nothing would ever cure me—not wind or flood or fire.

"I was thinking of what you might be like, if you were like a mountain or a boulder, some part of the land that's been here forever; and then I remembered the meteor—the one that came down to earth."

"Which one is that?" He brushed the hair from my face, and ran his hand down the my neck, tracing the curve of my shoulder and arm with one finger, and the wake of his flesh left a glowing blue line on my skin. I sighed in pleasure.

"You know—the meteor. It fell onto the Cordilleran Ice Sheet, but the Missoula floods carried it into Oregon, to Willamette. They say it's a fragment of a planet that was shattered by the sun, billions of years ago. It fell to earth thousands of years ago."

"Like this." Brett touched the scale at my neck. I felt it flare into life, and my bones vibrated. I drew away from his touch. It felt strange, like the whisper of radio waves snickering things into my ear that I couldn't understand. He didn't seem to notice.

"You think that's what I'm like." He rolled his fingers around a nipple, working my flesh into a hard red button. I felt myself squirm, and my toes curled as the pleasure trickled down my body. "You think I fell to earth like a star."

"I saw you that day."

"What day." He leaned into me, wrapped his lips around my tits as I moved onto my back. I closed my eyes, overcome by the pleasure of his lips, the soft wind on my skin and the warm blanket against my back. I slid a leg over his, letting the breeze rush over my cunt—it felt good to be so naked, so free.

"That day, the day I fainted in the scab lands." I caressed his hair, ran my hands down to his face, feeling the movements of his jaw as he suckled at me. "The day

I found the scale. I heard your car. And later, when I saw you on campus, I knew it had been you. You were out there."

"Clever girl," Brett murmured in between kisses. He shifted over me, lying flat above me, his pelvis and cock pressed between my legs. I stretched my legs wide, pressing up into his heavy flesh. His skin was so hot that when I ran my hands over his shoulders, little tendrils of smoke rose in the air.

"I see things," I said. It wasn't the drugs, I was certain. This was the way of the world and the lay of the land, and he was crashing into me like a meteor into ice, melting and releasing me like a flood across the world.

"I'll show you everything you ever wanted to see." His lips pressed onto mine, and our tongues thrashed against each other as he ground against me. I arched my back, squeezing my ass as I lifted him slightly. He rose up on his hands, and began humping me, wetting his shaft against the slick folds of my pussy. But his movements were gentle, not hard-edged and abrupt like they'd been before. This was what I'd always wanted, and I threw my head back and smiled, tasting the scent of our sweat and watching it rise in shimmering waves above our limbs.

Brett reached between our legs and grabbed his cock, and began rubbing the head over my clit in gentle circles. His skin was soft and smooth as wet silk, as soft as his tongue in my mouth. I ran my hands up and down his arms, through the thick layer of hair on his chest, over his hips and ass. The touch of his skin was gold, and when we gasped, bits of glittering fire sparked in the air around our mouths like fireflies. And every moment felt like a century. It took a millennium for his cock to slide into my pussy, and the push and pull of his shaft was an epoch unto itself. His thrusts were slow and methodical, and he bore down against me, his hard skin and thick hair rubbing against my clit until I felt all my muscles tighten around him, and the familiar conflagration of pleasure sweep through my bones.

My cry bathed his face in bright light—I stared up at him, his eyes grew dreamy with concentration as his below movements quickened. As he thrust deeper and deeper into me, Brett buried his face in my hair, his mouth pressed against my neck. I listened to his breath, how it quickened with each rough plunge of his cock, how the beads of sweat trickled like silver bells down his long spine. I lay still beneath him, my cunt raised slightly, and he fucked me endlessly, as if racing his car though the burning lands, while millions of scales fell sparking from the sun, endless and all-consuming. He spoke.

"I love you."

I said nothing, not believing my ears. His voice was barely a whisper, more grunting and moaning than actual words. He kept thrusting and panting, and

I closed my eyes. "I love you. I love you." Again, barely more than a trickle. I bit my lip, letting the tears run into my hair. I knew if I said anything, the spell would dissipate, the membrane would heal, and the world would be as it was before. I said nothing, and he came in me, a long and shuddering sob falling from his lips into the hollow of my throat, where it mingled with our sweat. I held him as he fell asleep, my arms and legs wrapped around his slick body. I didn't mind the weight. It was what I was born to bear.

"What did you see that day?" Brett raised his head from me, and the sudden loss of weight startled me.

"What?" Brett rose up on his arms, then to a sitting position. "What were we talking about?"

"Never mind. Here." He handed me the wine bottle, and I took a long swig, then stuck out my tongue for another hit. As I closed my mouth around the paper, it shifted, and I realized Brett had given me several, folded like a tiny accordion. My face must have given me away.

"You said you wanted to see everything. You will now." Brett stood up and walked into the woods to pee. I stood up, trembling in the sudden chill of evening, then walked to the river's edge. I was tired and cold, and I wanted a hot bath and my bathrobe. I waded past the fringe of fallen logs into deeper water, knowing it was stupid of me but not caring. The dragons were gathering at the edges of the boulders, and I wanted to watch up close. I watched as they crowded around my waist, slithering up and down my skin like hundreds of wet hands....

...and my hands were against a rock, my breasts dragging over the pitted, water-worn surface. It was day. My ass rose high in the air while the river stood still all around us, frozen in time. Brett grunted, his body pushed against me, and slammed me down hard against the ancient surface. I screamed as a red-hot lancet of pain slid up my ass, impaling me like an insect on a pin. Behind me, Brett's hands came down, gripping my splayed cheeks and forcing them even wider, until I felt the skin tear. I screamed again, and the sound hovered in the air before me, an indigo ribbon that spiraled in the slow wind before dropping to the frozen waters below. Another thrust, and more pain, and fear oozed out of me in shining drops, hanging in the air above the waves as time slowed and blackened like burning flesh....

...running through the dark of the woods, and branches chattered overhead while fingers slashed at my thighs, and the blood slicked between my legs in black gobs....

..."PLEASE OH GOD PLEASE!" The screams echoed back and forth among the trees, and I opened my eyes. Pink sunrise stained the skies, red

stained my hands, and clumps of dirt clung to my body like leeches. My cheeks burned—I wanted to cry, but my eyes felt swollen and dry. I lifted my hand to my face, delicately patting split curves of flesh....

...a metallic whine and click snapped through the midnight air, followed by a burst of bright light tearing across the space. I bowed my head, letting the strands of matted hair shield me from the harsh light. Something grabbed my jaw and pulled my head up, and the clicks and lights rolled through the air. *Smile for the camera.* I opened my mouth, but nothing came out except a whistle of breath, and the camera clicked again and again and again....

...the sliver of the sun rose up from my neck, into his hands. I thought of the dry desert, and the cleansing sun, but all I felt was the wet cold of the killing frost as it bled the warmth from my bones. His eyes slid over me, glacier-blue, and then the knife came down, a meteor carving a groove in the ice of my flesh....

....

...I stood in the middle of the clearing, watching the river rush by in the glow of early evening. Bright stars dotted the sky, and the moon waxed glossy and full. I wept. I was alone. But I was alive. I was alive.

He'd left the blanket for me, and I found most of my clothes in a sodden heap by the half-empty jar of jam. No shoes, though. I always seemed to lose my shoes in the woods. I scooped the dirt and bugs off the top of the jam, and sucked at the rest of it as I shambled down the road. Everything looked and felt gritty, tinged with a wash of pink. Blood, I realized. Blood, and the lay of the land. I'd never see him again. I knew that deep in my bones, without question. It didn't matter. I'd wanted to know that he felt for me. I found out.

Time passed in little increments of pain. I found the main road, and then the highway, and the twinkling lights of Leavenworth pulled me in like that deep-sea creature I'd thought I was so long ago. Cold night air pushed me forward, and I ignored the scream of nerves in my bare feet as I stopped and stood at the edge of the main street, watching the crowds walk back and forth under the holiday lights. Children, families, lovers and friends, all talking and eating, clutching packages of silver and gold, dressed in warm, bright clothing. The smells of Thanksgiving and Christmas filled the air—cinnamon and fresh-cut greens. Autumn was over.

Something gently brushed my aching cheek, and I raised my hand. I hadn't thought I was crying, and I was right. Flakes of snow, soft and lush, descended like lovers sighs onto my face, onto the town. I stumbled to the nearest pay phone, ignoring the horrified glances and shocked whispers. But no one stopped to help me—most people were so stunned, I was so horribly out of

place, I don't think they thought I existed. I didn't care, all I wanted to do was go home. I gave the operator my number, and wept like a child when I heard Richard accept the call.

"Oh god, oh jesus. You're alive. Oh jesus, Tesla, where the fuck are you?" He began to weep as well, and I felt terrible, as if I'd done to him what Brett had done to me.

"I'm in Leavenworth." Fresh tears rolled down my face as the wound in my cheek flared into life. "Brett left me here. I don't have any money, can you pick me up? If you have time, that is. No bother."

"But where have you been? I've been going insane! I wasn't able to file a report for two days. I thought—I thought—"

"But—I don't understand. What are you talking about? I've—" I broke off, and stared around at the streets. Christmas lights and cornucopias crowding the window displays. Snow in the air. The end of autumn.

"Richard, I've only been here one evening. Haven't I?"

"No. Brett came home six days ago, and left the morning after."

My mouth opened in a silent howl as he gave me the answer my body already knew.

"You've been gone two weeks."

MISSOULA

The naked chain at my throat shone like a sliver of the sun. I raised my face to the wide sky, squinting at the massive blur of gold dripping down beyond the horizon's edge. At the end of November, just when it seemed winter had finally settled in, one last burst of summer had descended on the land, a glorious flood of heat and blinding light. Indian summer. One last taste of freedom. One last chance.

A low growl of a car engine drifted across the plain as the wind picked up. "Déjà vu," I whispered. Something cold swept over my skin as I watched a thin line of dust kick up at the edge of the horizon, as if some great being had descended from that great space beyond, touched land, and was now racing toward me. Something relentless and all-devouring. I thought back to that moment four months ago, when I'd first found the scale, when I'd first felt that distant shadow pass over my grave. Now, everything I'd ever feared in that moment was coming to pass. No hallucinations, though. Not this time. A demon in his thunderous machine was bearing down on me, as real as sun on my skin, and this time he'd find me, and wouldn't let me go.

I shifted the open bottle of whiskey to my right hand, and with my left, reached back and pulled out three thick photo packets I'd crammed into the waistband of my jeans. Richard had given them to me the night he'd picked me up in Leavenworth—thinking Brett had killed me, or worse, he'd broken into Brett's sleeping alcove even as I'd been bleeding into the icy currents of the river. I'd only looked at them once, but once was all I'd ever need. The images still burned inside, blossoming where my love for Brett had died.

Faces, battered and bleeding. Bruised flesh, darker than the triangles of hair between splayed and broken legs. A tooth, balancing like a pearl on a red-stained breast. When I came to the photos of the girl who'd dropped out of school, when I saw how he'd used the handcuffs on her the second time around, I vomited. But that wasn't the worst of it. The third packet told me the story of a young girl, a girl with a golden scale hanging at her slender neck, and how her life ended in the heat and dust of the scab lands, at the edge of Ellensburg. *It could have been me, it should have been me,* I remember screaming over and over again. And Richard had held me and said *yes, it could have been you but it wasn't. And now you'll never forget, and you'll never let it happen.*

The engines howled, and plumes of dust coiled in small twisters. I let out a ragged sigh, trying to still my pounding heart, then took another swig of the whiskey. Richard had dropped me off at the gate an hour ago, and I'd walked out here alone. Despite his fears, I told him to wait. I told him I'd return.

The Mustang stopped about a hundred feet away, and the engine ticked loudly as it began cooling down. Gravel crackled under the weight of the tires. Then the desert was quiet again, except for the crack of the door opening and closing, crisp footfalls, and the swoosh of low brush against faded jeans.

Brett hadn't changed in the month he'd spent back in San Francisco. In fact, he looked much the same as he did the first day I'd seen him, at the far end of the walkway on campus—an animal in human form, as real and enduring as the flood-carved lands. His shirt flapped open, and I watched the roll of bone and muscle under the dark brown skin. I waited for his terrible beauty to hit me like it did before, waited for that wave of desire and despair. Some strange emotion did pass through me, but it wasn't the same as before. It couldn't be— the gold scale hanging at his throat told me so.

He stopped a few feet in front of me, and without a word, held out his hand. I couldn't play games and pretend I didn't have them—I was openly holding them. I held out the packets, and he snatched them from me, opening them up one by one to check the photos and the negatives. After he was satisfied, he closed them up, but still said nothing, only standing and staring at me. My

fingers clenched the neck of the bottle. I wanted a drink, but I knew it'd make me look weak and frightened.

"That scar looks good on you. It gives you history." I touched my face. A thin line ran from the corner of my left eye, ending in a curl in the middle of my cheek. It was dark from the gravel that Brett had rubbed into it—the wound had healed over tiny bits of the land, and now I carried a million years of history under my skin. There were other scars on my body, other marks he'd left, outside and in, but this was the most visible.

"It's not the history I wanted."

"It's not up to us. We get what the world gives us, and we make the best of it. How we deal with it, and the scars, that's our history." He ran his hands over the ragged lines of hard flesh on his stomach, and smiled in pride. "There's no say in the matter."

"I'm not here for history. You know what I'm here for." I held out my empty hand. Brett said nothing. Not even a smile passed his thin lips.

"What about the photos you took of me?" My voice sounded small and tinny in the open air. "You promised you'd give them back, that was the deal."

He turned and walked back to the car, again without a word. I took another long pull from the bottle. I didn't feel it going down anymore. I felt nothing. Brett tossed the packets through the open window into the backseat, then reached into the front. For one hideous second I thought he'd pull out a gun— but it was only cigarettes and matches. He walked back, and finally that sardonic smile began to surface. We both knew what I had to do to get the photos back. Brett stuck the cigarettes in his shirt pocket and stood before me, fingers hooked in the belt loops of his jeans. They shifted down, and dark straw tufts of hair sprung out in little tendrils.

"Yeah, I know what you're here for. And you know what I'm here for."

"And you're not just any man," I replied.

The land grew silent all around us, as the wind died. His eyes—glacial. And I thought of the great Missoula floods that once covered this land, scouring it free and clean, leaving behind great canyons and cliffs and coulees in less than two days. All that water breaking free, in the blink of the world's eye. We stood on the scar of a thirteen-thousand-year-old wound, and we were nothing at all.

I bent my knees, and I swear it was the hardest thing I've ever done in my life—it was my choice, but I had no other, and Brett knew it. He jutted his hips slightly, and I handed the bottle to him, then slid both hands up his thighs to the zipper. As Brett drank, I slid the metal zipper pull down, watching as the base of his shaft appeared between the shining teeth, turgid and quivering

in the thick tufts of hair. I pressed my lips onto his skin, in the deep curve of flesh where his torso ended and the heat and hardness of his cock sprang out. Despite myself, I once again marveled at all that latent power ready to spring to life.

Brett handed the bottle back to me, and I set it on the ground, then pushed his jeans down, letting his cock spring free. Brett didn't fuck around this time—he grabbed it, stroking it several times until it was as rigid as steel, then pressed it into my mouth. I didn't resist, letting him grab and hold my head in the vise of his hands while he slid himself in and out, faster and faster, grunting above me in small bursts of sound. He was doing most of the work, and I simply hung in his grip, mouth open as his cock banged back and forth against the back of my throat. My hands hung limp at my sides—I didn't need to caress or pet him. This wasn't about tenderness or pleasure—I was a wet and sticky bone-lined orifice, nothing more. All that was required of me was that I stay open and pliant as long as he needed, as long as it took for his cum to hit the back of my mouth and disappear into the slick of my insides, into my soul.

His movements sharpened suddenly, and his thrusts intensified. I could feel that white-hot moment coalesce and quicken, I could sense it in the frenzy of his movements. As I clamped down harder around his thick flesh, I let my saliva-soaked tongue run hot over the piston of his shaft like a flood of fire. A cry like gunfire exploded from Brett's lips, and he jerked and bucked in my mouth as cum spurted from his swollen tip. It trickled down my throat in little rivers—primal and antediluvian, like rich glacier-fed silt coating the bottom of an endless black lake. Brett shook slightly, adjusting himself in my mouth, and I accommodated him, running my tongue and lips around the tender skin as he gasped and stroked my hair. But I wasn't fooled. He wasn't going to pull out, not until every drop from the tip of his head had run deep inside me. I would swallow him as I had no other man.

We stayed in that position for a long time, with his cock resting in my mouth as the warm air of evening fled past us toward the horizon, and the sky flared purple at its edges. In a way, it was comforting for me to envelop him like that, in that strangely intimate way, even if we both knew it was false. But I wondered what it would be like to hold him like this forever, to always have him deep inside me, whether mouth or ass or cunt. It was only when men and women removed themselves from each other, pulled themselves free like the glaciers from the land, ejected and expelled them in a gush of climate change, that everything went wrong. Separation changed the lands, scoured them clean, left aching holes and hearts in earth and flesh alike. A revelation stole over me as his cock cooled in my mouth. I was as much a fixture of the land as Brett

was. I thought I was insignificant, that I was only a speck, a pebble. But even the shift of a single pebble could change the history of the earth.

Brett stepped back, groaning softly as he pulled his cock from my mouth. I watched as the long column of red slithered from my mouth, wet and smelling faintly of whiskey and salt. I pressed my hand against my stomach as my mouth contracted—there was always a moment after deep-throating when my body threatened to revolt, to send it all back up in a grotesque reversal of the act. I closed my eyes and sat back on my heels, ignoring the bite of rocks against my skin. I was grateful for the pain, actually. It goaded me into thinking beyond my immediate discomfort, into rising stiffly and brushing the bits of rock off my bleeding knees.

"You are good. I'll give you that much." Brett's voice sounded thick and satisfied. He reached for his cigarettes, smacking the pack against his hand in a neat crack until a slender white tube poked out of the paper. He caught it with his lips, and reached for his matches—I grabbed the bottle of whiskey at my side, hefting it like a dagger.

"You're not giving me the photos, are you?"

Brett only smiled and scoffed as he ripped a match from the book.

"You're not going to let me go. I'm never going to leave this place."

"What do you think, you stupid bitch?" His hand held the match to the book, paused as he stared at me. A sly glitter shone from his eyes. "Go on. Run. I'll give you a head start. Think of it as a thank you, for finally swallowing."

"I'm never going to leave this place," I dully repeated. The bottle rose to my lips, and I let the liquid pour into my mouth, dam up behind my lips and collect in the hollows of my cheeks. He struck the match and raised it to his cigarette—as the flame touched the tip, I expelled the whiskey outward in a gush of dark gold.

The girl with the golden throat. That's what I am.

He never screamed. I'll give him that. The ripple of flame exploded into a ring of blue-tipped fire, catching his hair and the edges of his shirt. It traveled over his body, caressing his flesh in ways no woman would ever master, swallowing him in ways no human would ever comprehend. Except I did. The fire came from me, from my mouth and from all the desire I'd ever had for him, all the unrequited love. It rippled over his flesh, dug into the crevices of skin and burned away the lies, curling back his skin and exposing his true self—black as the midnight sun. And still he stood before me, silent and unyielding, his hands in fists at his sides, the sockets of his eyes never turning from my face. We stared at each other, stripped to our true selves, as naked as we would ever be to anyone. I would have cried, if I hadn't felt such triumph.

But finally, blackened skin and muscle succumbed to flame, and then the bones themselves grew tired and gave in as the land sung him down. He died as I wanted him to—on his knees before me, collapsed in a deep bow, his burning head resting on the ground at my feet. Despite his protestations, he'd loved me after all.

My fingers reached down. The chain snapped as I ripped it off his neck, and placed the scale in my hand. It felt cool to the touch, for once, and my burnt flesh didn't mind. I let the chain slither from my hands like a bit of sun falling from the sky, and the flames crackled into renewed life as it landed on his back. Smoking fire gushed over him and spread to the bushes and grass, and I tipped my head back and opened my mouth, letting the scorching air flood my lungs as I placed the scale on my tongue, as I fed off the ashes of his flesh and bones. Red everywhere, the red of my hair and skin covering the earth and his crackling heart, and the lands boiled like the surface of the sun, until there were no edges left, until everything under the sun was itself the sun, everything was one.

And I swallowed it all.

Salishan Evergreen

Class: Pinopsida
Order: Pinales
Family: Cupressaceae
Genus: Cupressuceaohm/Cypress V
Species: Cupressuceaohm salishan nikola
Teslated Salishan Evergreen

APPEARANCE:

The Teslated Salishan is a slender tree approximately 50 feet in height, with minimal bark and dark wood. Branches mimic the appearance of telephone pole's tops—long and wire-like, with several larger flat branches extending several feet on either side. A massive knotty growth rests near the top of each tree trunk—these are wombs. Teslated Salishan are mobile, with thick, flexible roots that traverse almost any surface. In full flight, the roots extend up to thirty feet around the base, secreting electrical charges which allow for quick and efficient movement. If provoked, Salishans emit massive lightning balls from the larger branches that dissolve flesh and bone upon contact.

ECOLOGY:

These unique members of the Cypress family are the result of using living, stripped and truncated conifer trunks as utility poles for electrical wiring. Over the past ninety years, the combination of constant elec-

tricity along with airborne chemicals from encroaching suburban housing have
created a species that thrives on electrical currents. While some attempts have
been made to destroy them, thousands remain at wild in the Pacific Northwest,
able to adapt to the surrounding woods in secrecy—often blending in with
suburban communities for decades until they are discovered.

LIFE CYCLE:

Attracted to the high amount of utility wires surrounding ranch houses, Teslated Salishans converge upon neighborhoods in groups of ten to fifteen, attaching their top branches to outdoor wires and electrical outlets. The bark secretes
a creosote-like resin which, when exposed to autumn winds, hardens to amber
and discharges a subsonic current felt only in the bones of prepubescent girls.*
In response to this current, the girls, if not restrained, float into the air, until
caught and bound by the topmost branches. There the girls are subsumed into
the trunk itself, in essence becoming makeshift wombs. The trees then enter a
feeding/hibernation cycle of approximately twenty years. Left alone, they will
siphon energy off power grids with minimal disruption to surrounding houses.
It is for that reason—and the fact that the trees carry the living remains of
young girls—that many neighborhoods have adopted the practice of leaving
them alone, even protecting them against the authorities, and giving the trees
their daughters' names.

At the end of the cycle, the wombs drop into the circle of roots, where the
now desiccated girls split open, revealing a sapling Teslated Salishan. These
new generations of Salishans may therefore be hybrids not only of the common
Alaskan Cedar and raw electricity, but of Pacific Northwest girls. Understand-
able then is the reluctance of so many to destroy these dark and dangerous
trees.

As this species is still new to the scientific community, it is not yet known
how long they live, or what diseases they might be susceptible to. Long-term
observation through the University of Washington is underway.

---

* For this reason, many residents of the Northwest have built underground safety
   bunkers, where they can secure their younger daughters until old enough that
   they no longer hear those sound frequencies.

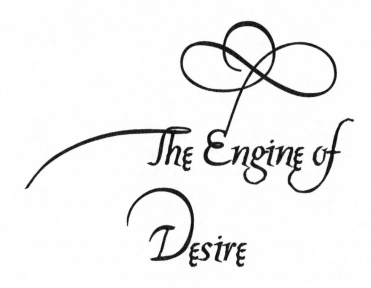

The Engine of Desire

FALL, 2002

Megan pulls the empty wine glass from her husband's limp hand. His fingers brush the shag of the living room floor, sway to the sleepy sigh of his breath. Clocks tick in the kitchen and hallways, and when she places the glass on the coffee table, the clink against the wood shoots like a falling star through the silent house. Outside, in the neighborhood, the engine throbs and waits.

Backing away step by quiet step, Megan creeps into the kitchen, where she pulls a sealed envelope from a hiding place in her mother's old roll-top desk. She props the card against the empty bottle, so Gary will see it when the drugs wear off. He'll read the letter, see his daughter, scream; but he'll move on, eventually. And he won't look for her, because he'll believe. They both know he's not the one Megan's wanted, for what seems like eternity. Although, she has him to thank for helping her through these sixteen years, his rough skin and questioning cock to thank, the press and push of his body over and into her, sloughing the lies of her life away to reveal repulsion and the aching void. A lifetime of enduring misplaced love? No, not anymore. After so many years, desire has eaten her hollow, and now it flows from her like burning oil. Megan walks down the hallway, and into her daughter's bedroom.

I met a girl in the cul-de-sac last week, Sophie had said. Such a simple phrase, yet all Megan needed to know that the time had come. She

picks knives off the sheets as she kisses Sophie's damp face—the same drugs
in the wine found their way into Sophie's glass of milk. Just, more of them.
Sophie's cooling body settles in time to the distant machine, Megan notices,
skin still flush with lust that once rose from her like spring mist. Megan runs
her nose over her daughter's skin, breathes the scent in deep. She smells the
girl on Sophie, that sharp undertone of fuel mixed with lemons and cigarettes.
And under that, the smell of the engine. Hot burning blood and smoking bone,
dismembered limbs whirling in a gasoline gyre. Megan locks the door behind
her, even though she doesn't have to, the knob slipping in her sticky hands. Her
daughter isn't for the taking, not tonight or ever; it's Megan's turn, and won't
the girl in the cul-de-sac be surprised. Maybe she'll be pleased.

Brass bells chime as Megan opens the front door, same as they've done for
as long as she's been alive. This little suburban rambler saw her grow up, marry,
give birth; it's led her through life like the faithful lover she never had. Mom
and Dad willed it to her years after that summer Lisa disappeared: with both
of them gone five years now, it's been hers alone, her rookery, her watchtower.
She stands on the stone porch, staring out at the purple glow of the setting
sun. Ravens cluster on wires and cables, glide from the tips of evergreens to
cedar-gabled rooftops. Driveway lights wink on and off, and wild dogs chant
at fast-appearing stars. All the signs of life are here, but this neighborhood has
long been dead. They're the only family left, and even they've fallen apart, like
rotting meat from the suburban bone. She walks down the driveway, her low
pumps clacking against the blacktop. As she steps into the street, her heart
races; and now she catches the faint whine, a sonorous metallic song calling out
in reply. After all these lonely years, it's returned.

From the far end of the cul-de-sac, a sixteen-year-old girl emerges from the
tangled overhang of rhododendrons framing a long-abandoned house. She
saunters into the street, tanned hips curving back and forth in waves as she
moves. Though autumn hovers in the air, she brings perpetual summer, shimmering all around her in rippling waves. One hand touches a lock of black hair,
then tugs at her striped tube-top—for a single sublime moment, a caramel-col-
ored areola peers into the rising dark. Megan feels the decades burn away like
ash in the girl's heat.

"Hey, spaz," Kelly says. "Got a light?"

"You didn't change," Megan murmurs. "Thirty years, and you're just the same."

"Yeah, I never change."

"But I *have* changed. Can't you hear?" Megan presses her hand against her
heart. "It's like it's inside me now, like I'm the engine, too."

"Oh really? You're the engine?" Kelly slips a cigarette into her mouth. "Are you sure?"

"You're not taking her. It's my turn."

Kelly runs a long tongue over wet lips. "She's already taken—it's what you made her for, right?"

Megan flinches, but the truth doesn't stop her from sliding the lighter out of her pocket, the one she's been carrying for years.

"Yeah, I guess," Megan says. "But she's gone."

"Really."

"It's just us now. No one else."

"No one else." Kelly hooks a finger into the waistband of Megan's skirt, drawing her near. Megan's heart hitches as Kelly leans in. "If there's no one else, you know what that means. I have to leave. I don't come for nothing, you know."

Megan raises the lighter, flicks it into life. The flame writhes in Kelly's dark eyes. "Tonight you come for me."

Kelly cups Megan's hand she passes the cigarette tip through the flame, sucking her breath in as she coaxes it into life. Megan slides her other hand around Kelly's warm waist, drawing her near. She drops the lighter, touches the cherry of Kelly's smiling lips. Her fingers come away red.

"What did I do?" she asks one in particular. The crows, the evergreens, the stars.

"It's not my blood, or yours. Who cares?"

"It's ok," Megan says. "It'll burn away." She clamps her fingers around Kelly's neck, and the girl melts into her like water through parched ground. Their lips touch, dance in through hot gasps for air. Megan pulls at Kelly's top, lowers her tongue. Soft warmth, and the hard press of trembling legs and jutting groins. Liquid fire rushes through her, and her bones bend like willows in a storm. She can bend Kelly as well, mold and rip through her like soft clay until nothing remains but desire, the exquisite pain of submission and defeat. She could feed off such things for eternity. Anyone could. Anything.

Kelly breaks off, flushed. "I have something to show you, in the empty house at the end of the street. Just the two of us." Her long fingers cup Megan's face. "Do you want to see?"

Reverberations bleed through the chilly air, relentless, exquisitely slow. Megan licks her lips, breaths deep. The air, her skin, all taste of Kelly, sea-salt sweet. What more will she taste of her, inside the engine of her desire—inside, under, below? Last time Kelly offered, she said no.

"Yes." Megan breathes the word and Kelly inhales, as if catching it on her teeth. Megan kisses her again, to press the promise deep inside, so it will keep

and never fade. Then, breaking away, she grabs Kelly's hand and they run, run like they did when they were both just girls and her world was bright and new, run through the end of night into the house, into the endless arms of her burning soul, and down.

SPRING, 1985

Megan stands in the center of the street, turning in a lazy circle under slate March skies. From here she sees one empty end of the street, then the other, and the ovarian rounds of the culs-de-sac, dilapidated and worn after so many decades of pushing out their young. She sees the things she's seen all her life—ranch homes and ramblers, cars and crows, and the thick stream of evergreens that seeps through suburbia like a leviathan's blossoming bones. She sees Gary, her husband of five months, carrying boxes into the two-car garage. They met in the Food King up the road, as he rang up her groceries, pleasant and slow. She saw her future that day, and the way to get there.

She does not see her sister. She hasn't seen her in fifteen years now: no one has. How many girls have been fished from the woods around Green River? And yet every time they show a new face on the news, her mother reaches for her heart medicine, and her father slips into the garden with his whiskey—as if Lisa had disappeared just yesterday, and the pain is still raw and new. They need to see her lifeless face, blue and speckled with gravel, to make it real. Without that, she wanders through their memories, a ship without moorings or berth, not dead or alive. If only they knew how very right they were....

Megan halts, dizzy, and looks at the house, *that* house, brooding under bushes and branches, still abandoned. All the kids in the neighborhood are gone now, grown up and off to college, other cities, other countries. The ones that escaped, that is. Most of them, like Lisa, went missing. The pretty ones, anyway, lush-lipped females all. She's the last one. And she's not a kid anymore.

It's been years since she heard the engine's rev. After Lisa, other girls disappeared—but soon there were none, and the engine faded. The neighborhood felt the loss, and soured. Families moved away, sometimes leaving overnight without a whisper. Her mom walked over to the Kerns, the Swensons, the Millers, for coffee or conversation—she came back every time, moving as if something wet and squalling had been ripped from her womb, and thrown far away. But still she won't leave. Lisa might come home, she tells Megan, tells anyone left who still remembers that the Morgans had two girls, not one. She's

her mother, and she'll never leave her daughter behind. Megan knows how that feels.

"Kelly." Megan whispers the word, reverent. Kelly's been missing, too, as long as the rest. Since that summer she and Megan snuck into the rambler—after that day, Megan never saw her again. There were moments, though. Out of the corner of her eye, as she walked home from school or sat reading in the backyard, as she opened or closed her bedroom curtains: a flash of girl-shaped movement, followed with a trace of lemon Jean Naté and cigarette-scented sweat. Sometimes she still wakes up at night, soaked in tears, Kelly's smell dripping from her fingers. She'll cry herself back to sleep, stifling the sobs so Gary won't hear. But it's not enough: her desire's a drop in the cup. All the cream has been skimmed, youth and desire siphoned away, leaving only human husks. Not enough left for the engine to feed on, and so it's gone, along with the mystery girl who charmed its prey and fed them bit by bit into its maw.

She can't bear to live like this, feeding off the fumes of girlhood love, dying before her parent's eyes while they mourn a better-loved daughter long gone. And yet, and yet…the engine sleeps, and this place is safe. No one to watch her do what she must do—a lengthy yet simple action, like the tick of a clock as it counts down the years before the alarm sounds out. Megan stares at the yellow and white eaves framing her old bedroom window as her fingers glide over her stomach, turgid and round. With her ailing father moving into the retirement home, and she and Gary moving in to take care of Mom, Megan can wipe her past clean, start over. Build a better web.

Gary waves at her as he heads back to the car for another load. She smiles and waves, a wan flap of her flesh. Megan goes through the motions with him, in all things. At night when he moves over her, she squeezes her eyes shut, pretends it's Kelly transformed, spearing her into sticky oblivion. The things she does, the images she sees…. Megan smiles as she walks back to the house, drumming her fingers over the mound of her unborn child—her third, though she took care of the other two before Gary and her parents ever knew. All the pain she endures will be worth it, in the end. They'll turn Lisa's old bedroom into the nursery, make a playground out of the weed-choked backyard. Maybe families will move into the houses again, the neighborhood will return to life once more, and the engine will return, Kelly swimming in its hot and fiery wake.

But if not, it doesn't matter. Megan doesn't need neighbors to do her work. She'll make the engine and Kelly return. That's why she's having a girl.

SUMMER, 1972

Megan opens her lips, and a perfect ring of smoke floats out. It rises up, widens, disintegrates. Megan's mouth stays open, her tongue slightly raised as if caught mid-question. She raises an eyebrow, knowing she's being watched.

Across the street, Kelly flashes a cool smile: the Queen of the Cul-de-Sac has approved. Megan takes another puff, staring up at the telephone wires as she sits on the flat-topped rocks lining the yard. Inside, triumph clangs like church bells; and the distant engine pounds in time, sending sound rippling like heat waves through the August afternoon air. Megan has been nothing if not patient, knowing well the reward. Golden-haired Julie left not long after Lisa, to join a commune up in Okanogan County, it was whispered. A few girls disappeared the following summer, and a few more slipped away last year as well. Teenage growing pains, signs of our troubled times, wild youth and drugs—mothers and fathers gossiped the pain away as they filled prescriptions and drank to oblivion. Megan kept her head down and waited, always with Julie's lighter in her pocket, resting low and hard on her hip. She's sixteen now: and now her time has come.

"May I?" Kelly motions, and Megan nods, trying to control her trembling legs. Kelly walks across the street, working the end of a bright pink popsicle in and out of her mouth. She stops in front of Megan, her shadow lying directly across Megan's body, matching her limb for limb.

"You still smoke?"

"Sometimes," Kelly says. "Not as well as you."

Megan parts her legs, slow and steady, as she leans back, resting each hand on the warm surface of the low rock wall.

"So." Kelly stares into the distance, as if concentrating. Listening, perhaps, to some unseen machine? "Lisa ever come back from her hippie trip?"

"Nope." Megan shakes her head hard, trying to act casual and cool. "You know, I was gonna go with her, but—you know. Parents." The last word shoots out of her mouth along with her cigarette, and she winces.

"Uh-huh. Parents." Kelly looks down at her, amused. Megan blushes. Kelly's eyes are brown, with little flecks of gold that dart and swim like trapped fish. When Megan stares into them, she thinks of when she locked herself in the garage one rainy afternoon years ago, when she was nine and her cat Sandy had just died. She sat in a corner, watching the shadows coalesce and creep, while in the opposite corner the house furnace rumbled, flames darting and swimming behind the metal like trapped fish. She wanted to scream and run, but she also wanted to open the door and watch the fire. She wanted to crawl inside.

"Do you think she'll come back?"

"I don't know. Probably," Megan lies.

"Your parents must be treating you like a princess, now that you're their only girl." Kelly reaches out, tugs at the end of Megan's neat ponytail draped over her shoulder. Her fingers linger, then slide away, brushing her breast in their wake. The sensation aches so much, Megan can barely breathe.

"Not really," she finally says. "They're still pretty broken up about it. My mom barely talks to me. My dad treats me like crap. Besides, I'm not a kid."

"No. You're not. You're all grown up like me."

A drop of pink falls from the edge of the popsicle and lands on Kelly's chest. Megan watches, mesmerized. Kelly drops the melting remains to the ground, then pushes her breast up as she lowers her head. The tip of her crimson tongue laps at the sticky droplet, following it all the way down to the elastic edge of her tube-top.

"Sorry about that," Kelly says.

"What?"

Kelly points, and Megan looks down. Between her legs, the popsicle pools on the driveway, little dots of pink decorating Megan's pale legs where it splashed up. But that's not where Kelly's pointing. A single bright dot rests on the crotch of Megan's white shorts, just below the zipper.

Kelly grins. "Want me to lick that off, too?"

Megan looks up, her face as hot as the sun.

"Come on." Kelly's accusing finger now becomes a hand, and Megan grasps it. With a quick tug, Megan's on her feet. Kelly keeps pulling her, and Megan stumbles forward, her breast bumping against Kelly's arm, her crotch against Kelly's thigh. The older girl leans in, whispering. Megan catches a whiff of sugar and blood.

"I found something, in the empty house at the end of the street. It has to do with the missing girls, and your sister. I think I know where they are. Wanna see?"

This is the moment. This is it.

Mute with love, Megan nods.

They walk in unison down the road. Megan's legs feel hot and heavy, and all the blood in her body sloshes around, spirals into a whirlpool of throbbing flesh and crackling nerves. Is the engine getting louder? No, just deeper, more intense, as though they are moving toward it. Overhead, birds wheel and cry in a contrail-laced sky of pure blue. Someone's mowing their lawn, and radios crackle and sing. Yet, they are all alone. It's just Megan and Kelly, and no other girl, the way it's supposed to be. Megan sees none of their neighbors as they

walk down the cracked driveway of the abandoned rambler, pine needles and dandelions carpeting their way to the faded green front door. Under eaves dripping with peeling paint and spider webs, Kelly grabs the brass handle and pulls. The door opens into cool darkness. Yet, further within the house, Megan sees light.

"Come on. It's just us." Kelly steps into the foyer, holding the door open. Megan stands outside, hesitant. Slight fear spikes her lust, dulling it.

"I don't know. Is it safe? What's inside?"

"You have to come in to find out." Kelly reaches out again, and this time her fingers slide between Megan's legs, cupping the space between. She squeezes, slow, and her thumb travels, presses down. "Come inside."

Megan's legs move, how she doesn't know, as Kelly's gentle hand leads her through the door. When it closes, she doesn't know, she only knows that now they're alone, and lips are pressed against hers, cold and bubblegum sweet. Her shaking hands move up, push the edges of the tube-top away. Kelly's flesh pours into her hands, pliant as clay. Insects drone and thump against the windows. Megan's fingers clutch at a diamond-hard nipple, and she moves her mouth down.

Kelly breaks away. "Not yet. I have to show you. Come on. Come on!" She smiles as she disappears into the living room and around the corner, almost dancing as she goes. Megan stands for a second, her body racked with blood-thick quakes. Underneath her feet, the engine purrs.

Megan finds Kelly in the room off the kitchen, a dusty den lined in fake wood and faded carpeting. She's on her knees before the sliding glass door, legs parted and skirt gathered in folds around her waist. Megan hangs back, watching in awe as Kelly's fingers dip and disappear into the thick black curls.

"Do you hear it," she breathes, her body rocking back and forth in time to the metallic bass below. "Do you hear the machine?"

"I thought I was the only one," Megan says.

"Help me up." Kelly raises her hand, and Megan grabs it, pulling the girl to her feet. Kelly wraps one arm around her waist, and they stand, swaying slightly as her still warm finger crooks itself into Megan's mouth and glides around her tongue, leaving behind a faint trace of salt.

"It's here," Kelly says, breaking away once more as she walks across the room and opens a door. Megan sighs in angry frustration.

"Why can't we—can't we stay here for a while? It's nice in here." Megan smiles, trying to look alluring as she fingers a button on her shirt, sliding it from its embroidered hole. What would her sister have done, or any of the other girls?

At a loss, Megan unbuttons her blouse all the way to reveal small, freckled breasts, unsure if she's doing any of this right at all. "Please?"

Kelly's only reply is to reach down, and rip off the tube-top in one lightning-fast motion. Her breasts tumble out of the fabric and against her chest, tanned with wide areolas. Kelly drops the top onto the rug, then steps back: down. Megan starts. Kelly steps back down and down, until the darkness swallows her, and only her voice remains.

"It's nicer down here."

Megan rushes to the edge of the door, and peers down. A flight of rough wood stairs leads into a basement rec room. More shag carpeting and paneling. From one of the corners, pale red light pulses, casting strange shadows that undulate back and forth. Kelly's skirt lies in a heap at the bottom of the stairs. Megan descends, one creaking step at a time.

At the bottom of the stairs, Megan sees the room in full, bunker-low concrete ceilings with thin windows looking onto the bushes surrounding the house. At the far end, Kelly leans, arms behind her back, against a set of folding utility closet doors that pulse and shake in time to the engine's reverbs. Her tan skin glows almost white in the ruby light spilling from the wood slats, as if she's melting into the house. She looks the same as the day Megan first saw her years and years ago, standing like sugar in the pouring rain, dripping smoke and secrets into her sister's ears. The engine sounds so loud now, so heavy and hard that Megan can't hear her own heart.

"Is this what you want?" Kelly thrusts her hips forward as she parts her legs. Red light spills from between them, as if whatever lies behind the doors cannot be contained.

"Yes," says Megan, "but, what does this have to do with Lisa? What did you want to show me?"

Kelly steps away from the doors. Megan's feet drag across the carpet, catching on nothing. Her fingertips touch the copper knobs, worn with age. Kelly presses against her from behind, pushing her blouse away as she cups Megan's breasts, pulling at the skin as Megan pulls at the doors. They accordion to the side. Hot fumes hit her face, stinging her eyes as they rise in the cool air. Little bolts of pleasure run through her body as Kelly laps at her ear, her fingers still working, working. From within the closet, a writhing mass sounds out a painful howl.

"This is the engine," Kelly whispers. "This is us."

Megan sees nothing at first, only dark red glowing from smoke and shadows. Gradually, the malformed outlines of a squat black furnace appear, the largest she's ever seen. Flames dart from crevices and tears, flick like tongues. Cables

thick as her body pierce the furnace from below and erupt transformed from its pulsing sides, spiraling around the beast in ropes of liquid-boned flesh stripped of skin, like a bloody fist squeezing until the prey has squirted from its grip.

"What the—" Megan begins, but another blast of sound cuts her off, and the floor shakes. Bits of white spackle drift from the ceiling onto their hair and arms, stick in the crimson mist spraying the air as one of the cables suddenly splits down the middle. Kelly's hands move faster, and down. Megan and the cables scream in unison—mouths open, tongues waggling in exquisite pain. The two halves of the cable crash together again, one thrusting inside of the other and fucking its way up until the faces appear together, two dismembered girls kissing themselves into one as they burrow back into the furnace, only to be eaten and extruded again. Another cable begins to split. Megan sees.

"Is it like looking in the mirror," Kelly asks, "or falling into the sun?"

More faces appear in the coils, luscious-lipped, wide-eyed faces screaming in toothless ecstasy: neighborhood girls. Megan mimics them as she kicks back. Kelly holds her tight, pushes her forward. Her hand moves down, under Megan's shorts, working the tender skin. Megan's hands grasp for the doors, then grasp for nothing at all as the rising pleasure slows her down. All those girls, all those wet bone bits…a face stretches out from the mass, blistered tongue snaking along the naked length of Megan's leg. Lisa. Her eyes are melted sockets, her nose pulp, her touch sublime.

"No—" Megan says, but the tongue lengthens, snakes up between fabric and flesh, taking over where Kelly's touch recedes.

"Yes, that's it," Kelly says. Megan grows limp in her arms, and she feels Kelly coaxing her forward, sliding her along the tongue into her place in the machine. "Just a few steps more, and we'll be together, all of us, forever—"

"No, not all of us! Just us, JUST US!" Megan snaps her head back, hitting Kelly's face with a sharp crack. Kelly cries out, a scream as full of pleasure as pain. Still, she loses her grip, and Megan falls free. Bits of shag come up in her hands, needle-hard like slivers of sawed-up bone. She sinks her hands into the putrid muck, clawing her way across the shifting carpet of rotting limbs and clothes back to the stairs.

"I waited for you," she cries over the noise. "It's only supposed to be us, no one else!"

Kelly looks puzzled. The tongue slithers around her leg, resting its tip in the soft black hair. Behind her, the engine of flesh and bone screams. "But it is only us, Megan. There's no one else here, not really. It's only ever been us."

"Liar! They're all here, all of them! Fucking cheater!"

"I can't be here without them. Without them, I won't come, and I won't stay. You can't have it both ways."

"I want it *my* way!" Megan slaps a hand against her chest, leaving a print of dirty brown behind. "I waited for you, and now you have to stay!"

Kelly rolls her eyes. "God, Megan, Lisa was right. You're such a spaz."

Megan crawls up the stairs, back into the quiet den. She rushes through the house to the bathroom, and turns on the tap. She soaks her face and head in the water, picks dirt and flesh from her fingernails and fingernails from her knees. The water pours over her, and she closes her eyes, sleeps for a few peaceful minutes. The sounds of the engine recede. When she wakes up, Megan slicks back her hair and buttons her blouse. The girl in the mirror is clean. She's calm. She's good.

"It's only supposed to be me," she says. "Kelly and me, and no other girls at all." Only after she leaves the house, though, does her reflection agree, nodding in time to the faint pulsing sounds of girls rotting under the house.

"She thinks she's doing bad things," the mirror whispers. The girl-shaped shadow in the basement wanders back and forth among the bits, smiling as it replies.

"That's what I love about her."

SUMMER, 1969

Megan hears the engine the night her older sister runs away from home, just a week after school was let out for the summer. She knows Lisa was angry because Mom and Dad wouldn't let her ride with some hippie college boy in his Volkswagen camper all the way cross-country to the Woodstock concert, even though she's seventeen and thinks she's a woman. Lisa spent that whole week raging against the world, and every night Megan fell asleep to her sister crying in the next room. Like rain, Megan grew used to the sound, and it stopped bothering her. Lisa was mean to her, anyway, and still treated her like a stupid baby even though she'd be thirteen next month. Let her sob, Megan told her pillow. It was only fair—Lisa made her cry too many times to count.

And then, tonight: no crying at all. Megan wakes from a dead sleep, sits straight up, and listens. No rain, not even a wind rustling the trees in the yard. Megan reaches out in the dark, her fingers spreading as if gathering up the night—somehow she can feel her sister's absence, as real and thick as the blanket against her legs. In the distance, the low rev of a car sounds out as it traverses the roads beyond their little Tacoma neighborhood. Megan waits for it

to fade. She lies back on her bed and listens, one hand sliding under her t-shirt and cupping a small breast.

"Lisa's gone," Megan whispers. "I'm the woman now."

The engine's soft hum washes over the house, filling the space that had belonged to Lisa, like a girl-shaped bass and pistoned song of love. It isn't a car engine, but it isn't one of the freight trains running down the coast to the sea. It's closer, deeper, and it doesn't stop. Megan thinks of Kelly, Lisa's best friend, and how angry she'll be that Lisa ran off to Woodstock without her. Kelly's sixteen, but she'll still cry, and Megan will take her into the wooded far corner of the backyard and slip her arms around her, rubbing her hands up and down her soft shivering back until Kelly realizes that Megan is her new best friend. Kelly knew how to French kiss, and had taught all the older girls on their street. Maybe now that Lisa's gone, Kelly will teach Megan, too—out of gratitude, under the evergreens, after the tears are gone and replaced with stars. Megan's other hand creeps into her panties; like the engine, she throbs. She falls asleep that way, to the sounds of her contented sighs and the vibrations of that far-off mystery machine.

Over the following days and weeks, the metallic thrumming never quite goes away, even though no one else seems to hear it. The neighborhood hums with summer life: mowers battling overgrown lawns, basketballs pinging against concrete and wood, stereo music drifting through backyard parties. And yet, Megan still hears it, threading into the low conversations between the adults in the neighborhood, sniffing at everything and everyone. Every early evening after putting dinner in the oven, her mother pours a large glass of whiskey and step out into the front yard for a smoke—Megan watches from the porch as the red dot of Mom's cigarette bobs over to the fence, where Mrs. Crabtree waits with more gossip, a red flame of her own at her Avon-orange lips. Teenage girls are running away from all of the neighborhoods in University Place. Lisa isn't the first, and she won't be the last. They speak the words to each other, and Megan can almost see the vibrations of that distant engine hovering around their lips, licking away at her mother's desire to find her oldest girl. Her mother is cream, Megan decides. They're all warm summer cream in this blacktopped bowl, and something is skimming them away.

Megan has her own routine. Every early evening, she wanders into the front yard, casual and limpid-limbed, and stands at the grassy edge, one hip jutting out as she surveys the small suburban kingdom. From there she sees clusters of boys and girls playing games, wheeling about on bikes, flirting and fighting. They converge and part like swarms of fireflies, fast and hot. Usually she doesn't

see what she's seeking. Tonight, though, at the end of this burning day in July, Megan sees the girl who fires her taboo fantasies, haunts her waking dreams.

Kelly, Queen Kelly of the Cul-de-Sac, leans against the mail box of the empty rambler at the far end of the street. It's the only house on the street that no one lives in, ever since the old woman died a few years back. The FOR SALE sign still dangles from a moldy post, as ignored as the building behind it. Kelly doesn't ignore it, though, and tonight, for once, she doesn't ignore Megan. She raises a hand, beckoning. *Come here,* she mouths, as she balances a cigarette on her wide red mouth. Megan's heart beats faster, and ozone fills the air. The engine's sounds lap at her lips, and everything turns faster, brighter.

"Me?" Megan chokes out as she takes a few stumbling steps toward the slender-hipped girl. Most of the older girls in the neighborhood smoke, stealing Virginia Slims from their mother's purses and lighting up in secret along the sides of houses. Kelly smokes in full view of all the parents and kids. But her light brown skin burns with a smoky sheen all its own, and short black hair frames her face in a thunderstorm of curls, curls that caress sharp features as she nods. *Yes.* Megan's stomach cramps in nervous anticipation. Her dream moment, just like she imagined. Maybe they'll sneak into the house. Maybe they'll be alone. Images of naked flesh wash over her, bodies filling the rambler's rooms with wet little sighs and sounds, and her legs buckle. Megan pushes the thought away, hard. No one can know, not even the girl of her dreams.

"You stand at the edge of your yard every day," Kelly says as Megan draws near. "Looking for something?"

"Yeah." Megan stares up at the trees, nonchalant. "Maybe."

"Looking for Lisa."

Megan shrugs. "Maybe."

"Maybe. Hmm." Kelly leans forward, and Megan catches scents of Jean Naté and sweat. "Got a light, kid?"

"No. I don't smoke."

Kelly steps away from the mail box, and raises her hand. "Didn't you see me, you freak? I said come here!"

Megan turns: further up the street, Julie Miller stands, flicking a lighter on and off, a curious smile at her lips. An ice-water anger sieves through Megan's chest. Kelly hadn't been calling out to her. Julie struts forward, flicking the light in time to the engine's heated throb, as if she hears it, too.

"That's ok, kid," Kelly says, as gold-haired Julie moves in, pliant supplicant to all of Kelly's needs. "Someday you will."

"Will what?"

"Smoke. Hope I'm there to watch. Know what I mean?"

Julie raises the light, and Kelly breathes the flame in. She glances up at Megan, winks, and grins. Megan reels, sees: hot burning blood and smoking bone, dismembered limbs whirling in an oily gyre. Behind Kelly and Julie, the windows of the rambler catch the final burnt oranges of the day, throwing light across the tangled yard as though someone inside had set the rooms to flame. Blood pounds in Megan's ears, and the engine reverberates in determined time. Under her naked feet, the pavement shivers. *Not enough*, Megan says to herself as she backs away. Watching Kelly, feeling what she feels—it isn't enough. She *will* have this girl, somehow, someway, someday.

And for one wild moment, a delicious and horrible sense of déjà vu washes over Megan, heady as the scent of gasoline. She's stood in front of this house, this girl, a million times before. No matter where she chases life to its lonely end, she'll find this moment again, this fierce and glorious desire.

Jetsam

"The part of a ship, its equipment, or its cargo that is cast overboard to lighten the load in time of distress and that sinks or is washed ashore."

I'm writing this down because I'm starting to forget. I may need to remember some day. The chemical air is already kissing my mind, biting my memory away. Something terrible happened at work today. Beyond imagining....

Jay stops reading the worn fragment of paper, and looks up. "I don't remember writing this. Where did you find this, again?" She speaks to the young man behind the counter, who's examining the creases of a jacket flap. His glasses slide down his nose as he stops to pull a book out of the thick stack on the counter.

"It was stuck in this one." The man holds up a worn copy of a short story anthology. It is one of about twenty books Jay has lugged into the used bookstore to sell.

"Oh. I though I searched all of them." Jay takes the book from him. It is old, as thick as a tombstone. Her hand trembles from the weight. "Wait. This book doesn't look familiar—are you sure it's mine?"

"It was in the box with the others. The paper was stuck behind the jacket flap. That's why I like to go through everything before you leave the store. Thought you might want it back."

"Thanks," says Jay, and walks away from the counter. She sits down on a worn upholstered chair and turns the paper over in her fingers. One side is crammed with writing, and the other is affixed with a single name tag, a sticker with a smeared red mark on it. She recognizes her writing. But she doesn't recall writing the words.

It was so still after all the previous commotion, as if the traffic and people had bled off the edges of the city. Emptiness, everywhere. Only smoke plumes in the sky, coiling like worms.

What day was this? What date? Nothing on the paper gives it away. Annoyed, Jay lets it drop to her lap. At the top of the torn edge, the name of the old publishing company she worked for stands out in crisp block letters. It's surely the thought of her former job that sends little shivers of distress sparking up her spine, and nothing else. That's what she tells herself.

"A lot of books from the same company," the man calls out. He is still methodically examining her offerings. "You're in publishing, right? I can usually tell."

"Not anymore," Jay says. "I work in finance now. Better pay."

Jay runs her finger along the jagged edge of the paper. She's really only told part of the truth. She didn't leave the company. The company left her.

"Didn't like the job, eh?"

"Didn't have a choice. They left the city," she replies. "The attacks. Some people jumped ship. You know."

The man is respectfully silent.

Everyone was in their offices, all cramming things into boxes, or staring numbly out the windows into space. Like I was.

The company did more than jump ship. It vanished. Jay and a few employees—the ones who hadn't been warned—traveled into the city one morning to find the building as empty of life as the smoldering ruins on the tip of the island. Whispers on the street said they'd fled to another country, leaving behind the detritus of their long history: piles of old books, unread manuscripts, and discarded employees. Just as devastating, in its own way.

"I have your total." The man holds another slip of paper, the credit for the books. "This is how much we'll give you in books, or you can take half that amount in cash. You can use it now or later—just don't lose it."

Jay takes the cash. Not much, as always, but it doesn't matter. Relief is the only payment she needs—relief that there is a little less crowding around her, a little less intrusion on her life. She needs to know that at home, at night, she has some space to think and breathe.

"Thanks. I'll come back next Saturday with the last load." Jay grabs her metal shopping cart and heads for the door. As she picks her way through dusty stacks, she shoves the receipt into her pocket. She stares at the fragment one more time, then slides it in as well.

> *From my office, I watched the apartment building across the street. Some windows were lit up in the rainy gloom like soft yellow candles, others were dark and tomb-like. Most had pale curtains drawn across the glass.*

As she walks back home, Jay sees herself reflected over and over again in dark storefront windows. In one tall pane of glass, a ghostly woman walks beside her whose face still flirts with middle age while her body has fully embraced it. In another she is thin and chic, a woman of the City, proudly urban in her clothing and demeanor. In a third pane, she's little more than a wraith. But her face remains the same in all those reflections: there's a furrow nestling between her eyes, a deep line of fear bisecting her brow. The sight of it shocks Jay. She hasn't seen that look on her face for almost five years.

That's how long ago her old life ended, how long she's kept herself from dwelling on her past. No reason to remember, Jay tells herself. It's over. But even now, part of her still wonders why the company left without a trace, while another part secretly rejoices that she escaped something worse than what had been intended for her. *What had been intended...?*

As she rounds the corner, her apartment building slides into view. It is thick and solid, comfortably utilitarian. From across the street her living room window is just one of many black rectangles, indistinguishable from the others. It doesn't have a view of the city skyline—she blocked it off years ago. She has no desire to see where she's been.

> *To the left of the building a massive clock tower rose like a cream-colored phallus, laced with delicate scaffolding from base to tip.*

The clock, the time—it was the last day she'd gone to work in the city, that was it. She'd been late. Only a week since the attack, and smoke still billowed in toxic sheets over the lower part of the island. Chemicals and flesh—the dead settled in their mouths and lungs. Jay hadn't wanted to step outside. But bills had to be paid. So she'd reluctantly crept down into the subway, taking her place within the throng of silent commuters. And when she emerged from the

underground, when she saw the company's triangular building, saw the dun of the sky—

No. She does not want to remember. To her right sits a battered trash can. Through the iron mesh, magazine covers press against thick seeping paper bags, sodden bricks of newspapers, strange dribblings of food. The fragment is a tight ball in her hand. It's only trash. But her fingers can't release it. She stares at the crumpled paper as it unfolds, an image blossoming in her mind…

Broken things pressing against each other, faces and bricks all jumbled into one terrible mass…. And a word—no. A single letter. Everywhere she had turned that morning long ago, she had seen that strange mark.

Jay crosses the street in quick steps. She pushes the shopping cart into the building courtyard, past the molding statue and stunted trees, toward her entrance. She stops to take out her keys, and the ball in her hand flattens out suddenly as her fingers work the paper open. It's a compulsion she cannot control.

> Between the buildings two inky smears of clouds slowly passed. They lingered briefly in the space before drifting toward the open square, as if surveying and cataloging the sodden masses below. If only I'd known—

She saw something that day. Not clouds, not smoke, not the ashes of her friends. Something *moved*….

Jay stands at the edge of the entrance, her body rigid. Her eyes slide up to the tops of the building and beyond, looking for the edges of the city, reassuring herself that she cannot see it. That it cannot see her. She runs her tongue around her mouth. It tastes as if something foul has just moved through her. There is more than the memory of ash in her mouth. She tastes *marked*.

The door swings out behind her.

"Could you—" says the janitor, and Jay grabs the door as he wheels his cart out. He gestures to the gaping mouth of plastic.

"Trash?"

Jay looks down at the fragment. "No. Thanks." She shoves it into her pocket.

"No books today? That's a first." The man smiles pleasantly at her. Jay sidles past him into the empty hallway.

"Not today. I've read enough already." She drags her cart up to the seventh floor.

> Giant bins of trash surrounded the building—the last remnants of the publishing company. Just twenty minutes ago, men were walking from bin to bin, red paintbrushes in their hands, marking them for removal.

Jay presses her back against the bolted door. The solid slab of painted metal makes her feel safe. Before her a cool and empty living room sits in silence. The lack of furniture and decoration comforts her profoundly. Owning nothing means nothing can be taken or thrown away, nothing can be forgotten.

She examines the sticker more closely. "**MY NAME IS**" borders the top in thick letters. The white space below is stained red, smeared and slightly cracked. Jay cocks her head slightly as she tries to interpret it. The original mark is lost to her. All that's left is on the paper.

Dropping her coat to the floor, Jay walks to a large, empty bookcase and pulls it aside with a groan. Behind the case, a grimy window looks out on the quiet street, the buildings, the sky. Breathing hard, Jay presses a finger to the glass, then, as if writing a secret language, slowly traces the tops of the buildings as they sprawl across the horizon.

The creeping skyline of this city both fascinates and repels her. No matter where she looks, the sky seems to stop at the rooftops—and there is a space, a thin crack where reality does not quite knit together. She imagines something pulsating at the edge, watching and waiting. Waiting for a sign, a mark.

Workers clustered in small groups, whispering fearful gossip back and forth. During the night a thousand companies fled. We had been abandoned.

"If I get rid of this, there won't be anything left of that day. Not even my memories. But you can't take things I don't have," Jay whispers. Her hand curls around the paper, crushing it neatly. "You can't take nothing."

A woman with a clipboard was shouting. "Proceed to your floor and pack your belongings—"

Her hand uncurls. It's no use. She still has the fragment. And now: trickles of memory, staining her soul like drops of blood in water. *Still marked*, she tells her reflection in the glass.

"—nothing will be left behind."

The sky looms overhead like a bowl of metal riveted to the edges of the earth.

Jay stands in the middle of an empty street, before her old employer's building. Beyond it, the island stretches out in one festering sweep of land. In five years, the corruption of the attack has spread outward and up the blocks. Now only smoldering piles of metal dot the landscape. Nothing whole remains, except the strangely triangulated building before her—a stone ship caught in a scoria sea.

A low boom catches her attention: in the distance a colossal wall, one hundred stories high, slices the island in half like a surgical scar. Rooftops of still-healthy buildings are visible over the top, while, at the base, tiny figures scurry back and forth in the thunder and wake of ponderous machines. Below, subways gag on hardening concrete. Jay had to bribe a man at the borough docks to ferry her across the water to the island. There was no other way in.

"Why not you?" Jay asks her old building. It cannot be coincidence that it alone remains. Rows of windows grin at her like blackened teeth, revealing nothing. Pink stains the worn stone. Some brighter color once ran down its sides, then faded with time. Jay's fingers grasp the wrinkled paper.

> *The woman slapped a name tag on my coat while a man shoved an empty cardboard box into my arms. "You have fifteen minutes to get to your floor," he said. "Put your personal items in this, and wait in your office to be escorted out." As I made my way through the lobby, my fingers slid over the tag. They came away red.*

She picks her way past the rounded tip of the building and tries the lobby door. After a few pulls on the handle, it swings open. The landscape behind her reflects as wavering ribbons in the thick glass and brass. Jay looks back over her shoulder.

Two dark grey clouds float along the eastern shore. They creep over the rubble as if they are snuffling and rooting their way inland. Jay slips into the building and pulls the door firmly shut, then presses her face against the glass. One cloud rises slowly, thinning out as it catches the sluggish wind. The other pulses slightly—the ruins beneath it shift.

Jay backs into the lobby until darkness envelops her. More drops of memory trickle through her. Outside, the grey mass of air spreads itself farther out and up, until it is beyond her vision.

At the far end of the lobby, beyond the elevator banks, there is an open door to a brown stairwell. Jay hesitates, listening for any sound. After a moment of silence, she begins to climb. Her footfalls sound distant, as though her body is walking somewhere she can't yet see. She knows something terrible happened that day, to everyone who entered the building. Somehow, she escaped so thoroughly that she even escaped the remembering of it. Her bones remember, though.

My floor was a wreck. I picked my way through broken furniture, crushed bookcases. Dust choked the air. And everywhere, papers and books crammed in boxes, all marked with the same red paint. The same letter.

The water fountain is dry. Jay clenches her jaw, and air shoots out of her nostrils in tortured bursts. Fourteen floors—twenty-eight small flights of steps. A quick glance to the glass doors of the old office space: the glass doors are open slightly, one large crack running down the right side. Beyond lies empty office space.

Jay walks through the doors into the reception area. The silence is profound. As she makes her way down the narrow hall, Jay marvels at how stripped and spare it all is. No boxes or books anywhere, no furniture, no light fixtures. She moves through bands of muted light and shadow—even the blinds were removed. As she passes each office, she glances at the sky.

At the thinnest end of the building is her little nook. It's not really an office, just a space made out of bookcases and file cabinets. Jay stops before the opening. Her desk is gone, but two thick indentations mark the carpet where it once rested. She steps in and runs the toe of her shoe along the groove, then turns to the bookcase, placing her back to the window.

I packed my box in minutes, then sat on the desk and pulled the name tag off. It stuck to my fingers as I held it to the light. What did this red mark mean? As I lowered it, a movement caught my eye. I glanced out the window.

She swivels around and stares at out the window. Five years ago, clouds had reflected off glass buildings, cold and clean.

The sun shifted, and light threw red reflections across the glass. I watched the color intensify in waves—red sunset in midday. And then....

"I saw," Jay says, although the words mean nothing. She still can't remember. "I saw."

That's when I realized what it was. What I had become.

Jay imagines herself five years ago, suspended in cold air, mouth open and slack, eyes huge with the sleepy pull of the clouds as they drift from left to right. She imagines pulling the layer of past over the present, moving one grey sky onto another, matching the clouds one by one....

> *I saw*
> *I don't remember the name*
> *remember remember*

But she cannot, and there is nothing more on the paper to help. The last sentence ends in an illegible scrawl of repeated pencil marks, smudged beyond recognition. She squints at the last word, larger than the rest, in the darkening light, then frowns. The letters are barely distinguishable, but still. It looks like her name.

Jay rubs her eyes. She has no idea what happened that last afternoon. But does it really matter? Will it change anything? She came here for an epiphany, for understanding and resolution. There is none. She has a new life now. Everything else is trash. It will only drag her down if she clings to it. She crumples the fragment into a ball and throws it against the window with a papery ping. Her eyes continue up to the top of the frame.

A wet red line oozes down the glass.

Everything fades and falls away, except for the line, suspended between her and the sky. It grows thicker as it descends, as if an invisible hand is marking where she stands. Another line joins it, and a third. The buzz of blood and fear nips at the back of her neck and down her spine, until her body flushes it out in a thin stream of urine. Behind the red line, the horizon grins wide, hiccups, then splits.

"I knew," Jay says. "I knew."

Where the sky has stopped short at the edges of the horizon, hundreds of cloud-like creatures blossom and spill forth like sea anemones expanding to catch the currents. One cloud darts forward shockingly fast. The blunt end expands. Ropey spirals of wet flesh unfurl and catch the rotting ruins, suckling them up.

"Were you waiting for me?" The words barely pass her lips. Jay sees giant chunks of buildings work their way through the tubes into churning pockets. Sides bulge outward; bodies expand and adjust. They fan out across the island. The largest stretches leisurely and shoots out toward the building.

"Yes," Jay says to the floating beast, "I think you were."

Red explodes across the glass. Jay leaps back into the hall. Moving in slow strides toward her are figures in white biohazard suits. She backs up into the final office, all the way to its very end, to the prow of the building; she's trapped. The window is painted shut. Below she sees more men in suits move an undulating hose back and forth. Red bursts forth from it like fire, dancing intricately around the coils, forming the mark they once had five years ago.

"Stop! I'm still in here!" She pounds on the window, but they can't hear. Above, the creature pulses, and tiny veins of lightning run down its sides. Something slides around inside the mass, bending the grey flesh without breaking: the tip of the old clock tower. She punches the glass, ignoring the blood and pain.

"Turn her around!"

Figures grab her from both sides and pin her arms against the walls, while a third holds up a clipboard. An electric voice pours out of a black faceplate.

"Is this you?" He thrusts the clipboard into her face. One thick finger points at a word on the page.

"No." Her voice is firm over the rising wind, with only a tinge of panic. They will listen to reason, she tells herself—they have to. "That's not my name, there's been a mistake. Please get me out of here."

"I didn't ask if this was your name. You don't have one! This is you, right?"

"No! That isn't me. I told you. I have a name!"

"What are you, then?" The man raises his voice. "Come on! I don't got all day—tell me what you are! What's your 'name'?"

Jay's face hardens.

"My name is—my name—"

I'm writing this down because I'm starting to forget, I may need to remember someday.

Her name. She cannot remember her name.

"My name is Jay?" she asks.

"Hey, wadda ya know? That's what this says." Even with the creature growling outside, she hears their laughter float through the room.

"She's the last of the trash, boys—let's do it."

Someone steps forward with a small machine and presses it against her right arm. Shafts of metal tear through the bone and flesh, impaling her to the stone wall. Her head snaps back against the glass, and the window finally breaks. Too late.

Gloved hands rip open her blouse, and another machine appears. Thin lines of light embroider her skin, searing through the flesh. Someone is screaming—is it her?

"Yeah, she won't escape this time." More laughter.

The entire building shudders. Everyone falls silent and looks up at the ceiling. From above, there is a crackling, then a thunderous roar of ripping stone and metal.

"It's started—everyone out!" The figures grab their equipment, jostling with each other to be the first from the room.

"Why?" Her howl bounces off their backs. "Why are you doing this? What's happening?"

From above a second wave of destruction pounds down through the building. The man with the clipboard looks back at her but doesn't stop moving for the door.

"Nothing personal, lady. I'm just the garbage man."

He turns and runs.

Vibrations burrow deep in her bones—they travel up from the stone and through the metal pins. Bits of ceiling break away. With a waterfall of sound, everything around her rises. Something smashes against her side, then rips away. Jay no longer feels her right arm. She no longer feels. She stares up into the sky. There is no sky, only the pulsing grey. Membrane and ridges curl back to reveal a mouth as wide and long as her blood-stained eyes can see.

"This isn't my name." She wants to point to the mark but cannot move. "I'm Jay. I'm Jay—" She lets out a small sob, almost a laugh, as the weight of her name drags it downward. It seeps through the skin, nestles into her soul.

Jay is a letter. It is the *mark*. It is not her name.

The grey sky inhales, and she rises.

Jay is a traveler now, squeezed through tubes and shunted from one contraction to the next. Shapes flood her eyes and graze her skin: bones, granite faces, bits of carved railing and brass fixtures.

Trash.

Flashes of light ripple across her vision—the grey membranes holding her become translucent as they rise. Below, she sees another creature move in to finish the job. It spreads great sails of skin and strands of flesh as it rides an unseen current. Jay would sigh at the terrible beauty of it if she were able to breathe.

Now they skim in silence over the top of the massive wall. The rest of the city appears, healthy and alive. Jay's severed right arm lies slightly below her—spires of steel sift between the fingers. She sees the city, a slow-moving river of rooftop gardens and secret alcoves, silver windows and neon smears, resting like the body of a lover, safe in sleep. For now. One calm moment of beauty, worth the price of Jay's pain.

The creature tilts. Trash rumbles about her as Jay is thrust forward through hooked membranes. Mucus uncoils from her throat. Everything shifts. Jay plummets into darkness like a blood-tipped comet, the remnants of the building her silky-stoned tail.

Nothing is left behind.

My name—

"What are you looking for?"

Jay looks up at the sound of the boy's voice. She is unaccustomed to being spoken to, unaccustomed to anything other than the sound of her hand sifting, sorting, pushing aside, and breaking. She pulls a cardboard box to her side, and opens her mouth. But the words fail her, as always. If she could just find the fragment, she might remember what to say....

The boy steps back and watches as Jay shoves her hair back from her face and stares into the valley. Jumbles of skyscrapers fill deep pockets in the land, separated only by occasional trickles of rivers and accidental bridges. Up where they are, blind horses canter down cracked streets with deformed dogs nipping at their sides. Here, potter's fields and wooden shanties cling despondently to each other, and the people do the same. Perhaps they are afraid if they let go, they will drift away. From where she stands, she sees no difference between the brown of earth or sky. There is no up or down in the universe's midden.

Jay and the boy both crouch as a wind rises. Heaps of trash stir and hitch around them, great stinking piles of garbage—old toys and dishes, broken lamps, bits of magazines, clothes. It is their history. It is everything they ever jettisoned in life, before life jettisoned them. Her box is full of paper. She reaches inside with long, dirty fingers. They curl around like dark worms. Papers crumble. If she could only find a fragment, a piece, a certain word.... She doesn't remember. She only remembers the wind and the search, and that sometimes the sky will open up and vomit more broken memories across the land.

"What's your name?"

My name—

The boy is speaking again. She tries, tries to mold the feelings up out of that festering sore in her chest, to trick it from the darkness in her mind. Her fingers creep, searching for inky triggers. But they find nothing, and the only word that comes out is the only word she knows. It cracks open her mouth and hovers before them, then floats away in the filthy wind, nothing more than what it is—which is everything around it, everything she has ever been.

"Jetsam."

The Four Hundred Thousand

I stand on the balcony outside my parent's cinder-block apartment, watching contrails drift apart in slate skies. My left hand grips a just-delivered letter, crushes it. I can't help it, the tracking device that the officer has shot into my hand makes it impossible to uncurl my fingers just yet. It burns.

By direction of the President…the following personnel are ordered to active duty…on that date, the named will proceed to ███████████ *Military Facilities for the retrieval of said personnel out of Jet Oberaan(yr-15)/ovaries-2:*

In the living room, a printout of number and letter combinations sits on the couch: four hundred thousand, one name for each egg follicle inside me, one name for each potential soldier. I'd stopped reading after the fourth page—there are one hundred and nine pages more. By my calculations, and the doctors' latest report, I'm twenty-six healthy divisions full of death to our enemy. No surprise I've been called. I always sort of knew. I just thought I had more time. I have five days.

Inside, Mom still shouts with joy. She's been waiting for this moment since the day I started my period, when she dragged me to the registration office. She'd said if I got picked, we'd all get rich. A credit for every vat-grown baby forced into adult soldierhood within a year of conception, a credit for every soldier shipped into space, with a bonus if they were modified. Then I'd have a room of my own instead of sleeping on the couch, and Mom could buy us real food. Dad could get a new heart, which they couldn't afford because all the money from

Mom's factory salary was going to me—for pills to jump-start all the plumbing and for doctor's fingers poking inside me every six months, from the time I turned five. It was my fault he didn't have the right pills or the right heart. That's what Mom said. Of course I signed, the day my period started. I didn't know any better. I was nine.

My neighbors across the way are staring at me. Faces peer out from a grimy square of glass, barely large enough to see out of. They're surprised I'm out here—there's not much of anything to see. Their balconies are the same as ours, the same grey concrete and steel. If I stood on the railing and jumped, I could almost reach them. To my right and left, hundred-story high apartment buildings sit in rows, bits of laundry fluttering from tiny open windows. Eighty stories below, a neon-lined strip of street glows in shadow. I've walked for miles and never seen the end of our street, never seen the end of this metal canyon, the beginning of somewhere else. Somewhere up above me, a war is being fought, has been fought for as long as anyone remembers. My made-to-military-specification sons and daughters will cram themselves into ships, soar past the curve of the planet. Will they crowd the windows, stare at the dwindling city before space and time swallow them whole? Will they see the end of my street before I do? Probably.

It's so quiet out. I pull the oxiclamp from my nose and sniff the air. Metal and fuel.

Building by building, row by row, lights flicker and wink out. Airbase sirens sound through the chilly air. The city sobs. The latest corps are about to launch—little more than one hundred thousand in all. Rumor has it, something terrible happened with the deep space travel modifications to the last draft. They had to destroy half the crop. And the last two female draftees disappeared—ran away, or killed themselves. That's why they needed me so soon, I bet. I stare at my hand. Under the brown skin, a dot of garnet winks at me as it burrows deeper. No one's taking chances this time.

"Jet, get inside." Mom reaches out from the doorway, plucking at my sleeve. I go in and lock the door behind me, sealing it airtight. Mom bangs the thick steel shutter over the window. Everything has to be protected. The burn-off of battle cruisers floats through the air for days, bright cinders of liquid fire, beautiful and deadly. Sometimes it burns right through the walls. I grab my pack off the couch, fastening it to thick rubber straps at my side. Everything I need to survive is in it: food and ammunition, credits and bullets, tampons and hemlock. For barter, or for use.

"What about the list? Jet, take the list!" Mom struggles with her own pack, trembling hands snapping the locks into place. It's hard to see anything in the garnet glow of the single emergency light over the door.

"It's too big, I only need the letter."

"Put that away, and get the list! It's military property, we need to bring it with us when you go to the hospital."

"No, we don't!" Mom never listens to me. She rips her pack off and opens it, trying to cram all the paper inside. The hall alarms kick in, and we wince. My earplugs are somewhere in my pockets. We have two minutes to get to the inner stairwells.

"Mada, we don't need the list," Dad shouts from the bedroom doorway. His pack is crammed with plastic bottles: heart pills, all my vitamins and supplements. I see how his hand presses against his body. I recognize the stance. He's holding a knife.

"Dad, I won't need those anymore." I hold out my hands to take the pills. "Not after next week."

Dad stares at me, open-mouthed. He hasn't thought about it. None of us really have, until this moment. We're so used to doing the same things, over and over again. Now it's all changed. He shakes his head, no. He stares at my winking wrist. I say nothing.

The building trembles.

"She's right, Essam." Mom looks up from her pack, pulls loose strands of her hair away from her shiny face. The air is getting hotter. Or maybe she's been crying. I realize I don't know how old she is. Mom could be close to fifty, or no more than thirty. She stands up, the pack slipping to the floor. Behind us, the safety override on the front door clicks on. We're in here for good now, for at least a day. One less day of freedom left for me.

I press my hands against my body. Everything depends on two small, soft sacs of flesh and all that they hold inside. The vibrations of the battle cruisers crawl up my legs as their engines reach full power. I wonder if the egg follicles feel it, wonder if my children will crowd the curved walls of the ships a year from now, remembering that they first felt that thunderous power from within their mother's flesh.

"If I went through all this for nothing," I scream over the noise, "I swear I'll—"

"I'm sorry, I'm so sorry." Mom's face crumples as she speaks, and I feel my heart stopping. "I didn't mean to— I wasn't thinking. I'm so tired. I'm just so tired of this, this life. I only wanted us to be happy. That's why I did it." She

stretches out her arms, so thin in the black fabric of her unisuit, and I reach out mine. But she walks into Dad's embrace. She wasn't talking to me.

I fit my earplugs in, adjust the clamp at my nose, making sure the oxygen still flows. Lift-off: the engine scream hits us, and we drop in the hot air. They built the airbase a few years ago, less than half a mile away. No one bothered to relocate us. There isn't anywhere else to send an entire ghetto to.

Dad lifts me up, carries me to the bedroom. As he lowers me to the bed, his fingers press against my flesh, trapping the tracking device before it sinks any further inside. The blade lowers, presses against the veins.

You can't. I see his lips form the words in the red-tinged darkness. *There is no war. You'll be murdering your children.* I've heard his lies before, but still I freeze. He waits for me to nod my head, yes or no. Mom's hands reach out, grabbing him, grabbing me. We lie in a huddle on the thin mattress, our hands clasped in a circle, waiting for my answer. Engine after engine roars into the air. It's raining black and red now, pocking the metal balcony doors with burn marks. The walls hiss. Despite the noise, I hear Dad's heart, or think I can—the soft fluttering of something that's been dying for years. We're all dying, I realize. It will always be this way, for us. But it doesn't have to be this way for my children. And despite the noise, I know they both hear me when I scream over and over until I almost pass out from the roar and heat of my own anger, *yes I'll do it yes I'll go yes I'll give them up yes I'll save us all—*

Only then does Dad let go of the knife, and my wrist. The garnet dot disappears. He never wanted this for me. He'd say anything, any lie, to stop me. He just wants us all to let go, to stop making soldiers and guns, to lay down and let them come, let them bring death, or bring peace. Anything other than this life. But it's too late. It was too late the day I turned nine, the day I signed. Mom falls back on the bed and smiles. I close my eyes and hold him. He cries.

Outside, battleships rise and burning fuel falls.

Mom sits at the kitchen table, under the dim light of the bulb, carefully turning the pages of a pamphlet. The pages are glossy and stiff, crowded with fancy writing and bright photos of apartment buildings covered in sheets of light blue glass. I bet the people who live in those places have never seen their stairwells.

Dad sleeps in the bedroom. It's been a few hours since lockdown ended, and after thirty-six hours in the stifling apartment, burning debris pounding against the outside walls, you'd think we'd want to be anywhere except here. But there's nowhere else to go.

"We're out of food." I stare into the metal cupboard. All I see is half a tin of crackers, and two cans of soup. Dad may get hungry later on, so I shouldn't eat them. For once, I can go without.

"Then go downstairs. Take Essam's prescription with you."

"Do you want anything?" I stand in front of the table. Mom doesn't look at me. She pushes her hair behind her ears as she turns another page. I sigh. She looks up, annoyed.

"What do you want, Jet? Do you want me to tell you to be careful? It won't matter what I say. You never listen to me."

She stares down at the pamphlet again, then picks up a pencil and draws a circle around an apartment floor plan.

"I've never understood why you hate me so much." My tongue feels dry and swollen in my mouth, and the words are hard to pronounce.

Mom doesn't look up. "I don't hate you. I'm tired of you."

At the end of the hall, half a block down from our door, I push the swinging door into the eightieth floor communal bath.

The air smells of mold and disinfectant, sloughed-off skin.

Steam rises in thin wisps from a single nozzle—Thabit stands under a stream of light brown water. I slip off my unisuit and pad across cracked tiles to the next nozzle.

"You look lovely," says Thabit as he points to my red nose and bloodshot eyes. "Heard you spent lockdown in your apartment. You missed Solomon bugging out in the stairwell. Took four shots to take him down."

"The stairwell's for pussies," I say, pushing at a small soap dispenser on the wall, then activating the shower head with the circuits in my wrist—wiring given to each occupant of our building. The water is hot, but there won't be much. The timer is ticking, I have three minutes to find some semblance of clean. Thabit's shower shuts off, and he shakes the water off his long pale hair onto my face.

"You love living on the edge, don't you?"

"I don't live on the edge. I *am* the edge." We laugh. It's our old saying, our old routine. Stupid, but it belongs to us.

"Draft girl!" Thabit's sister Badra emerges from a toilet stall, naked and smiling. Her spiked white hair glistens with traces of soap. She pulls on her suit, fastening hooks and clamps, sliding weapons back into place. Badra was my first, and then I was with her twin brother, who was just as gentle and cautious—because of the draft and the doctors, there are things I still can't do. Thabit and Badra are cool with that. They're two years older, but we've always gotten along. We're family. As soon as I turn sixteen, we'll make it permanent.

"It's no big deal." I point my head into the stream, let the water push the soap out of the stubble of my black hair. Dad buzzed me last week. No hair is ugly, but easier. "How did you find out? I haven't told anyone."

"Your mother made sure everyone knew the second the doors unlocked." Thabit says the words lightly, but I wince. Already, she's dividing us from the rest of the floor.

"Sorry," I mutter.

"I have to go downstairs, get some food, fill some orders. Are you with me?" Badra locks her gun into place. There used to be minimarts on every floor, but when the elevators stopped working last year, they shut down. Now every trip to the street and back is an exercise in planned pain, especially for those higher up. Badra is paid to shop for others, for things on the market and off.

"Yeah. I need to get my father's prescription refilled anyway. But I have to be back by tomorrow. In three days—" The water shuts off. I stand, naked and shivering, hands clasped against my breasts. Three more days before a knife splits my skin, and the four hundred thousand report for duty. Thabit and Badra stare at me. I feel bad. They have no idea what to say. Neither do I.

Two more people wander into the bathroom, adults from the other side of the hall. They're trying not to stare. Everyone knows. Badra stands up, hand on weapon, a sweet smile on her face. They walk to the benches on the other side of the room, acting like nothing's changed. Thabit throws me his damp towel as I step off the wet tiles. "We'll get you back by morning, no worries," he says.

An hour later, we walk outside. I try not to gag as I turn my oxygen feed on. The air is soupy down here, rancid garbage, urine and human sweat mixed with the unyielding tang of soot and gasoline. No one looks at each other. Everyone rushes along, anxious to get their things, to get home, to stay alive one more day. I stare down the street. The neon-tipped end disappears in the rows of buildings, as always. I don't know what I expect this time—perhaps that the horizon will open to me because it knows that I've changed. I just want to know where it is my soldiers will be going, what they'll see.

Someone jostles me as they push by, and I reach for my arm blade, ready to give them a little "lesson nick." Thabit's hand stills me. He shakes his head. He's the calm one. If Badra had seen, there'd already be blood hitting the sidewalk. I frown, but stand down. Thabit's right, of course. He's seen what Badra hasn't yet, what I realized twenty flights down. In the shadow of signs and storefronts, two soldiers in civilian unisuits stand, nonchalant in pose but aware at all times of who they guard, and how many. They're letting me know I'm surrounded. Safe.

Thunder rolls through the canyon. I look up. Light flashes in thick clouds. As the first dirty drops of rain hit my cheeks, Badra grabs my arm and spins me off the sidewalk, into the shops and bazaars making up the first floor of the block. Most stores are shuttered, out of business for good. We wander poorly-lit corridors, listening to the distant boom of the storm. Badra picks out square packs of food, slips them into a mesh bag at her side as she swipes the credit bar on her sleeve. She doesn't steal. No one does. I'd shoot her myself if she dared.

"The prescription." I remember the disk in my pocket. "I should go ahead, the lines will be long."

"I still have a list of people to shop for," Badra says to Thabit. "I'm going to be a while. Go with her," He nods, and we walk together out of the store, his hand resting lightly against my waist.

"So soon," he finally says. I was wondering when the subject would come up. I've been dreading it ever since I got my orders.

"I'm old enough. We knew it would happen sooner or later."

"Sometimes, I hoped—" Thabit doesn't finish that sentence, but I know how much he wants children. I know what he wanted to say.

"Do you know who's been drafted to fertilize the eggs?" Thabit stops at a kiosk, running his fingers through loops of brightly-colored plastic tubing for oxygen masks. I can tell he didn't want to ask.

"They won't tell me. I don't think I get to know."

"So it could be anyone. Someone you already met, or a complete stranger."

He doesn't know what I do, that soldiers sent into space don't look like us, that they're monsters. Half human, modified into half something else. "It's not like I'm getting married. It's just an operation. They pick parents for compatibility, nothing else. I'll still belong to you two." I touch the dingy grey tubes snaking out of my nose clamp, then lift bright red strands from the pile and hold them against my face.

"How's this?"

Thabit laughs.

"You'll look like your nose is bleeding."

I drop them back down. The man in the kiosk glares, but says nothing.

"A daughter." Thabit pushes his goggles into his white hair. Pristine circles of skin surround his blue eyes, untouched by the gritty air. "That's what I'd like. I want to be the father of the daughter of divisions. A girl just like you. You are going to ask them, right? Ask them to hold back an egg?"

I imagine holding something small and squealing as it's pulled from my flesh. Will it look like Thabit, or its space-bound brothers and sisters? Guns for hands? Will it even have a face? My stomach turns.

"We've talked about this before," I say. "You know I don't know if I want my own baby. I still haven't thought about it."

"Well, it's time you *do* think about it. If we're going to be together, if we're going to be a real family, we have to decide together, and soon. In two days, there won't be any more time."

"I told you I haven't decided, so back off!" My voice echoes off the exposed ceiling pipes. Thabit blanches, but he doesn't back down. He takes me by the arm, leads me around the corner to a dead-end. The lights are low here, no one else is around. The soldiers, always discreet, are nowhere to be seen.

"I'm sorry, Jet," Thabit say, "I know this is rough for you, but you don't have the right to yell at me or command me. I've done nothing wrong. I deserve better than this."

Angry and ashamed, I nod my head. He's right—but he's also not. He has no idea what I'm going through. No one does, not even me.

"You also don't have the right to decide for us, even if it's by not deciding at all," he continues. "We're supposed to be together. You know, I'll never get the chance to choose how many children I get to have with you, or when I can have them. Something's been taken away from me, too. I'm just saying, we all have to deal with this. Me and Badra both, as well as you."

"I know." The muscles in my face stiffen as I try not to cry. "You're right. I shouldn't have freaked. I'm sorry." I sound just like Mom. Thabit pulls me close, holds me.

"I know you're frightened. But we'll get through this. This is what families do, we get through things together."

My body feels unbalanced, swollen. I don't want him to touch me. I pull away, staring into his face as I speak.

"I'll find out about having my own baby, I promise. If I'm allowed, I'll have an egg set aside and frozen. Then we can make a decision later. No matter what happens, the three of us will decide. I promise."

"You're not alone. Don't forget that." Thabit kisses my forehead, then my lips. I feel bad for him, for us, but I don't know what else to do. Badra's voice crackles softly, and Thabit breaks off, speaks softly into his headset. "Yeah, we're still in line for her dad's medicine. We'll be about—fifteen minutes?" He looks at me, and I nod, glad to do anything but stand here and pretend to know what to say.

We walk to the drugstore and stand in line, acting as if the conversation in the corridor never happened. The pharmacist behind the counter doesn't need to tell me what to do. I've known him since that day I turned five. He nods in greeting as I insert Dad's medical disk into the groove in the bulletproof glass.

The pharmacist removes it and disappears behind a door, then reappears with a small flat package wrapped in recycled brown paper. Right away I can see: it's not Dad's usual prescription. The pharmacist puts it into the hollow space under the counter. Our eyes lock as I open the door to remove it.

"I should offer my congratulations, but I'll miss your visits," he says. I guess he heard the news, too. "I've known you since you were a little girl—I almost think of you as one of my own daughters."

"I'm sure I'll be back, after, you know," I say.

"Tell your father he needs to inject this once a week, otherwise it won't work. The side effects are immediate. Read the paper."

"Ok." I turn the package over. No instructions. "What kind of side effects—"

The pharmacist turns and walks away without another word. Something's wrong. I feel Thabit's eyes fixed on me as I slip the package into the folds of my unisuit. Behind him, Badra hovers in the door, and behind her, the soldiers hover in the shadows. Everyone watches me, everyone's waiting for me to bolt, to run, to slash my wrists, to stab my stomach. To do anything they don't want me to do. They don't know I'm already doing it, and I don't even know what it is.

"Come on," I say, grabbing his hand and pulling him to the door. "I'm starving. Let's get out of here before I put a bullet in someone's head."

"That's my little trooper," says Badra as we head for the exit.

I hate it when she calls me that. When I get back from the hospital, I'll make sure we all decide to never say it again.

The living room is dark when I open the door. I'm careful to keep quiet, it's still night, and Mom and Dad are probably asleep. I put my pack on the couch and unbutton my lapels. The package is warm from the heat of my body. I turn on the light over the table, and sit down. I'm careful, I don't make a sound. My kids will be good soldiers. They'll know stealth.

The paper is easy to open, the tape slits apart with just a touch of my blade. It's a miniature syringe kit. I can tell before I open it, I've seen them before. Inside, two syringes made of hard plastic nestle within molded foam, needles already in place. They're ready to go. I rock the kit back and forth. A thick silver liquid slides back and forth in the tubes. The whole thing looks like a child's toy.

"It's not for you."

I drop the kit onto the paper. Dad stands in the room, tying his bathrobe with shaking hands. I didn't even hear him close the bedroom door. So much for stealth.

"But it's not for you, either," I say. "So who's it for?"

"It's heart medicine, for dissolving clots if I have an attack." He picks up the kit and closes the cover, then slides it into his bathrobe pocket.

"I don't believe you," I say. "It's poison, isn't it? You're going to kill me, or try to kill the soldier who's supposed to fertilize the eggs."

"Don't be ridiculous," Dad says. "You're my daughter, and I love you. You drive me crazy sometimes, but I'd never harm you, or your soldiers. Hand me the wrapping paper."

I slide it over to him. Dad smooths it out against the table. For a moment, his face relaxes, and I see something of the father I remember from when I was young, when he taught me how to read and write, took me for walks in ancient parks under dying trees. Now all the parks are gone.

"You know, your mother took the hormones, too. She registered for the draft, but they didn't pick her."

"What?" Shock slides through me, prickly cold. "She never told me."

"She didn't want you to know. She was so ashamed. Her parents went bankrupt from the cost. After that, no one would have her, she was damaged goods. But I saw something in her, so beautiful, so—" His voice cracks. "I should have know it wouldn't last. Nothing that fragile ever does. Greed always wins."

Dad folds the paper into neat squares, and the softness disappears.

"She didn't get her money, but that didn't stop her from finding another way. That's why she gave birth to you. As far as she's concerned, you're her second womb. Nothing more."

Outside, night rain pelts the window.

"You're lying," I declare. "I don't know why you're saying these things, but they won't make me change my mind. And if you think that that needle or your disgusting lies will stop me, you're wrong."

Dad reaches across the table, pressing the folded paper into my hands. I try to drop it, to pull my hand away, but he won't let go. I've never seen him look so old, so worn.

"I've changed my mind. I don't plan on stopping you." His voice is low and gravelly. He has trouble speaking, as if he's about to cry. It makes me ashamed. "When you see what it is that you've been responsible for creating, I'm hoping you'll realize that all this has to be stopped. I want you to make that choice yourself, because then you'll be acting as an adult, not as a child who simply does as she's told."

"What I'm responsible for is creating soldiers that will help us win the war. *My* soldiers, not my mother's, not yours."

"I keep telling you, Jet, *there is no war.*" Tears trickle down his face. "Open your eyes. There's never been any war. We send our men and women into space, and nothing comes back? Not a single message? Not even a bomb from the enemy? Nothing?"

"But then where do they all go? We send soldiers to their death, just because? I don't believe that."

"Don't be so naïve. I taught you better than that—I've told you time and time again, this is a war-based economy. There probably was a war, a long time ago. But it's over, and we're forced to keep pretending, simply so that a corrupt military government can remain in power. We live in coffins and crowd in stairwells, barely alive, while we pour all our resources into sending our children into space only to shoot them down."

"I don't believe you, that's just more lies!" I struggle again to get away, but Dad tightens his grip, drawing me up and toward him. His face glows.

"It's not just burning jet fuel that falls on us. It's broken battle cruisers, broken bodies. From *our* ships, not the enemy's. Remember the time I snuck you out of the stairwell, when you were ten? I showed you. You saw—"

"I saw nothing! I was little, I don't remember anything!"

"I remember." Dad's voice grows calm, and his hands slip from mine, fall slack at his side. His stare is distant, cold. It frightens me.

"I remember how the ship split apart like an eggshell. I remember men and women falling like comets over the city. Their burning flesh left contrails in the air. They didn't scream. All you could hear was flame, wind, impact."

He unbuttons his nightshirt. I've never seen my father undressed before. Melted folds of flesh appear, scars upon scars, with an angry red line running down the middle.

"I remember how they came through the buildings and streets, putting bullets into every body, every heart. I thought if I lay still, they'd think I was already dead, and pass by. I was wrong."

We stand silent in the dark. Through the distortion of my tears, for a moment I see a younger Essam, the shadow of what he used to be. And then his shoulders slump, and he covers his chest.

"Does Mom know?"

"No. And she never will." His voice is firm.

"How many—"

"How many died? I don't know. How many are alive? I don't know that, either. The men and women who saved me, they said there were others. But we keep

apart, we blend in. It's safer. I'm one of the lucky ones, I wasn't augmented. I can pass."

A small spark of understanding— "The pharmacist," I say. "He's one of you, isn't he? Oh. He's your brother...." Now it really hits me. I sit down.

Dad doesn't answer. I realize he never will. He's still loyal. But I have to be loyal, too.

"Nothing will change if I say no, if I run away, even if you use that needle." I hold up my wrist. The tracking device swims somewhere below the surface. "They'll just find me, kill me, take out my ovaries. Then they'll kill you and Mom. I can't let that happen."

"Everything can change, and without anyone knowing. Without anyone firing a gun or saying a single word. No one will die."

"I'm doing this for you, you know. So you can get a new heart, so you *won't* die!"

"I'm already dead, Jet. This isn't being alive." Dad bows his head and shuffles back into the bedroom, leaving me alone.

I grab the paper and unlock the balcony door. Light rain lashes my face as I lean against the railing. It's freezing outside, the street below barely visible. A few kitchen window lights glow, weak sparks of life in the blue-black of early morning. I think about how easy it would be to climb onto the railing, to spread my arms and leave everything behind. Somewhere in the silent rows of buildings, tucked into invisible spaces, soldiers stare at me, watching. They'll never let it happen. They're loyal, too.

In two days' time officers will come to the apartment again, disarm me and strip me down. I'll be clean. They'll do the same with Mom. But Dad has a history of heart problems. He's an old man, and his hands tremble. They'll let him keep his medical kit. If I tell them what I think is going to happen, they'll put another bullet in him, and this time they'll get it right. If I don't— Someone is going to die, no matter what. And despite what my father said, I can't say it won't be me.

I straighten from my hunched position over the railing, and open my cramped hand. The folded paper is wet, and threads of blue ink stain the brown surface like spider veins. I unfold the squares. The writing is smeared and blurry, but I can still read my father's name in neat block letters: *ESSAM OBERAAN.* Larger letters bleed through the surface, from writing on other side. I turn the paper over.

Someone has drawn an eye, large and almond-shaped. It's filled in completely with deep blue ink, no pupil or lid to be seen. It stares up at me, unblinking. I hold my breath and wait.

Nothing happens, of course. A gust of wind throws more rain against me, and the eye dissolves into indigo oblivion. I ball the paper up and throw it high into the air. It disappears. I feel powerless, stupid. The daughter of a soldier, and I'm useless.

I speak to my armed guardians, silent and surrounding me.

"Tell me what to do."

If they answer me, I can't hear them. All I hear is rain.

The last two days burn as fast as rocket fuel, and taste much the same. I say my goodbyes to Thabit and Badra. We pay a kid to stand at the bath door and chase people to the other floors, while we spend several hours alone. I tell them the truth, the thing they don't want to hear. There will be no egg left behind, no spliced-gene daughter for the three of us. It's Thabit who cries, but I expected that. Badra tells me they'll wait for me, that we'll talk about it again when I come home, but none of us believe what she says. "Are you with me?" I ask, and they say yes. Yet Badra's voice is ozone cool, and so are Thabit's lips. Already, they've moved on.

The escort guard lets Mom and Dad come with me, when they come. It's their right, as I'm technically a minor, even though I'm now in the army. People gather around my door, but I don't see Thabit and Badra. I didn't expect to. I recite the loyalty pledge to my city and planet in front of everyone, and there's polite applause, and then I'm whisked down the long hall. People stand in their doorways, whispering and watching. Someone's been making curry again, the smell of it seeps through the walls. One of the officers activates the supposedly-dead elevator, which causes a small riot. Dad helps me past the surge of people, but he won't look at me. I assume that somewhere in his unisuit, the little syringes wait. I don't want to know. The elevator rushes past the basement level, and I'll admit I get a thrill when I realize where we're going. I've heard there are underground transports, but no one gets to use them anymore. Well, except for military. That's me, now. Private Jet Oberaan and her four hundred thousand. The sirens sound, faint and mournful, as we stand on the sub-level platform. In a year, they'll sound for my children.

More papers. I sign until I think my hand will fall off. The train rushes through tunnels so fast, I can't see what's outside. Mom wants to know when we'll get the credits for the eggs, and almost passes out when they tell her they'll cut an advance against conception right at the hospital. I try to get Dad's attention, but he stares out the windows, ignoring us both. My gun and blade are gone, they disarmed me back at the apartment. I feel light-headed and off-bal-

ance. I think of Thabit and Badra. I sit up suddenly, knocking the papers to the floor. I'm hungry; no, I'm thirsty. I don't ask the woman in uniform if they'll freeze an egg for me. I do ask if the soldiers will have faces. I don't remember anyone's answer. I can't stop thinking, I can't stop asking questions, I can't stop pacing back and forth, I can't oh god I can't I can't oh daddy don't do this don't do this don't make me choose—

White.

The color is beautiful. Pure white. No dirt, no grime. I never thought any wall could look so clean. The woman sticks an inhaler against my nose, and I take another breath as she pats my back. I'm calm now, I don't even remember when we got here. Drugged to the gills. Panic attack's over. I feel good.

We're escorted through the hospital corridors, on our way to meet the man who'll be the father of my twenty-six divisions. Not man, the doctor said. *Male.* The male who'll contribute the second half of my little army. He's not human, that much info they gave me. I'm so high. I smile at my father, a loopy grin that he doesn't return. Mom stayed behind the waiting room. She wore makeup today. There'll be booze and black market food, and lots of handsome men congratulating her on her daughter's plentiful ovaries. "I bet the apple doesn't fall far from the tree", one will probably say, and she'll blush and laugh, not knowing what he means. Dad never took her to the parks. She's never seen an apple, or a tree.

We pass through weapons sensors and wide walls of x-ray machines, past doors four feet thick and twenty feet high that take ten minutes to swing out. We're sprayed for stray bacteria, and little badges with foreign symbols are placed on our chests. "I hope that's not a target," I joke as a woman fastens it to me, but she doesn't smile. She looks pretty damn scared. She makes me take one more hit of the anti-panic gas before she runs back down the hall.

Behind the last door is a room, bigger than all the rooms I've been in, put together. All along the walls, stories above us, men and women in white coats peer down from observation windows. The walls are dotted with lasers and cameras. Hundreds of soldiers—half-human, bristling with machinery in their ugly faces—surround us, weaponry sweating in the heat. The air stinks of oil and cement dust and chemicals. At the center stands a cube of two-foot thick glass, and in the center of the cube stands the male. The officers draw their weapons and escort me to one side of the cube, to the metallic round of a speaking window, then back away.

The creature's eyes are long, almond-shaped pools of mercury. They widen as I step forward, and his lips pull back, revealing a dog-like set of fangs in a jutting muzzle. That's what he is, he's a dog with the thick body of an over-

muscled soldier, coated in bristling black fur. Except, he's not a dog, or a man. My father stands beside me, disappointment washing over his face. He can't get to the creature behind all that glass. He can't use the syringe on it. Of course, there's no glass surrounding me. Guess I know who gets the poison now. Under the haze of the drug, I giggle.

"What is he?" Dad asks.

"This is the future of the military." Behind me, one of the officers steps forward. I can tell he's memorized his answer by the way he stumbles over the words. "By combining the high intellect and reasoning skills of humans with the brute strength and longevity of this species, we've been able to create the perfect space-faring military weapon. Excellent for stealth missions, almost telepathic in communications skills, and blind in loyalty to their commanding officers. Loyal to the death. This is the future of the military. You'll be pleased to know that the divisions you and he create will be the first wave of that future—a future that will ensure us both victory and peace."

The officer stands beside us now. He looks satisfied. My father mouths, *prisoner of war*. I pretend not to see him.

"What is he? Where is he from?"

The officer smiles. "That's classified."

I ignore Dad's "I told you so" smirk.

"Does he have a name?"

"He has a number."

"That's stupid. He needs a name. I'm going to call him Sidabras. For the color of his eyes."

Now the officer looks a bit pained. I think he's getting tired of giggling girl before him, even if she is the mother-to-be of twenty-six divisions of death. I swallow down another nervous laugh, and try to look serious.

"Will the babies—the soldiers—look like him?"

"Not quite. A bit more human, more like you, less—" he waves his hands, as if unable to express the disgusting alienness of the creature standing before us. "You'll be quite pleased. And I think your darker skin tones will help."

"What?" I can feel Dad's anger as he speaks, his hands gripping into my skin.

More hand-waving. "No, it's not that, not at all. The last two batches with this male were produced with lighter-skinned females, which led to problems with the stealth capabilities of the fur and skin. Someone with coloring closer to his will correct that. We can't afford to destroy any more batches."

"Have you already, you know—" I glance down.

"Oh yes. It's harvested and good to go." The officer pats me on the shoulder. "We're all just waiting for the four hundred thousand to report."

The creature's snarl has faded. I can't tell what he's thinking. His children, maybe, destroyed or sent to space to die. "Does he understand us?"

"You can speak to him," the officer says. "We've wired him with a communications system." He flicks a small switch by the metal circle, and an intercom crackles to life.

We stare at each other.

I lean forward, open my mouth. But I don't know what to say.

Wide hands rise, both large enough to cover half my head with just the palms. He places a finger against his neck, flicks a switch with a sharp nail. A delicate movement—I bet he's good with weapons. Small wires run down one side of his neck to the front of his throat, ending in an electrical plate bolted on an armor-like chest of calloused skin. He opens his mouth again, and several short bursts of harsh sound shoot out. Seconds later, I hear the translation.

ARE. YOU. LOYAL.

"Yes," I say, not sure what he means. I look him directly in the eyes, and he does the same in return. It's what you do with animals. I think we both know that. "Are you?"

The translator crackles, unable to understand the sharp bark. I jump at the sound. My heart pounds faster, and it's getting hard to breathe. The anti-panic gas has worn off, I'm freaking out. "I'm so sorry you're in here."

COMMAND. THEM.

He must mean his children. Ours. "I can't go into space with them, if that's what you mean. I would if I could." The lies come babbling out. What does he want to hear? "They won't let me go. I'll never see them. If I could—"

The glass fogs as ivory fangs appear from the red of his mouth, and his face distorts in the steaming air. His growl sounds like thunder in the canyons.

I step back. "Can we go now?" Dad reaches out with his hand to draw me away. I see a flash at his fingers.

"No!" I grab his wrist, and we struggle. The officers watch, dumbfounded. They don't see the syringe, they only see a stubborn old man resisting his daughter. "I won't let you kill them!"

"You stupid girl, it's not for you—!" We collide, and I cry out: something just punched my heart. Dad pushes me away.

The syringe sticks out of my chest. It's empty. I stare up at Dad. He points to one eye, his finger tearing the lashes as tears stream down his cheeks.

"Be loyal," he says.

I say something, but my voice sounds so small and distant, I can't hear the words.

Behind me, the creature roars. I hear him slam against the glass, and several hundred soldiers start as the entire cube shifts forward with an ear-splitting shriek. I scream—hands pull me back and under the cover of limbs. Doctors are shouting at the soldiers, trying to push through the wall of weapons and armor to get to me. Dad pitches sideways, hits the cube and slides down. I see him clutching his chest as soldiers surround him, weapons clicking.

"Don't kill him!" I grab my throat—it burns. My heart is on fire from the poison, and the fire is spreading up. I press forward as the soldiers jostle their guns in confusion. They're waiting for orders to shoot or save my father.

The dog soldier looks out, down, and our eyes lock. All that storm-cloud mercury fills my mind, and I feel the words drop out of me like bullets or babies newly formed, even as the doctors finally pin me to the floor.

sidabras. don't let him die. be loyal.

I don't think I spoke.

The creature rages. Plumes of white gas curl from the cube's ceiling, even as soldiers surround it like beetles on rotting food. The glass cracks, shatters all around us in sharp rain. Gunfire and sparks in the smoke—

I disengage.

I've done it before, like when I was jumped during an all-night party that turned into a riot, several years ago. I shot three men. Didn't feel a thing. There's a part of you that shuts down, and the lizard part blossoms, cold and bright and uncaring. There's a man trying to rape you: stab him to death. The doctor straps you to the gurney: don't fight it. Wake up, feel the gauze at your waist, you're not a woman anymore: forget it. Ask the officers about my father—they don't know anything about a syringe or a shot. You were high, hallucinating, remember? They do know something about a heart attack, but your father refused treatment: you say nothing. They tell you your mother left the base with a suitcase in one hand and a pamphlet in the other. She remembered to take your money, but forgot to leave her new address:

Disengage.

And now I stand on the apartment balcony, gripping an honorable discharge. Inside, Dad runs a hand down the front of his mended unisuit. Underneath, a new heart beats—a chop-shop job I got on the street, after he collapsed again on the train ride home. It was that, or let him die. Guess I'm not loyal. Dad hates me for it, says he loved the old heart better. It was the heart he fell in love with his wife with, the heart he loved me with. The heart of a soldier. Now the wife's gone, the heart's gone, the money's gone, and I'm the monster.

I open my hand, and the wind whisks the papers away. I stare at the distant buildings, silver and slick. I fall to my knees, fall asleep. I dream of mercury, and unblinking eyes.

Sirens wail as I run the tip of the pen over the last white square. Black fills up the space, and now the calendar is complete. One year gone. Outside, battle cruisers prepare for lift-off. Already the buildings vibrate from the engines springing to life. There are more cruisers this time, three times as many. Whatever was in that syringe, it didn't affect the eggs. The dog soldier and I, we did good. The letter on the table, delivered today, tells me. Four hundred thousand, every damn one of them grown up, armed, and ready to go.

"Mom should have waited before she dumped us. She'd have twice the money now." I push the letter across the table toward Dad, then hold the bank chip up to the light. A credit for every soldier shipped into space, with a bonus for "extensive" modifications. Just like they'd promised. Not that it matters much now. Things are bad—food supplies low, water dwindling, medicine nonexistent. The power is off half the time or more. Everything tastes and smells like rotting metal. Something's gone wrong in the world, but no one knows what it is. This time, there are no rumors.

"Are you listening to me?"

Dad stands at the balcony door, a silhouette in the pale morning light. He doesn't want to admit it, but he's been waiting for this day as much as me. He's their grandfather.

"Fine. Whatever," I say to myself. Dad doesn't talk anymore. He hasn't spoken to me since we left the base a year ago. Not one word. He's healthier with the new heart, he even walks downstairs once a week. But he can't forgive me for not stopping the war—for not dying when he stabbed me, for not dying when he stabbed himself. At least he didn't kick me out. I have no place to go. Thabit and Badra don't live in the building anymore. It seems they weren't with me, after all. They were with a girl from another floor, the one I heard Thabit knocked up. I can't blame them.

Something whispers in my ear, little half-caught words I can barely understand. It's Dad, muttering under his breath again, whenever I look away. This is what he does instead of speaking, and it drives me crazy. I slap the chip onto the table, knocking the chair over as I stand.

"I am so sick and tired of your mumbling. If you have something to say to me, just say it!"

The light bulb fizzes, and winks out. I can hear the power dying in the building, all the ticks and hiccups of machinery shutting down. The sirens fade.

"Great. Just great." I stumble into the living room, feeling around for my pack. "Come on, close that door and let's get going. If we go now, we might still find a good place in the stairwell." Silence, of course.

"I swear it's like talking to a child…." I find my pack and strap it on, then feel my way into the bedroom. Dad's pack is on his bed. I reach for it, then stop and cock my head, hearing the absence of engines. The battle cruisers. Have they already gone? Have my children already gone?

The pack slides off the bed, contents clattering onto the floor. I reach out, grab—

My hand shoots back, stung by the tip of a needle. As my eyes adjust to the dark, I see syringes. Empty syringes and full ones, too many to count, roll around my feet. I pick one up. It's the same type that entered my chest. Even without a light, I see traces of silver glowing inside the hollow tube.

Everything tastes like metal, smells like metal.

"You son of a bitch." I run to the kitchen, clutching the syringe. He's not there. "You bastard! What did you do to me?" I kick the fallen chair aside, and step out onto the balcony. In the strange silence, my clumsy movements sound like thunder.

Dad sits on the railing, one leg thrown over the edge. His body leans into empty air, as if he's looking for something in the distance, the right place to jump to. I don't move.

"If you want to jump, fine. I'm not going to stop you," I say. "But first you tell me what you did to me. What is this shit and what does it do? You owe me an explanation!"

"I never used them on you, not after the accident, at the cube—" Dad's voice cracks, and he stops. It's been so long since he's spoken, we're both surprised at the sound. He clears his throat before beginning again. "I told you they weren't for you, you never needed them. They were intended for me, only for me. I'm sorry." He leans out, raising his free hand high.

"Wait, don't jump! Please—" I reach a hand out to him, slow and deliberate in the chilly air. "I promise I believe you, whatever you say. But please just tell me what why you're doing this. Just *talk* to me for once."

i've never stopped talking to you.

I drop the syringe, staring.

what did I tell you? do you remember?

His lips aren't moving.

everything will change, and—

"No one will say—"

Dad raises a hand to his lips. He points one finger up, just below his right eye. Flecks of silver swim in the brown, like neon in the night, like open doors.

a single word

I don't even have to concentrate. All I have to do is be still.

"It won't last. Before the pharmacy shut down, I bought as much as I could. But it's not an endless supply, it was never meant to be. Eventually you'll have to do it."

"Do what?"

"Command them."

Whispers, behind me. Inside me. Familiar and soothing, like when I hold Mom's pillow to my face and breath deep, inhale the faint fading scent of her skin. I pull the oxiclamp from my nose. Smoke from burning trash lingers in the air. Somewhere beyond hundreds of miles of crumbling city blocks, the sun rises. I lean over the rail, stare at the dark thread of the street. I follow the line to the horizon, and look up.

One building ripples with movement, then another, and another. It spreads, as if the canyon is a wound, bleeding drops of water that take on the colors of concrete and sky. The droplets spread, pouring themselves toward me, growing larger with every second. Not water, but iron, bone and blood, camouflaged to move like rain in the wind. But this place is too narrow for the stealth of so many, and the quiet of morning reveals their sounds. They push the air before them, and it carries the rustling of weaponry, the soft click of claws and guns, the scent of singed fur and leathered skin. Hundreds, then thousands, then tens of thousands. They keep coming. Hundreds of thousands. Four hundred thousand. Four hundred thousand, and one.

He appears in midair as his stealth armor deactivates. I watch the creature—Sidabras, that's what I'd named him—soar in a graceful arc, claws striking into steel-plated walls. Sidabras holds, pauses, then leaps again. Once there were birds, and they flew, and never had to walk. Is this was it was like, before the war? To watch creatures fly above us, and not cower from burning fuel and fuselage?

Several low explosions echo back and forth down the canyon, rattling balconies. "Bombs," I say, panic creeping over the wonder. "This is really happening. They're destroying the base." Dad steps up behind me, gripping my shoulder.

"This had to happen."

"There'll be nothing left but chaos."

chaos is change.

Engines concuss the neighborhood—the battle cruisers are springing to life. And now the stealth armor of all the soldiers fades, and everything around me turns black. I gasp and cling to Dad. All of these people came out of me. Soldiers hang all around us, cling to balconies and ledges beside us, above, and below. Male and female and other, dark-skinned and muscular, four hundred thousand in all. Silent, waiting for me to command them. I can see their wide eyes—dark brown pupils floating in silver seas. They have something of me in them, after all. How much of them do I have in me?

The balcony edge blurs, flickers, and he is there. Sidabras stands, tongue lolling from the edges of his fangs in a soft pant. Blood dots his strafed armor, oozes in a sticky line from the fur of his upper arm. I didn't realize how large he is, how much space he takes. There's no glass between us now.

Dad pushes me forward, gently. I smell singed flesh, sweat, steel. Sidabras lowers his head, and I stare in his mercury eyes. His breath smells of the long-gone parks, of damp black earth beneath trees. I reach up, touch the matted fur of his muzzle. He doesn't move away.

you are loyal.

Command them.

His words sound clear and crisp this time. I notice that the communications device has been ripped from his throat and chest, leaving raw wounds. I turn to Dad, but he steps back, as if handing everything over to me.

Command them.

I look around us. In the clear morning air, my children stare at me, open and expectant. I catch the eye of one, a young man almost as large as Sidabras. He stands on the balcony opposite us, a large rifle in his hands. He has hands. He has a face. He smiles. My heart feels like it's on fire again.

"My son. He's my son."

"He's your soldier," says Dad. "They all are. And so am I. Tell us what to do."

All around me, the four hundred thousand watch as the world opens up before me. I can leave. I can stay. I can destroy the city, maybe the world. I can disappear into the great mystery of space. I can stand here and do nothing, until the buildings crumble down. I feel Sidabras' hot breath on my face, feel the distant vibration of the cruisers. Feel my children, feel Sidabras and Dad, waiting.

"Are you with me?" I ask my father. He smiles.

"I've always been with you, sweetie."

I decide.

I turn to Sidabras, but he's already raising his hand, signaling to the rest. He knows my thoughts as I think them. Movement, all around. Dad gathers his

pack and the remaining syringes, and I wrap my arms around the father of twenty-four divisions, lash myself to his armor, hold tight.

"Mom should have waited," I whisper into his fur. I'll never see this apartment again, never sleep on the little couch, never huddle in the stairwell, trapped in sleepless fear. A large hand steals over mine, and some delicate emotion seeps from Sidabras into me, comforting and warm. There will be other trees, it seems to say, other families. New possibilities. New loyalties and love.

Sidabras jumps.

And now the moment of sorrow is gone, and so is everything old and tired. Only the empty space before us exists, space and the rising sun. Behind me, I hear Dad laughing, like he used to long ago. I'd look back, but I don't need to, ever again. I see how we move in the world. We unfurl like the wings of some long-dead god, resurrected and in flight, to the end of my street, and up, and beyond. We will all of us wear the stars—father, daughter, four hundred thousand, and one.

Brimstone Orange

The tree was a gift to her mother on the day of Cyan's birth, but it was barren. In her fourteen years, Cyan had never seen the stark, mean limbs bear anything, save for a creeping fungus. She didn't even know what kind of tree it was.

"I don't remember," said her mother, uneasily. "It's tropical, it wouldn't grow in this part of the country anyway. It was a mistake."

There were other trees in the yard—apple and pear, each laden with fruit by high summer. But her mother wouldn't speak of them, just like she wouldn't speak of the two locked rooms in the house. She never let Cyan enter the rooms, or touch or eat the fruit. It rotted on the ground; and the flies grew fat.

Cyan seethed. And she labored. She cast stones, mixed potions, held afternoon vigils with her girlfriends. They serpentined round the tree, long toes ripping grass as they swayed and chanted dreamy nonsense. She ran her tongue against the trunk, wove strands of her hair in the branches. But the gnarled wood remained lifeless.

Summer came and went; so did autumn. Her mother brought home oranges and sugarcane. Cyan spent evenings at the window, sucking sweetness till her lips cracked. In soft moonlight, the trees were equally beautiful, from tips to base. As her fingers traveled down the smooth length of cane, Cyan smiled....

Midnight found her kneeling in grass, thick clumps of dirt all around. One by one she peeled and plucked segments of orange from its skin, then passed them between her legs. In the secret crevices of

the tree, she gently tucked away the red-stained pulp. After, Cyan cradled the slender trunk, her fingers buried in its roots.

"Bear something for me," she pleaded in her sleep. "Bear me."

Hot lips and a smoking tongue woke her as slivers of orange pressed into her mouth. Cyan stirred—the creature moved with her, sliding rough arms across her naked flesh. She shivered, swallowed the fruit. They kissed again, and she fed from him. After a while, she didn't know where she left off and he began, only that he was inside her and she in him, that even in the rings of his cold splintered flesh, her belly felt ripe as the sun.

The sloe-eyed neighborhood girls gathered, and whispered. After her daughter disappeared, the woman took to crawling round the yard, scratching and weeping at the roots of her trees. "Don't eat the fruit!" she howled. The girls asked why, but the woman couldn't give them any reasons. They asked about Cyan— "What's Cyan?" she said. The girls' firm vows to guard the fruit consoled her, even as strange men bound and whisked the woman away.

But after a while the girls forgot, and flocked to the trees like birds. The cherries and pears were all right, but the salty-sweet oranges won their hearts. They stained their lips bright crimson.

And inside, how they burned.

Take Your Daughters & to Work

Sadie smooths down her long brown hair, then fastens a choker around her neck. She stares at herself in the mirror. Today her father is taking her to work, and she must be perfect. There will be other girls there, other daughters brought to work by their fathers. But her father runs the company, and so she sets the example. All who look on her must see perfection—otherwise, her father will be shamed.

From the darkened master bedroom, weeping rises. Sadie adjusts the heavy gold at her throat—her mother gave it to her this morning. It's been in the family at least a thousand years. She leans close to the mirror, and smiles.

"Don't worry," she tells her quicksilver self. "You'll do just fine."

The train station swells with the chatter of a thousand excited girls. Sadie walks slowly, her head held high. Her father's fingers trace patterns in the air as they climb the metal steps to his private car, fathers and first-born daughters crowding into the rest. Beneath her feet, engines throb. A lurch and a thrust: now the city parts as the train flows inside.

Sadie perches on the stiff horsehair seat, watching rooftops sail past the elevated tracks. Young men in brown livery pour tea into porcelain cups, and Sadie remembers to hold her little finger out, like a lady. The tea is the color of the sky—sulphur tinged with whorls of cloudy grey. It is the color of the webbing between the young men's fingers, the color of milky pupils in their lidless eyes.

"Will we see the ocean behind the factories? You promised."

Sadie's father smiles.

"I did indeed. You'll see all the waters of the world."

Sadie sips her tea, touches her throat with nervous hands. Outside, the horizon rushes toward them, a forest of massive smokestacks pumping out fire and haze under a burnt orange sun. The liveried men bow and sway, strange words bursting in wet pops from their lips. Fire makes them nervous. Sadie understands. She's nervous, too.

Her father leads her to the observation car as they pass the first edges of the factory. Sadie stares in wonder at blackened brick rising all around her, at steel pipes tangled around cauldrons larger than her house. Red sparks float in the air like weightless rubies. The factory is the only ocean she's ever seen, and it crashes against the city like a storm. Every year, another row of crumbling homes is eaten away. This is the way of the world, *His* way, her father has explained. If they cannot raise the old city with the old ways, they will bring it up from the deep, piece by piece, and the factory will rebuild it. Sadie cranes her neck, staring at thick columns blotting out the sky—she can see their fixed surfaces, but feels the walls bleeding through other dimensions, dragging a bit of her soul with them. Nauseated, she swallows hard.

"Remember what I told you, Sadie?" Her father touches her lightly, and she turns away.

"Never look directly at the edges," she recites, and he gives her shoulder a quick squeeze.

"That's my girl." He fingers the choker, moving the interlocking hydras into place. Two small rings hang down from either side, like gaping mouths. His fingers hook them, gently. "You're the reason I work so hard. You're our future. I know you'll make me proud."

Alien emotion swims up from Sadie's heart, and catches in her throat. The skin beneath the metal swells and chafes.

"I know," she replies. "I know."

Deep within the heart of the factory, Sadie shakes the scaled hands of many important men. Secretaries slither before her, leaving trails of damp that evaporate quickly in the factory heat. They give her gifts of seashells, and lovely historicals of the factory's beginnings, bound in gilt-edged skin. Sadie eats lunch on a courtyard crowned by pyramids of slag, at a coral table set just for the daughters. Metal fines cling to their skin, settle in their food. Sometimes, Sadie lays down her fork and gasps for a bit of air. Just nerves, she tells herself, and wills herself to breathe.

Afternoon fades, as small trams whisk them down mile-long shafts to a room of pale rib and abalone, where dry air gives way to plump humidity, ocean-sweet.

Sadie licks her lips, and tugs at the heavy gold around her neck. Her father holds her hand as they cross the floor, and when they reach the double doors at the far wall, it's as if she's traveled to the end of Time. Behind them, vice-presidents and company managers hover, their daughters clinging anxiously to their coats.

"Open the door, Sadie."

Sadie wipes the sweat from her hands, and pushes. Brisk wind and the roar of surf rush in as Sadie leads them onto the balcony. Below, black sands speckled with skulls descend in jagged dunes down to the endless sea. It is everything her father promised, and more.

"Can we go down?" Her lungs expand, and baleen inside her corset snaps.

"Lead the way." He points to wide steps plunging into the coarse sands. Sadie skips down the steps and into the dunes, all the girls following behind like a veil of trailing flowers. Overhead, pipes larger than the train thrust from the factory walls, plunging straight into iron-grey waves. As she reaches the beach's edge, factory horns sound one by one, great spine-shuddering cries that send the waters rushing back. Sadie stops and turns. All along the curving coast, green light explodes from pockets of the factory—signal fires lighting the way.

The men spread out across the beach, directing their daughters to the edge of the tide line. Before them, dark shapes rise from receding waves—cobblestone roads slick with foam, low houses clustered like rotting mushrooms, and beyond…. The sandy ridge breaks off and free-falls into the rift. Sadie spies chimney stacks peeking up from the depths, bioluminescent smoke coiling in the air, freed of the weight of water. Soft movements appear, as flippers and webbed feet emerge from gaping doors. More employees of her father, ready to greet them all. Sadie spies the liveried young man from the train car, and her heart skips a beat.

Some of the girls cry as their fathers pull chains up from the sands, attaching them at the loops in their golden hydra chokers. The chains stretch out along the ancient roads and over the edges of the rift, ending in the city below. Sadie trembles slightly as her father stretches out his hand, links of black metal dripping off his palm. Beneath her choker, skin stretches wide, half-developed gills sucking at the moisture in the air as they vaguely remember what to do.

"I'll always love you. Remember that, in the last moments." Her father looks down at her, the tentacles of his beard coiling into a hundred tender smiles.

"Of course." Sadie covers his hand with her own. In the dying light, the silver of her bones shine through the flesh, luminous and pure. "When my bones are added to the city, you'll see me. We'll never be apart. It is my honor to join the work."

"You are my greatest gift, my greatest sacrifice." As he kisses her forehead, his tears fall onto her skin. Sadie feels the chain slide through the hydra's mouths as he carefully hooks it in place. Somewhere, beneath the rift, strong tentacles hold the other end. Sadie prays to the Mother that whoever accepts her, he is vast and terrible. After all, her father runs the factory, and she is her father's daughter. She sets the example till the day her chained bones, heavy with spawn, are pulled back from her bridal grave.

"Our work renews our world," her father says. "Our daughters renew our lives. In His name we bring them together. In His name, we take our daughters to work."

Sadie steps onto the slick cobblestones, and the employees of New Y'ha-nthlei Steelworks follow, each of them walking their daughters into the rising waves.

Omphalos

Vacation doesn't begin when Father pulls the Volkswagen camper out of the driveway, and speeds through the sleepy Tacoma streets toward Narrows Bridge. It doesn't begin on the long stretches of Route 16 through Gig Harbor, Port Orchard, and Bremerton, your twin brother Jaime fast asleep beside you on the warm back seat, his dark blond hair falling over his eyes. It doesn't begin with the hasty lunch at the small restaurant outside Poulsbo, where your father converses with the worn folds of the Triple-A map as your mother slips the receipt into a carefully labeled, accordioned envelope. 16 whittles down to 3, blossoms into 104 as the camper crosses Hood Canal onto the Olympic Peninsula, and still your vacation does not begin. Discovery Bay, Sequim, Dungeness: all the feral playgrounds of vacations and summers past: no. It is in Port Angeles, under a storm-whipped sky, against the backdrop of Canada-bound ferries gorging their wide, toothless mouths on rivers of slow-moving cars, when Father turns away from your mother, thin-lipped and tearful from the forced confession that another envelope holding four passports sits on the quiet kitchen counter back in Tacoma. You roll your eyes. Why do they go to such trouble of pretense? Oh, yes: for the neighbors. For the pastor, for colleagues and relatives, for all the strangers and passers-by who wouldn't understand, who want to hear only the normal. Father sees · the look on your face, and takes you aside as his large flat thumb rubs against your cotton-clad arm in that old familiar way, that way you've known all of your fifteen long and lonely years, the way that always

sends your mind into the flat black void. Old Spice tickles your nose, and you rub the itch away as Jaime scowls, the color fading from his perfect face like the sun.

"Don't worry, June-Bug. I know a place. Better than Victoria. No distractions, no tourists. Where there's nothing at all. You know the place. You've been there, before. It's where you always go." He places his calloused finger at the center of your forehead, and you almost piss yourself in fear: does he know?

"Where we can—you know."

Your mother takes Jamie aside, her fingers sliding around his slender waist as she spins her own version of the same tale. Father winks and parts his lips, coffee and cigarette breath drifting across your face as he whispers in your ear.

"Be alone."

Vacation has begun.

Salt ocean air and the cries of gulls recede as Father guides the camper through Port Angeles. You wish you could stay, walk through the postcard-pretty gingerbread-housed streets with Jaime, shop for expensive knick-knacks you don't need, daydream of a life you'll never have. Father drives on. Office buildings and shopping districts give slow way to industrial parks and oversized construction sheds surrounded by rusting bulldozers and dump trucks. None of it looks permanent, not even the highway. 101 lengthens like overworked taffy into a worn, three-lane patchwork of blacktop and tar. Campers and flatbeds, station wagons and Airstreams all whoosh across its surface, with you and against you. Port into town, town into suburbs, suburbs into the beyond. The sun has returned in vengeance, and all the grey clouds have whipped away over the waters, following the ferry you were never meant to take.

"Once we're off the highway, we can follow the logging roads," Father shouts over the roaring wind as he steers the camper down the Olympic Highway. He sounds excited, almost giddy. "They'll take us deep into the Park, past the usual campgrounds and tourist spots, past the Ranger Stations, right into the heart of the forest. And then, once the logging roads have ended—well, look at the map. Just see how far we can go."

You stare at the silhouette of his head, dark against the dirty brilliance of the window shield. One calloused hand rests on the steering wheel, one hand on your mother's shoulder. His fingers play with the gold hoop at her ear, visible under the short pixie cut of grey-brown hair. She turns to him, her cheek rising as she smiles. They remind you of how you and Jamie must look together:

siblings, alike and in love, always together. Father and you used to look like that. Now you and he look different. You clench your jaw, look away, look down.

"It's not even noon, we should be able to make it to Lake Mills by this afternoon—"

Your mother interrupts him. "That far? We'll never make it to Windy Arm by then, it's too far." So that's your destination. You've been there before, you know how much she loves the lake, the floating, abandoned logs, the placid humming of birds.

"Not this time, remember? We're taking Hot Springs Road over to the logging roads. Tomorrow we'll start out early, and we should be there by sundown."

"But there's nothing—wait, isn't Hot Springs closed? Or parts of it? I thought we were going down Hurricane Ridge." Your mother looks confused. Evidently, they didn't make all the vacation plans together. Interesting.

"It's still drivable, and there won't be any traffic—that's the point. To get away from everyone. Don't worry."

"Aren't we going back home?" Jaime asks. "Where are we going?"

"We're not going all the way to the end of Hot Springs, anyway," Father continues over Jamie. "I told you we're taking the logging roads, they go deeper into the mountains. We already mapped this all out, last week."

"We didn't discuss this." Your mother has put on her "we need to speak in private" voice.

"Take a look at the map. June has it," Father says.

"I don't need to look at the map, I know where we planned on going. I mean, this is ridiculous—where in heaven's name do you think you're taking us to?"

"I said we're going all the way." His hand slides away from her shoulder, back to the wheel.

"All the way to where?"

"All the way to the end."

The map Father gave you to hold is an ordinary one, a rectangular sheaf of thick paper that unfolds into a table-sized version of your state. Jamie scoots closer to you as you struggle with the folds, his free hand resting light on your bare thigh, just below your shorts. His hands are large and gentle, like the paws of a young German Shepherd. You move your forehead close, until your bangs mingle with his, and together you stare down at the state you were born in, and all its familiar nooks and crevices. In the upper corner is your small city—you trace your route across the water and up the right-hand side of the peninsula to Port Angeles, then down. The park and mountains are a blank green mass, and there are no roads to be seen.

You lift the edge of the map that rests on your legs, and dark markings well up from the other side. "Turn it over to the other side," you say.

"Just a minute." He holds his side tight, so you lift your edge up as you lower your head, peering. The other side of the paper is the enlarged, fang-shaped expanse of the Olympic Mountain Range. Small lines, yellow and pink and dotted and straight, fan around and around an ocean devoid of the symbols of cartography, where even the logging roads have not thrust themselves into. You can see where your father has circled small points throughout various squares, connecting each circle with steady blue dashes that form a line. Underneath his lines, you see the lavender ink of your mother's hand, a curving line that follows Whiskey Road to its end just before Windy Arm. Over all those lines, though, over all those imagined journeys, someone has drawn another road, another way to the interior of the park. It criss-crosses back and forth, overlapping the forests like a net until it ends at the edges of a perfect circle—several perfect circles, in fact, one inside another inside another, like a three-lane road. Like a cage. The circles encloses nothing—nothing you can see on the map, anyway, because nothing is in the center except mountains and snow, nothing the map-makers thought worth drawing, nothing they could see. The circles enclose only a single word:

Χάος

Someone has printed it in the naked center of the brown-inked circles, across the mountains you've only ever seen as if in a dream, as smoky grey ridges floating far above the neat rooftops of your little neighborhood, hundreds of miles away. Letters of brown, dark brown like dried-up scratches of blood—not Father's handwriting, and not your mother's.

"Do you see that?" you ask Jamie. "Did you write that?"

"Write what?" He's still on the other side of the state. He doesn't see anything. He doesn't care.

You brush a fingertip onto the word. It feels warm, and a bit ridged. "Help me," you whisper to it, even though you're not sure to who or what you're speaking, or why. The words come out of your mouth without thought. They are the same words you whisper at night, when Father presses against you, whispering his own indecipherable litany into your ears. Your finger presses down harder against the paper, until it feels you'll punch a hole all the way through the mountains. "Save me. Take me away. Take it all away."

The word squirms.

Goosebumps cascade across your skin, a brush fire of premonition. As you lower your edge of the map, Jamie's fingers clench down onto your thigh. Perhaps he mistakes the prickling heat of your skin for something else. You don't dissuade him. Under the thick protection of the paper, hidden from your parents' eyes, your fingers weave through his, soaking up his heat and sweat; and your legs press together, sticking in the roaring heat of engine and sun-soaked wind. Your hand travels onto his thigh, resting at the edge of his shorts where the whorls of your fingertips glide across golden strands of hair, until you feel the start, the beginning of him, silky soft, and begin to rub back and forth, gently. His cock twitches, stiffens, and his breath warms your shoulder in deep bursts, quickening. You know what he loves.

"Do you see where we're headed to?" Father asks.

Hidden and unseen, Jamie's hand returns the favor, traveling up your leg. You feel the center of yourself unclench, just a little. Just enough. Raising the map again, you peek at the word. After all these years and so many silent pleas, has something finally heard? Face flush with shock, you bite your lower lip so as not to smile. You stare out the window, eyes hidden behind sticky sunglasses, watching the decayed ends of Port Townsend dribble away into the trees, watching the woods rise up to meet the road, the prickly skin of an ancient beast, slumbering and so very, very ready to awaken.

You want to believe, but you shouldn't. Belief is an empty promise. Belief just leads back to the void. You shouldn't want to believe, but you will. This time, just this once, you will.

"Yes," you say. "Yes, I do."

The beginning of a journey is always deception. The beginning always appears beautiful, as a mirage. Once you fold the map away, there's laughter and music, jokes and gentle pinches, and the heady anticipation of traveling someplace new, all of you together, a family like any other family in the world. Sunlight drenches the windows and you laugh at the sight—so many prisms and prickles of color, glitter-balling the camper's dull brown interior into a jewelry box. After half an hour, your mother unbuckles her seat belt and makes her way across the porta-potty, wedged in between the small refrigerator and the tiny bench with its fake leather cushions that hide the bulk of the food.

"Something to eat—a snack? We had lunch so early." Your mother raises the folding table up, fixing the single leg to the camper's linoleum floor, then pulls sandwiches and small boxes of juice from the fridge, passing them up to Father. She's a good wife, attentive. Jamie drinks a Coke, wiping beads of sweat from its bright red sides onto his t-shirt. You pick at your bread, rolling it into hard balls before popping them into your mouth. The camper is traveling at a slight incline, and the right side of the highway peels away, revealing sloping hills that

form the eastern edge of the Peninsula. You think of the ferry, of all that cool, wide ocean, waters without end, in which all things are hidden, in which all things can be contained.

"Can we stop?" You point to a small grocery stand and gas station coming up ahead to the right, overlooking a rest stop and lookout point.

Your mother points to the porta-potty. "You need to go?"

"No." You feel yourself recoil. "No, I just—I just thought we could stop for a while. I'm getting a little queasy." It's true, you get carsick, sometimes. You think of the curved slope beyond the rest stop, and how easy it'd be to slip over the rail guard as you pretend to be sick. You think of the water, so close you can almost see it. "While we can."

Your father doesn't slow the camper. "Sorry, June-Bug. We need to keep going."

You nod your head. "Sure. No problem." You think about what you've just said, and decide that it's not a lie. Running away would mean you didn't really believe that the word moved, that something out there in the mountains is weaving its way to you, some beautiful, dangerous god coming to save the queen. You want to stay. Just this once, you want to see your miracle.

Outside, 101 splits off, part of it flying off and up the coast to Neah Bay as the newly-formed 112. Now the landscape morphs, too, sloughing off yet more buildings and houses. A certain raw, ugly quality descends all around. The highway curves away, and with it, the store, the land. You're going in a different direction now. No use to think of ferries and guard rails anymore.

Jamie pulls out a deck of cards. They fan out and snap back into themselves as he shuffles them again and again. Your mother leans back against the small bench, watching him deal the cards. Go Fish—their favorite game. You've never liked games. You don't believe in luck or chance. You believe in fate.

Reaching to the floor, you pull a fat book out of your backpack, and turn the pages in an absentminded haze, staring at nothing as words and illustrations flow past. Ignore her, you say, ignore the two small feet, bare and crowned with nails painted a pretty coral, that appear between you and Jaime, and nestle in cozy repose at his thigh. You press yourself against the edge of the seat, forehead flat against the window, legs clamped tight, ignoring the low hum of their voices calling out the cards. It's not as if you hate your mother—you have long talks with her sometimes, she's a good listener. And she's never touched you, never like that. Sometimes, she even comes to your defense, when you can't—just can't do it anymore, when you're tired or sick or just need a break, just need an evening to yourself, to sit in your pink-ruffled bedroom and pretend you're a normal girl in a normal world. Still, though. She's your mother, not your friend,

and Jamie is her favorite, just as you are Father's favorite. Sometimes you wonder if Jamie might love her more than you. That would kill you. It would be like,
she's rejecting one half of you for the other, without any real reason why.

"Where did you get the map?" Why did you ask her that? You curse yourself silently. Always too curious, always wanting to know everything, and more.
Like father, like daughter.

Your mother looks up from her cards, mouth pursed. Clearly she doesn't like
being reminded of the map, and doesn't want to answer—or she's going to answer, but she's buying a bit of time. It's her little not-so-secret trick, her way of
rebelling. Jamie does the same. Like mother, like son.

"It's just a regular map," she finally says, adjusting her hand as she speaks. "I
don't know where your father got it. Maybe the car dealership? Or the 76 station on Bridgeport." She lays down a card, as you wait for the shoe to drop.
Your mother is often more predictable than she'd care to admit.

"Why do you want to know?" she asks.

"Never mind."

Your mother sighs. "You know I hate it when you say that. Why did you
ask?"

Jamie looks up from his cards. "She wants to know who drew the third map
and the circle on it."

"The third *what?*"

"Jamie." Your voice is calm, but the biting pinch of your fingers at his thigh
tells him what he needs to know. "Nothing, I meant nothing," Jamie says, but
it's too late, he's said too much.

"Did you draw on the map?" Your mother's voice is hushed, conspiratorial.
Together, your heads lean toward each other, voices dropping so that Father
won't hear.

"No, I swear. I thought *someone* had drawn on it. That's all. That Father drew
over it, where we were going to go, and someone else drew another map over
those two."

"Juney, there's no third map—there's no second map. What are you talking
about?"

"I—"

Now you're the one who's said too much. She places her cards on the table,
and holds out one hand. The diamond on her wedding ring catches the light,
hurling tiny rainbow dots across your face. "Let me see it." Her voice is low. You
realize she's not just angry but afraid, and it unsettles you. Your mother is often
cautious, but never afraid.

"I didn't write on it, I swear."

"I hope to God you didn't. He'll kill you—"

"What's going on back there?" Father, up in the driver's seat.

"Nothing, honey. We're playing Go Fish." She motions for the map. You pull it out from underneath your jacket, and hand it over. Your mother opens it up, spreading it across the table. Cards flutter to the floor. She stares down, hands aloft as if physically shaping her question with the uplift of her palms. From where you sit, you can see what she sees, upside down. You look up at the front of the camper. Father's sea-green eyes stare back from the mirror, watching.

"Sonavu*bitch*," she whispers.

"What do you see?" I don't want to know, but I have to know. What map does she see?

"June." She throws up her hands, as if exasperated. "I have no idea what you're talking about. I see my map, which obviously your Father can't see because he obviously is ignoring everything we've been planning for the last two months, but there is no second or third set of drawings here."

"How can you not see that?" You know you see the lines, drawn over her directions and Father's. You know you see the word in the circular void. It's right there, on the paper, right in front of her. And, you know you don't want her to see, you want it to be *your* destination, the secret place only you can travel to. But you place a trembling finger onto the middle of the circle, just below the word. You have to confirm it, that your map is unseen, safe. "All these new roads, leading to this circle in the middle, leading to this word—"

Your mother raises her hand, and your voice trails away. She stares down, her brow furrowing as if studying for a test. You want to believe that the small tics and movements of her lips, her eyelids, are the tiny cracks of the truth, seeping up from the paper and through her skin. Her fingers move just above the lines, and then away, as if deflected from the void in the middle. She moves her fingers again, her eyes following as she touches the paper. Again, deflection, and confusion drawing lazy strokes across her face, as her fingers slide somewhere north. Relief flares inside you, prickly cold, followed by hot triumph. She does not see your map. She sees the route and destination only meant for her.

"June, honey." She leans back, thrusting the map toward as if anxious to be rid of it. "It's just coffee stains. It's a stain from the bottom of a coffee cup. See how it's shaped? Probably from your father's thermos."

"Yeah, you're right. I didn't see it until now."

"All that fuss for nothing. What were you talking about, anyway—what, did you think it was some mysterious, magical treasure map?" She laughs in that light, infectious tone you loathe so much—although, the way she rubs at the small blue vein in her right temple reveals a hidden side to her mood. "Come on, now. You're not five anymore, you're too old for this."

"Ah," you say, cheeks burning with sudden, slow anger. She's done this before, playing games with you. Long ago, like when she'd hide drawings you'd made and replace them with white paper, only to slide them out of nowhere at the last minute, when you'd worked yourself into an ecstatic frenzy of conspiracies about intervening angels or gods erasing what you'd drawn. You'd forgotten about that part of her. You'd forgotten about that part of yourself.

"It just looked like," you grasp for an explanation, "it just looked like you'd drawn your own map of our vacation, and Father drew another, and the circles looked—I mean, look…." The explanation fades.

"Sweetie, calm down." Your mother tousles your hair, cropped like hers. She appears bemused now, with only a touch of concern. She doesn't believe in miracles or the divine, and sometimes she thinks you're a bit slow. "Honestly. You read too much into everything, and you get so overexcited. That's your father's fault, not yours. All those damn books he gives you—"

"I'm sorry," you stutter. "It was stupid, I know—it's so bright in here. The sun."

"Are you feeling all right?" She places a cool palm against your forehead. She does love you, as best she can, in her own way. "Maybe we should have stopped. Do you want some water? Let me get you some water."

"Don't tell Father," you say, touching her arm with more than a little urgency. She pats your hand, then squeezes it.

"Of course." A flicker of fear crosses her face again. "Absolutely not."

As your mother busies herself in the fridge with the tiny ice-cube tray, you fold the map back up, turning it around as you collapse it into itself. Your hand brushes the surface, casually, and you close your eyes. The paper is smooth to your touch. It's just our secret, the circle, you tell yourself. It's between us, between me and the void. That's what you call it: the void, that black, all-enveloping place you go to whenever Father appears in your doorway, the place where you don't have to think or remember or be. After all these years of traveling to it, perhaps now it is coming to you.

"Are you ok?" Jamie touches your arm. You shrug.

"I'm fine. Help me pick up the cards. I want to play Old Maid."

"June, it's getting dark. How can you read that—scoot your chair over here before you hurt your eyes."

"It's ok. I can read it just fine," you lie.

If there's a sun left in the sky, you can't see it from the makeshift campsite, a small flat spot Father found just off the one of the dead-ended offshoots of Hot Springs Road. He says that according to the map—his version of it—there's a lake nearby, but it's hidden from view—wherever it is Father has parked the camper, you get no sense of water or sloping hills, of the space a lake carves for itself out of hilly land. The earth is hard and flat, and piles of stripped logs lie in jumbled heaps at the edges, as though matchsticks tossed by a giant. The woods here seems weak and tired, as if it never quite recovered from whatever culling happened decades ago. You sit on a collapsible camp stool, watching Father set up a small table for the Coleman stove and lanterns. No fire tonight, this time. Father says there isn't time, they have to be to bed early and up early. "It's ready," he says to your mother, as he lights the small stove. "I'll be back in a bit." He turns and walks off with the lighter, disappearing between tree trunks and the sickly tangle of ferns. His job is finished, and he's off to smoke a cigarette or two, an ill-kept secret no one in the family is supposed to notice. There are so many other secrets to keep track of, he can afford to let slip one. Besides, it calms him down. You note that the map is in his back pocket, sticking out like a small paper flag.

Your mother has become thin-lipped and subdued over the past hour—you know what she's thinking, even if she doesn't. No matter where the family goes, a vacation for all of you is never a vacation for her, only the usual cooking and serving and cleaning without any of the comforts of home. Jamie knows how she feels, and as usual, he helps her. Beef stew and canned green beans tonight, and store-bought rolls with margarine. Chocolate pudding cups for dessert. If she was in the mood, she'd make drop biscuits from the box, or cornbread. She's not in the mood tonight. It's more than just cooking, this time. Father and your mother are divided over the vacation, over the destination. This is a first for them, and a first for you. Usually they are united in all things, as you and Jamie are, because so much is always at stake for all of you, because everything must be done in secret, away from the eyes of those who wouldn't understand, which is everyone in the world. But things are off-balance, tonight. You stare up at the trees, trying to see past them to the heart of the mountains. Your mother couldn't see the brown ink lines, the map within the map. Does he? You think you know the answer. Otherwise, why would he ignore his own vacation plans, his own map and dotted blue lines, why would he take you all here?

"June." Your mother, her voice clipped and tired. "Go get your father. Dinner's ready."

You stand up, looking around. Nothing but trees. It's peaceful here without him, brooding over everyone. You don't see the need to change that.

"I don't know where he went...."

"June, please. It's been a long day. Just go get him."

"I don't even know where he went to!"

"Just follow the smoke," Jamie says.

"Hush!" Your mother slaps at his arm, a playful smile on her face. For a moment, her dour mood has lifted. You use it, slipping into the woods unnoticed. You'll follow the smoke only as far as you need to, before going in the opposite direction. He can come back on his own.

Five feet in, and the darkness seals up the space behind you, as though the cozy camper and the soft lights never existed at all. Up above, the sky is still blue, but starless and without light. There are no paths or trails here, only ground thick with fallen pine needles and cones, and large ferns that brush at your face as you push through them. No trace of smoke is in the air, you smell only wet earth and pitch and leaves. You should have grabbed a flashlight, but you've never been afraid of the dark before, so you push forward. After several thick strands of webbing lash your face, you raise your arm, holding the book up high before you like a shield. It's a crumbling cloth-bound volume Father gave you years ago, for your seventh birthday. *Mythology of Yore.* Mythology of your what?, you'd joked when you unwrapped the book. Father stopped smiling: later, when you started reading, you stopped smiling as well. The stories are old, very old, and deliciously cruel, and when you touch the illustrations, red and silver bleeds off onto your skin. "This will explain everything," Father had said when he gave it to you. "This will explain why we do what we do, and why it is not wrong. Why it is as old as mankind itself, beautiful, divine."

He must not have read all the stories in the book.

"You know where we're going, don't you?" Father appears from behind the trees, and you let out a small gasp as you lower the book. He's barely visible in the gloom, the red tip of the cigarette the only real part of him you can fix your sight on. Yet, you can tell, even in the dark, even from a distance, that some strange mood has seized him, morphing his face into a mask. He wants something, he's seeking something. You remember what he told you on the piers at Port Angeles. Now is not the time for a smart-ass reply.

"We're going to the mountains. Into the center of the Olympics, like you said."

"We're going into the center." Smoke billows from his mouth as he speaks, and he crushes the remains of the cigarette with his finger and thumb, carefully so as not to create stray sparks. You watch him slip the butt into his front pocket—Father never approved of littering—and his hand is upon your throat, lifting you up and back into the solid wall of a tree. The book tumbles from

your grasp, away into the dense brush. It's gone, you'll never find it in the dark. Once again, he places a finger at the center of your forehead. Small coughs erupt from your lips, wet with spittle, as you struggle to breathe, as your feet slide up and down the rough bark, trying to find some place to come to rest.

"And where are you going, where do you go?" Father asks. His voice is a whispered snarl, hard and tight. What little air your lungs clutch at is tinged with warm smoke and rank sweat. "Where do you go when I'm with you? Where are you when the light leaves your eyes and all that darkness pools out of them as you beg me to take you away? What do you see?"

"I—don't—know." The words are little more than croaks.

"You don't know? You don't know? I treat you like a goddess, like a queen, and you slip away like some backstabbing little whore?"

"No—never."

The finger at your forehead disappears, and you hear the rustle of paper. The map. "Is it here? Oh yes, I see it. I don't know how you did it, when you drew it, but there it is. I drew my road to where I wanted to go, and she drew hers, and then your little web appeared, shitting itself all over our destinations. Except, I couldn't figure out how to get my road to the center of your map, to that nice big space inside you, no matter how many roads there were, no matter how many times the lines crossed. I always lost the way to the center of your little Tootsie Pop. *And it's just a fucking piece of paper!*"

"Guess—it's not—you stupid—fuck."

The map slams against your face, and there's a *crunch*. Blood streams from your nose, and pain explodes like lightning through your skull. And then Father wrenches your shorts and panties down and off your legs in a single motion and his zipper is down and your legs up as he parts them wide and he's against you and inside you in a single painful thrust, his cock spearing you against the tree like a butterfly.

For a moment he doesn't move, only breathes hard against your face as the branches rustle overhead, catching the evening wind. It's true night now, and there is no moon and there are no stars. What is he waiting for? You realize the map is still stuck against your face, stuck in the sweat and tears and blood. You move, listening to the rustling of paper so close you're your open eyes, your open eyes that see only liquid primordial night, and he begins to thrust. Long, hard strokes slamming your back and head against the rough bark, in and out, again, again, and you can feel it but you can't help it but you can feel it the old familiar vortex of pleasure forming somewhere deep down inside your traitorous thrusting body and you would give anything to not go there to not feel that and the words form silent in your blood-filled mouth *take me away take it away take it all away*, and even though you can't see, you feel it, you feel the blood-brown word expanding, burning through the layers of map, burning through bone and skin. Somewhere, a chain is being pulled, a hole unplugged, and your muscles slacken as the dark of night whorls around, thickens and deepens, as the flat black void opens wide to take you back in, even as something begins to spill out—

The map disappears, and the hand comes down hard against your cheek. You're back.

"I go everywhere with you. *Everywhere!* Do you hear me?" Your father's grip tightens, and you spasm against the tree, struggling as he pins your arms back against the trunk with his hands. Tears and snot drip down your face, plop onto your breasts.

"I go *everywhere*," he says. "You don't get to leave me behind. And the next time, the next time?—I go with you. The next time, I see everything you see." He leans in, kissing you hard as he thrusts deeper, harder, his tongue pushing into your mouth, filling it up until all you taste is him, all you breath is the air from his lungs, all you feel is what he feels, what he wants.

He lets go.

You fall, choking on your spit and pain, into the roots of the tree, your shorts and panties bunched at your feet. Father walks away, thin branches snapping under his feet as he zips up his pants. Then the metal rasp of his lighter, followed by the solitary blue-orange flame singing the tobacco into red. "Tomorrow night, when we get there, I'll be with you. All the way to the end." A moment of silence as he takes a deep drag, and exhales. You stay huddled in the knotted arms of the tree, hand at your throat, afraid to breath.

"Dinner's waiting, June-Bug. Hurry up." He walks away, crashing and cursing as he tries to find his way. It would be funny, if— When you no longer hear the sound of his footsteps, you crawl to your feet, clinging to the bark of the tree for support, then pull your shorts back on with trembling hands. The map is stuck to the bottom of your right sandal. You wipe the blood and dirt off with great care, then fold it small enough to tuck into your panties, small enough to not be noticed by anyone. He's done for the night, and you're not touching Jamie again tonight, not with your mother's smell all over him.

Off to your left, that's where the campsite was supposed to be, except, you don't know what left is anymore, or where it used to be. You walk forward, toes curled and back hunched as if worried that a single noise will bring him flying out of the darkness at you again. Your sandals slide over blacktop, flat and smooth. Overhead, the stars, and a sudden feeling of space and distance: the road. It's the same road Father drove down two hours ago, before he turned off

onto the dirt road into the woods. You turn, looking back into the woods. All of
the trees look the same, you can't tell which one Father pressed you against. All
you know is that when he first did, you and he were not at the side of the road,
there was no road at all. You closed your eyes and you traveled. You escaped,
but you took him with you, and only this far.

Is this what he was waiting for?

How much farther can you go?

Dinner is a dream. Your mother pinches your nose and wipes the blood away
without a word, then gives you cold water with miniature ice cubes from the
tiny freezer, saying nothing as she hands you the glass. She must know what
father did. Maybe she made him do it. Father has two beers, and your mother
doesn't hesitate in bringing them to him. He's mad at her, which is when he
drinks. She's subservient when she's mad, which makes him angrier, because he
knows she's just pretending. Jamie's eyes look a bit puffy, not enough for anyone
except you to notice. Your mother did or said something to him, that he didn't
like. He touches his bangs constantly, keeps his head down. You eat your beef
stew in small bites, careful to grind it down to a paste your tender throat can
swallow. It all tastes the same. And as you force down your meal, you realize
that all the things you know about your world, the normal things, aren't the
right things. They aren't the things that are going to save you. You think of the
book, lonely and cold, heroes and gods already festering in the damp of the
undergrowth.

But the map…. The map is folded into a tiny square, shoved deep into your
underwear. It's your map now, it's not his or hers, he threw it away, and besides,
it was never his map anyway. It was never his journey, his destination. He had
his own, and besides—isn't what he gets from you enough? Does he have to go
everywhere, see everything? Is there no place left for you and you alone? You
bite down on the lip of the plastic tumbler. There's nothing you can do, really.
It's not your fight, what they fight about. You, like any good map, can only
point any number of ways. But if he wants to see everything, he's going to be
surprised. Everything is not where you're headed. Everything is never where
you go.

After dinner, it's quick to washing up and then to bed. You and Jamie each
get five minutes alone in the camper to change before clambering up into the
camper's upper bed. Father and your mother argue quietly in the front of the
camper, behind a small plaid curtain your mother sewed. I can't believe you lost
the map, she says. We don't need a map, I know where we are, and I'll know

when we get there, he says. That doesn't even make sense, she says. We agreed to go to Windy Arm, we agreed to go where I wanted to go for once, she says. Wherever we go, we go together, he says. We do it for the family. That's how Mom and Dad taught us, it's how we survive. We do it as one.

Jamie and you lie on your sides in a shallow imitation of spooning, his arm draped across your waist. At first you didn't want him touching you, afraid they'd stick their heads up into the pop-top for a last good-night—you've long suspected that they know what you and Jamie do, what you are to each other. Still. You don't need them to have it confirmed. Finally, the lights click out: the night is so dark in contrast, for a second it seems bright as noon. You slide your hand across Jamie's, bring it up to between your breasts, as if to shield your heart. Your breath is shallow. Father and your mother zip themselves into their sleeping bags, and the camper settles into the ground, little creaks and ticks sounding out like metal insects. You wait. And, after what seems like half the night, gentle snores and deep breathing fill the small space. They're asleep. Nothing more will be needed of you and your brother tonight.

Your lips part, and you close your eyes, letting anxiety sieve out through the netting into the cool night air. Still, though, you don't move a muscle, and neither does Jamie. Let them fall asleep peacefully below, undisturbed. Let them lie together, like they should. Sometimes, after the school day was over, Jamie would whisk you into one of the crumbling old portable classrooms, unused for years since the new additions were build. There in the soft of the chalky air, he'd press you against the plaster walls, his body fitting neatly against and into yours. It was so different than with Father, it felt so good, so right. There was no need for the void with Jamie, no need to escape, because you wanted to be there, you wanted to remember every sigh, every moan. It's like Jamie was made for you, made to fit you, made to taste and smell exactly how you like. He was made for you, though, he was a part of you once, inside your mother's womb. Making love to him was the only way you could love yourself.

Jamie's hand opens, slides down around your right breast, cupping it gently. You feel protected, safe. And yet. And yet.

Another hour passes, and another. Jamie drifts off, you can hear it in the rhythm of his breath, feel it in the dead weight of his limbs. Below, Father and your mother are lost in sleep. Do you dare? Even as your mind asks the question, your body is answering, your hands slipping up to zip, inch by careful inch, the hard mesh that surrounds the pop-top of the camper. Jamie stirs, turns over and away. You stop, listening. Somewhere in the woods, a branch cracks, sharp like a gunshot, and silky rustling follows. Here, in this part of the world, the moon is of little use to you, and the stars are nothing. Here nothing can pen-

etrate the blanket of wood and branch and needles. You move forward, sticking
your face outside. You see nothing. You are blind as a worm.

The zipper moves again, and now your entire upper body is exposed to the
night. If you try to climb down the camper's slick sides, you'll only fall, and that
will mean noise, unnatural human noise, the kind that wakens other humans.
This is the most you can do, the most you can be free. Hidden at the bottom of
your sleeping bag is the map. Your toes grasp the folds of paper, and you bend
your knees up, reaching down at the same time. Slowly the map travels into
your hands. You hold it out into the open air, outside in the world, your finger
brushing across the bumpy ridges of the circles and into the center, where it
once again rests on that strange, lone word. Is this truly the place you travel
toward, when Father visits you in the night? Do you really hold the map to that
invisible place, and if so, how and when did you draw it? Or was it you? Perhaps
there is more in the flat black void than sublime nothingness. You move your
finger back and forth, coaxing the letters to respond.

The brownish ink, invisible in the night, leaps against the whorls of your
fingertip, as if tracing a route, an escape from the center and into the world. The
paper crackles, and you stiffen, holding your breath in. Again, you listen. Silence.
For a wild second, you imagine Father and your mother, awake and perched at
the edge of the bunk, pupils wide and oily-black as owls as they stare down at
you and your sleeping twin, younger versions of themselves, when they were
brother and sister, before they were husband and wife. You ignore the cold fear
as you send your plea, your command, out into the mountains, wherever in the
night they are. *Save me. Take me away.*

But nothing happens, and your arms become stiff and cold. Soft hooting
punctuates the silence, followed by another passage of the wind through the
ferns and trees. Resisting the temptation to sigh, you curl your arms back into
the camper, and fumble for the zipper. As you close the mesh screen, the wind
picks up, and small cracks sound throughout the clearing. It's a familiar sound,
but you can't place it. Something flaps against the screen then whooshes away:
startled, you shiver and slide back from the netting, images of insects and bats
filling your mind. Jamie stirs, turns away. Another object hits the mesh and
slides away—this time you recognize the sound for what it is. Stretching one
hand out, you press against the mesh as hard as possible, fingers outstretched,
wiggling as if coaxing. When the page hits the flat of your hand, you grab and
reel it back in. The wind dies down, and the flapping of loose paper fades.
What's left of the book is gone for good, scattered into the sky. You take the
page and insert it into the folds of the map. You fall into restless sleep, paper
clutched against your chest like a rag doll. In the early morning before everyone

else awakens, when the sky is the color of ash, you'll wake up and study the pen and ink drawing of an ancient maelstrom, its nebulous center leading somewhere you cannot see.

The road Father drives down while you fall asleep is smooth as silk compared to the road you wake up to. It had been beautiful before—unbroken lanes of blacktop, with perfect rows of evergreens lining each side, wildflowers of crimson-red and white crowding at their roots. The magazine slipping from your hands, you'd grabbed a pillow from the storage area behind the bench and snuggled against the window, bare feet resting flat against Jamie's legs. You slept hard, so hard you didn't feel the vibration in your bones as the road shifted to gravel and dirt, pitted with potholes and large rocks. You didn't see the forest fall away, dissolve into ragged sweeps of ravaged land, green only in the brush and grasses sprouting around stumps of long-felled trees. You didn't see the land itself fall away, until all that remained of the road was a miserly ledge, barely wide enough for any car, clinging to the steep sides of barren hills. You only woke up when you heard your mother screaming.

"Don't ask," Jamie says, before you can. He's sitting on the porta-potty, ashen-faced and shoulders hunched over, methodically placing one green grape after another in his mouth. You rub your eyes, trying to make sense of the ugly, unexpected landscape. To your right, the hill rises in a steep incline, tree stumps clinging for their lives to the dirt like severed hands. To your left: nothing. There is more desolation in the distance, but right beside the camper, there is nothing but jagged space.

The camper lurches down and shoots up, sending books and backpacks sliding across the floor. Your mother screams again. "Turn around, goddamnit!" Tears stain her face in shining streaks.

"I can't turn around," Father shouts. "There's nowhere to turn!"

"Where are we?"

Jamie shrugs. "A logging road, somewhere. It's not on the map. Dad says it is, but—" He shrugs again, and shoves several more grapes in his mouth, barely chewing before they're gone. He always eats mindlessly when he's stressed out.

"When did we leave the real road?"

"I don't know—an hour ago? It didn't get really bad until about twenty minutes ago. I can't believe you slept through all that. I thought you were dead." The camper lurches again, swaying wildly. Jamie stares out the window, a grape at his lip. "Yeah, I don't want to talk anymore. I just want to be quiet for a while, ok? I need to not—I need to be quiet."

"Yeah. Sure." Reaching for the grapes, you start to rise, and Jamie shoots out his hand to block you. "Stop, ok? Just—don't. Fucking. Move. Sit down." The camper lurches again, and for a wild second, you get the impression that there is nothing under the wheels, that you're all about to topple over and fall. The shriek is out of your mouth before you can stop it.

"Goddamnit." Father, at the wheel. "Sit down, June, both of you sit down and shut up!" Your mother covers her face with her hands. You've never seen her cry. You've never seen her lose control of her emotions, or of Father. They've always done things as one. Now she's sobbing like a child. Father turns back to you, motioning.

"Come up here."

"I—" You're paralyzed.

"Look at the road—" your mother shrieks. Father's hand lashes out like a snake. You can't hear the slap of his hand over the roar of gravel and rock under spinning wheels.

"June, get up here *now*. Jamie, get off the goddamn toilet and help your mother to the back. Everybody, now!"

Jamie stands up, legs shaking, and grabs your mother's hand as she sidles out of the passenger seat. Mascara coats her face in wet streaks, except for where Father slapped it away, and her lipstick has bled around the edges, making her mouth voracious and wide. Jamie helps her across the porta-potty, while you stand to the side, fingernails biting into your palms. There'll be raw red crescents in the skin when you finally unclench your hands.

"Come on," Father snaps, and you crawl across the toilet, hitting your head against the edge of the refrigerator as the camper slams over a log. Father curses under his breath, but doesn't slow down. Sweat the color of dust dribbles down his face, collects at the throat of his t-shirt and under his arms. If his jaw was clenched any tighter, his teeth would break. "Sit down. Open up the map."

Up here, in your mother's seat, you see now how bad it is. The road before you is barely there, crumbling on the right side back into the mountain, gouged with giant potholes—more like depressions where the road simply dropped away. No guard rails or tree line, just a straight drop hundreds of yards down, the kind of fall the camper would never survive. And the road curves, so steep and sharp that you can't see more than ten or twenty yards ahead, assuming there's even a road ten or twenty yards beyond that. No wonder your mother was hysterical. Father's going to kill you all.

"June, the map."

"You threw it away in the woods, I don't have it—"

"Never mind the fucking seatbelt. Take out the fucking map!"

Reaching into your blouse, you pull out the warm square of paper.

"Open it up."

You do as he says, refolding it so that only the folds showing the Olympic Peninsula show. It fits perfectly in your lap, the land and the void.

"Tell me where we are."

"Ok, I—" Your finger traces over the hand-drawn roads, so many of the brown-red roads that start and end with each other as abrupt as squares of netting. Below them, somewhere, is Father's dotted blue ink line, along with your mother's wishful scrawl of lavender road. Frantic, you move your fingernail along Father's road, following, following— You lost it. No: it's simply gone.

"Where are we, June-Bug?" Father manages a tight smile. "How much further do we have to go? I'm counting on you to help us."

"I'm looking—it's hard to see, it's like a furnace up here." Panic sharpens your voice. Again, you find the start of Father's road, and you follow, follow—it disappears. And it's not like it simply stops, and you can see the end. The road is there and then it's not, and your gaze is somewhere else on the map, on another map altogether, on the one that was meant for you.

"I'm sorry." The words barely leave your dry mouth. "I just can't find it. It's not on here. I'm looking and I see all these lines but there aren't any logging roads, and I can't find the road you drew—"

Father puts his foot on the brake, and the camper grinds to a hard halt. When he cuts the engine, the silence almost makes you groan with pleasure. Only the ticking of the engine now, and the whisper of wind and rolling gravel outside. Father places a hand on your shoulder. It sits there like some cancerous growth, hot and heavy, pressing down until the bones grind together. "You can do better than that," he says. "You know what map I'm talking about." He leans toward you, his eyes still on the ever-thinning road ahead. "Look at your map, June-Bug. I want you to tell me where we are on *your* map, not mine. Because every time I try to read it, I can't quite make out the roads. You know what I mean. Read your map, and tell me where we are. How far we are from the center."

You look back at your mother. She holds Jamie in her arms. His face rests at her throat, lips on her skin, pressing gently, whispering words you cannot hear because they aren't meant for you. Those beautiful large hands, around her waist and thighs. He didn't love you most, after all.

"June-Bug." Father stares at you, and you return his glance. There can't be any lying now. He already knows, and you're so tired. You just want this all to be done.

"It's not my map. I didn't draw it, you know. I don't know how it got there."

"I know. We didn't draw those other maps, either, your mother and me."

"What?" You lean back in the seat, astonished and angry as you stare at the limp paper. You wanted divine intervention for yourself, not for him, because you were the one who needed it, not him. Did the void betray you? "Why didn't you tell me?"

"It doesn't matter."

"Do you know how it got there?"

"I don't know. I got it at a gas station, I didn't open it till I got home, and there it was." He stares at the dusty windshield, beads of sweat matting his brown-grey hair. "I think—I think they appeared because that's where we wanted to go more than anywhere else in the world; and I think something in the world heard us and showed us the way. To a place where we can be ourselves without anyone else's eyes on us, to where we can be free to do and act as we please."

As animals, you think. As monsters. But you remember Jamie in the same breath, curving over you in the quiet corners of the school. Like father, like daughter. Animal, monster, too.

"Why can you see my map? Why can't we both see yours?"

"Because your map, that's where we both most want to go now. Because I love you, and I want to be with you. We need to go there together."

"All of us, together?"

Father's hand moves from your shoulder, gliding over your breast as he lowers it onto your thigh, the fingers rubbing hard against your sore crotch. "Us, together. Just the two of us. That's how it's supposed to be."

The sun boils the fabric of the seat, searing your skin. You stare out your window at all the desolation, feeling his hand, working, working. You barely see a thing in the glare, but you don't need to. You don't need to see anything at all. The cool, black edges of the void nip at the edges of your conscious, small nudges that leave smears of black in your vision, as though ink is trickling into your tears.

"I know the way to the center," you say.

"Good girl." Father leans in, kissing you on the cheek, almost chaste in his touch. "Good girl."

The engines roar, and the wheels whine as Father shifts into first, sending the camper rattling back up the small ledge. It's not that much further, you tell him, just a few more corners to round, and we'll be at the top, and the road will even out. You stare at the map as you speak, fingers moving back and forth as they trace the roads to the nothingness in the middle. Another corner comes and goes, and another, and you can see the anger in his face start to rise again, anger and impatience because he thinks *no he knows* that you lie, and you move your hand to his shoulder and squeeze it, then place it on his thigh. He smiles, takes your wrist and moves it in and down, wrenching the small bones in his haste. Repulsion fills your throat as you slide your hand past the folds of fabric, but you grab tight, grab as you slide to the edge of your seat, place your other hand on the wheel and your foot on the gas, down hard. And the road becomes a blur, the cliff is a blur and the screams and Father's fist against your face are mere blurs, and only the momentary silence under the wheels before the sharp weightless flip of the entire world strikes you as having any substance or weight, just the right weight and terror to send you into the flat black void, into the nothingness of the center, as you whisper to Father and Jamie and your mother and to anything else that can hear:

Can you see everything now?

You open your eyes.

You stand in an open field on a hill. Beyond this hill, more hills—small moun-tains bristling with dark green trees. Beyond those, the Olympics rise up from one end of the horizon to the other—endless, imperious, cold and white, their jagged peaks tearing through passing clouds like tissue. Until now, you never thought they were quite real. You never knew anything so colossal, so beautiful, could actually exist. Behind them, the sun is lowering, and long shadows are creeping toward you and the hill. The light is wrong: thin and pale. The air is cool, almost cold. It doesn't feel like summer anymore. It doesn't feel like June.

Both your hands are covered in clotted scars and blood—your right hand clutches a long, pitted bone. Many of your nails are gone, the rest have grown out hideous and sharp. It takes a moment to recognize the filthy strips hanging from your body as the remains of your pajamas. Your skin is deep blue: hands, arms, torso, legs, feet. Dye from small septic tank in the porta-potty. You smell like shit and death.

An animal-like grunt sounds out. Startled, you turn. To your right, a small herd of elk graze on the short grass. They are large and thick-furred, the males with antlers high as tree branches. They pay no attention to you. To your left sits the camper, monstrously dented and mangled, windows shattered, sliding side door long gone. Inside, it's dark. There's no movement in or around it, save for several birds perched on the pop-top. Scattered all around you are bits of clothes, empty cans and boxes, plastic bags, with a larger pile by the front tire of the camper, like a large nest. The hill. The road. The fall. The camper should

not be here. You should not be here, alive. This is not the remains of the logging road. This is the interior. This is the center. But of what, you do not know.

Turning to the camper again, you wait.

You wait for Jamie. You wait for anyone. You wait until the sun begins to lower behind the range. Waves of nausea roll through you, sending drool and bile spilling out from between your lips, and your muscles spasm and twitch. But you are not ill, and you are not hungry, and you hold a long clean bone in your hand. You raise the bone to your face. It's been scratched and scoured clean.

You know they will not appear. You know where they've gone.

As you lower your hand, you notice how rounded your belly is, like a little pillow, and how your naval sticks out like a round fat tongue. You're thin but not starved. Bending over slightly, you study your inner thighs: they, of all places on you that should be caked with blood, are clean. "Oh." It's the only word you can form. You know what this means, and you now know you've been on this mountainside longer than just three months. The tight, blue skin of your stomach is dotted with a latticework of markings as intricate as lace. You touch the blood, a roadmap of brown ink—it's the map, you realize, it's your map made flesh. You run your finger in a spiral around to your naval, circled three times in dried blood. Press at the soft nub of flesh, the place that still connects you to your mother's womb, and to all the women before her, to the beginning of time, the first woman, the first womb. It was always going to be like this. It has to end like this. It cannot begin again.

Behind the mountains, the clouds and skies deepen into vivid pinks and purples, rich and wonderful. A wind barrels down, sharp and stiff: the herd raise their heads from the grass in a single movement, then shoot off down the slope. You smell the change in the air, see the shimmering dark gather around the high peaks as the first thread of lightning splits down and away. Shivering, you sit down in the grass, balancing the bone at the crest of your mounded stomach, and carefully, firmly, run your wrists across the sharpened edges. And the sunset begins its slow dissolve, while lightning dances around the mountaintops, as all light fades from the world, and you start to cry. It's not a mirage, you see it: a separate, circular mass of black flowing up from the heart of the mountains, up and over the peaks like a tidal wave. Clouds and lighting curve toward the darkness, sliding into the mouth of the maelstrom and away. Near the edges of the whorl, uprooted trees begin to swarm into the air like locusts, disappearing with the earth itself. The ground beneath you shifts, and the entire hill jerks forward: the camper topples over and rolls out of sight. This is it. This is it. Raising your arms high, you inhale as much as your cracked ribs allow, and shout as hard as you can.

Take me. Save me.

It's not very loud, or hard, and your broken voice can barely be heard. But it doesn't matter. It's widening, consuming everything, and it doesn't even care or know that you exist because this is chaos, this is nothing and not nothing, and this is where you want to go more than anyplace else at all, because inside that, there is no sorrow, there is no pain. Only everything you ever were, waiting to be reborn.

And while you can still feel, you feel joy.

Within your belly, movement—a deep watery ping of a push, like someone beating down against a drum, over and over. You cover the mound of flesh with your weeping arms, and crouch before the rising winds. Everything's going, this time. Nothing will return. Cherry red ribbons cover the blue stains and black scars, erase the circles, the roads. No new map this time. Only a river rushing into itself, only a girl striking out on her own, with no directions left behind that anyone can follow.

Which is as it should be. Where a girl goes, the world is not meant to know.

Her Deepness

PART ONE
Sometimes There's No Poison Like a Dream

In a corner of the great southern metropolis known to its citizens as Obsidia, in a sprawling district known to its inhabitants as Marketside, a squat, hollowed-out block of a building sits at the edge of a roaring traffic circus, windows gaping like broken teeth in an ivory skull. In the center of that century-old pile of stone, a young student named Gillian Gobaith Jessamine stands under the drooping brown leaves of a lemon tree, a frisson of *morriña* trickling through her as she observes a canary groom itself in the sticky summer air. The canary is bright yellow under a layer of soot, and a small ivory ring marked with a row of numbers and letters binds one leg: this tells her that the bird isn't some wild passerine but a domestic, bred for a specific anthracite mining company, several hundred miles away. Gillian knows because she wore a ring just like that, a scrimshaw bone collar fastened tight around the pale brown of her neck when she was young, when she worked in the deep of the earth. How it came here, all the way from the industrial heart of the city into the dank inner suburban courtyard of her school, is a mystery. Then again, she took that same journey when she was merely twelve. Is that the reason for the jolt of *morriña*? It unsettles her to feel sudden nostalgia for such an ugly, terrifying time and place, a place she's tried so hard to leave behind. Then again,

nothing in Obsidia is impossible, Gillian has found. Everything, both wonderful and horrifying, can be, and is.

The canary hops from the tree, flying over to a half-finished obelisk of pale limestone. All across the rectangular courtyard, pallets of tombstones are scattered, flat slates of stone ready to be hauled into the school workshops, where names, dates and lyrical bits of *memento mori* will be carved into their blank faces. Gillian rubs the scars on her hands, then picks at the dirt under her short nails. She's spent the past five years learning how to draw—first on crisp onionskin, then balsa wood, and finally stone—folded hands and flippers holding prayer books, mining and Masonic symbols, skulls encircled by elaborate borders, clusters of violets and rose blooms grasped by stately demons and leviathans. She even carved herself once, as an impassive-faced angel of death gliding across the cool surface of silver-shot *Dark Emperiador* marble, lifting the departed soul into an endless sky. She doesn't know who the tombstone was for, if it now resides in one of the vast cemeteries scattered throughout Obsidia, and if so, who or what lies beneath it. Still, it pleases her to know that it's out there, somewhere. Like most of the working-class residents of the city, Gillian can't afford a plot of land and a neatly-carved marker. When she dies, she'll burn like the coal she once helped rip from the lands, and her ashes will find their final resting place in a holding pond of toxic sludge. All that will remain will be her face etched in marble, until time itself wipes that away, too.

"Another year without lemons. Shattuck will be furious." Emanuel Pallesynd, her teacher for this last year, and her lover for the past four, walks up to her, one hand lightly touching the small of her waist as he reaches out to the withering tree, and tugs a deformed nub of fruit from a branch. "Great God, look at it. It's almost obscene."

"What did he expect?" Gillian examines the folds of the fruit, her fingers caressing the rough skin of his hand. "We told him it wouldn't work. The courtyard doesn't get enough sun, the soil is full of chemicals, and lemons are tropical, anyway. We're too far south." She smiles as his hand slides down the folds of her limp cotton dress. The lemon falls to the ground with a weak thump as she touches his wrist. "Too far south, Mr. Pallesynd. Someone might be watching."

Emanuel removes his hand but leans in, and Gillian feels his grey-flecked beard brushing the back of her neck. Heat drifts from his body through her dress, and despite the stifling air, she welcomes it. Emanuel speaks in measured tones against the curve of skin, as if imparting another lesson. "Everyone else is gone. In ten minutes, you'll have your certificate and your placement. We're free to do as we please."

Gillian watches the canary lift from the tip of the obelisk. It circles once, then darts into the rectangle of the sunless workshop door, as if the shadows had swallowed it whole. The sun pours down, sending beads of sweat trickling underneath the limp black curls of her bobbed hair, all the way down her scarred back. The rectangle throbs and looms in the light, grows larger. Images erupt from long-forgotten memories. A sunless city, an empty train track, a silent tunnel opening wide.... Gillian looks away from the door, blinking hard until the dark breaks up into sparkling fireworks behind her crinkled eyelids. She hasn't thought of that nightmare in years.

"Free." She smiles at her lover, at his handsome face and soft brown eyes. Emanuel is almost twice her age, yet the boy still lives so lightly on his skin, in his heart. If she told him how she felt, how little she felt, that boy would die. She's sure of it. "As free as one can be in Obsidia."

Emanuel bats at the dying lemon tree with his worn Panama hat. Dead leaves drift like feathers to the bone-dry ground. "Not very free, is it?"

"Free enough for any human," Gillian says.

Emanuel nudges the hat back onto his shining forehead. "Free enough for any Obsidian, you mean."

"Well. Yes, I suppose."

"Like I said, then. Not very free."

"And like I said," Gillian says as she hoists her heavy tool satchel onto one shoulder, "free enough."

Distant clocks chime the half-hour as they walk across the courtyard, passing through shadows of half-carved statues and disassembled mausoleum friezes. In the far corner, an aging priest from the local parish gives a benediction to a completed tomb, his webbed hands shaking as he recites the words first in the city's own language—a mish-mash of English, Welsh and Spanish, which they all speak—then in the Old Language. Gillian has never truly believed in the Gods, but nonetheless she bows her head as they halt, listening in respectful silence with Emanuel. For a moment, the river of heavy traffic outside the building fades, and there's only the voice, the harsh Language, the glossy drone of flies. And then the ceremony ends: the priest drops heavily onto a half-carved column, panting several times before taking a sip of aguardiente from a glass straw while a young novice squirts warm ocean water from a gilded spray bottle over his scaly face and cenote-round eyes. Gillian leads the way, almost skipping through the workroom and into the brown tiled hall that leads to the upstairs offices.

"What's your hurry, Miss Jessamine?" Emanuel laughs.

"I want to find out where I'm going," Gillian calls back as she dashes up the stairs to the warren of offices on the fifth floor.

"You don't need to run—you always know where you're going."

"No, I don't," Gillian says to herself. "I just don't want to go back to where I've been."

Headmaster Shattuck's office is at the northernmost corner, overlooking the chaos of the seven avenues that merge into Marketside Circus. As Gillian pauses at the top of the stairwell to catch her breath and compose herself, Hingham Pitts, a fellow student, appears in the narrow doorway before her, grim as the statues in the courtyard. Down the hall, a stack of yellowing papers collapses onto a pile of ledgers like dandruff flakes.

"Where did they place you?" Gillian asks. Pitts only snorts and shakes his head—it's enough of an answer to know it wasn't where he wanted. "You're last," he says as they pass each other. "Best for last, right? Good luck." He disappears down the stairs, and Gillian proceeds to the crooked end of the hall, mulling over his fate. Like many of the students, he's not much more than a competent carver. Most will end up as caretaker's assistants, sweeping floors and mending damaged markers. That can't be me, she tells herself. After all I've been through to get to this moment, I deserve more.

"Enter," a voice calls from inside before she can knock. Gillian pushes the protesting wood door open.

"Miss Jessamine." Headmaster Nathanial Shattuck stands at the closed windows behind his desk, staring through the greasy panes onto the streets below as he cleans his glasses with the edge of his coat. Gillian lets out a discreet cough, though she knows it's useless. Shattuck rarely opens the windows, preferring to marinate in the furnace of stale air.

"Are you well? You seem pale—paler than usual."

"It's the heat, sir. It's usually not this warm in June." Gillian closes the door and stands with her hands clasped at her waist, a penitent pose that has served her well in the past, when she's been in trouble—and she feels like trouble hovers somewhere close.

"And your son, the tailor's apprentice—Jasper, is it? I haven't seen him in some months, is he well also?"

Jasper Ioen. Her thirteen-year-old ticket out of the mines, born when she was only twelve. She never told him he was born a half-mile underground, that her last act as a canary was carrying his naked, bloody body to the surface of the world. "He's very well, sir, thank you. Still a tailor's apprentice, but his skills are quite advanced for his age. He's hoping to become salaried by summer's end."

Shattuck nods his approval and perches his glasses back onto his nose, then motions to a carved coupe glass on his desk, filled with a clear yellow liquid.

"Go on, take it. To celebrate."

Gillian picks up the coupe, and takes a sip. Cheap champagne—sour, warm and flat. "Very good, thank you," she says, wiping her grimace against the back of her wrist.

Shattuck picks up the bottle, and drains it into his glass. "Lemonade would have been better. Goddamn tree. Well, next year."

Trying to hide her smile, Gillian walks to the side of the room, where twelve headstones rest on wooden easels. Each one is a commission, carved from start to finish by each of the twelve graduating students for a paying customer. Above the stones, onionskin sketches and mock-ups are pinned to the flocked velvet wall.

"It's like a private museum exhibition," Gillian says. "Or an art gallery."

"I suppose," Shattuck answers, his voice hesitant. "A few of these slabs might make the dead rise in protest—not all of your classmates have the skills for carving, I'm afraid."

Gillian gulps down the rest of the champagne, embarrassed to admit she agrees with him.

"Mr. Pallesynd tells me you have an inordinate talent with marble," Shattuck says, "and I concur." Shattuck walks over to her piece, and runs his hands across the polished slab of *Afyon Violet*, covered in a tangling of trilobites, ammonites and gastropodes resting under a canopy of shooting stars—her final project for the school. "He says you're able to speak to the stone, to bring it to life even as you're slicing into it."

"Oh, I wouldn't call it speaking. More like coaxing." It's a joke, but Shattuck doesn't seem amused. His fingertip runs along the lettering of the *memento mori* phrase she carved in the center.

"'I ride the wings of the morning sun, and dwell in the uttermost arms of the deep.' Did you come up with that yourself?"

"Yes, sir."

"Quite moving. The lettering is exquisitely fluid, almost cursive, like a pen wrote this instead of a chisel and hammer. 'Of the deep'—you were a canary in your childhood, right?"

"Yes, sir."

"Sent ahead of the miners to make sure there were no poisonous fumes?"

"I—yes, sir." She was going to tell him more, tell him how they would send her into the newly-made tunnels, after the colossal drilling machines had pulled out of them like satisfied lovers; how she wandered the subterranean labyrinth searching for coal seams with no light, no mask, no water; how her hands pressed against stone walls still smoking from the bite of the drills, how she heard and felt and smelled the living earth; how she always found the coal. How she woke up screaming at night, dreaming that the seam had somehow seen her, had found her first....

"Miss Jessamine?" The headmaster sits at his desk now, files and ledgers spread out before him. "I think you've wandered away from me."

"Oh." Gillian blushes. "I'm sorry. Memories of the mines—they took me back. I try not to think about that part of my life anymore."

"Then I should apologize. I didn't mean to bring up such painful times." Shattuck appears genuinely concerned, and Gillian believes him. He's something of a crotchety old man, a bit eccentric at times, but he's never been deliberately cruel to any of the students.

"I'll be fine, sir. That's all in the past. I'm ready for my assignment. I'm ready to start something new."

Shattuck holds up a round finger. "Of course you are, and of all in your class, you most deserve it—no, no, don't be embarrassed, you know it's the truth. Now let me see, where did I...."

Now he's the one who's lost, in a blizzard of memos. Gillian downs the rest of the champagne in one open-throated pour while the headmaster shuffles through the sleeves of a brown leather portfolio. He draws out a folder with her name on it, and holds page after page to the low light of the banker's lamp, occasionally glancing up at her. Gillian feels the scars on her back throb with a phantom ache—the heat and press of her corset always aggravate them so—but she resists the urge to hunch against the back of the chair like some animal satisfying an itch. The scars are the remnants of a mine explosion that happened when she was seven, an incident she remembers only in liquid gold flashes, and even then only anymore in troubled dreams. They cover her body from scalp to soles in a patchwork quilt, some fine and spider-thin, others thick and brutally jagged, as though the mine had tried to sew her back together even as it tore her apart, a recalcitrant creature of coal fixing a broken human toy.

"Excellent! Here it is." He lifts a file with the name *HELLYNBREUKE* scrawled across it in green marker, and opens it up. Gillian clasps her hands together into a tight fist. Her middle name, Gobaith, is Welsh for "hope." She has spent much of her life hoping, and much of her life suppressing that emotion— it so rarely transforms into reality. And yet. Dare she give into hope now?

Shattuck sees her reaction and smiles. "Yes, Hellynbreuke. Tell me what you know of it."

"A private necropolis, very historic," she begins, keeping her voice *Roman Sicillia* calm—chilly, creamy gold. "The most perfect examples of funerary art in the world are located there, created by the most skilled artists in Obsidia. Family mausoleums carved entirely of single, seamless blocks of anthracite and amber, monuments created from giant geodes and other rare mined crystals—or so I've heard. There are no photos or drawings of it that I've been able to find. I've heard rumors that it's located somewhere within El Torres del Pain, accessible only to the highest levels of government and industry officials. I've also heard—" Gillian stops.

"Go on."

Gillian shakes her head. "No, it's stupid. Just rumors."

Shattuck smiles. "Such as?"

"Oh. Artifacts and creatures ripped out of the mountains and ocean, kept in collection rooms and holding pens. Objects of profane power, doorways and portals to other worlds—" Gillian breaks off once again. Shattuck stares at her, visibly impressed.

"Well. How did you find all this out?"

"When something interests me, I become—determined."

"Evidently. Tell me something else, have you ever heard of Wormskill?"

"No, I'm not familiar with that name."

Shattuck waves an aging sheaf of papers in her direction. "It's a small company cemetery up north in the middle of Feldspar—the first district, the humble birthplace of our vast city. At its peak of production, Feldspar produced two hundred thousand tons of coal a day, and hundreds of thousands of ties for the railroad tracks, as well as the great engines that would begin burrowing through the mountains to the ocean beyond. It was only when a fire, most likely started by the illegal practice of burning trash, spread underneath most of Feldspar, destroying the mines and rendering the city limits uninhabitable—"

Gillian interrupts his lesson. "I know about Feldspar's history, but I thought it was quarantined."

"Oh, it has been, for over a hundred years now, along with the cemetery. However, about twenty years ago, several descendants were given permission to move their ancestors' bodies from the city limits."

"So, Wormskill no longer exists, then."

"Yes. However." The Headmaster hands her a slip of parchment and turns to the window. Gillian reads the spidery words. *One carved quartz or metal*

reliquary, which may or may not contain the partial remains of an employee of New Y'ha-nthlei Steelworks.

Outside, clouds move above Avenida Providencia and Marketside Circus. The room sinks into murky grey.

Gillian's mother was a cool creature, not one to grace her daughter with compliments or smiles. She gave Gillian nothing, not even a history, not even her father's Tehuelche name—assuming her mother had even known it. The woman disappeared in the middle of summer, the last Gillian spent above the ground. Gillian holds that image close to her heart: silver-haired Morwyn Jessamine giving her half-breed daughter a tight-lipped nod of farewell before slipping into a flame city sunset choked with black telegraph wires. Was it relief on her mother's imperious face that she'd seen? Regret? The image, like an empty grave, holds no knowledge to illuminate her with. She only knows how it made her feel even to this day, to think of her mother, like hope, abandoning her with the setting sun.

Shattuck opens his mouth, but Gillian already knows what he's going to say.

"You want me to retrieve what was left behind. That's my new job. You want me to go to Wormskill."

The Headmaster holds an envelope up, near to the lamp's weak flame, so that she can see the writing. MISS GILLIAN GOBAITH JESSAMINE, HELLYNBREUKE NECROPOLIS is typed on its cream front, the flaps sealed by a dark oval of gold-flecked wax, imprinted with the official city seal.

"Not me, my dear. The Minister of Necropoleis wants you to retrieve the item, and deliver it to Hellynbreuke, after which you will remain there permanently, as director of Hellynbreuke's carving and restoration shops. All those beautiful monuments, and you'll be in charge of them all." Shattuck leans forward, sliding the letter toward her fingertips. His watch chain clicks against the desk. She recognizes the metal, knows its qualities, its name.

"Gillian Jessamine of Hellynbreuke, the cemetery queen," he says. "How does that sound?"

It's pyrite.

On certain nights in the city, when all the stacks of the factories are venting their smoking spleen, noxious fumes wash through Marketside District, rousing people from sleep long enough to reach for their ventilators. Gillian learned at an early age how to bind and fasten the straps around her head, adjust the long cylindrical nose against the lower half of her face, how to breathe and speak and sleep with charcoal-filtered air seeping in minuscule amounts through her gasping mouth. She learned to ignore the stench of her own breath, the vomitous tang of air that rose from her stomach in coughs and belches, only to slide into her nostrils and lungs. Later, she learned to fuck with the mask on—over time, it became less of a hindrance and more a clever means to disengage, an excuse to stare mindlessly at water-stained ceilings or unfamiliar skies while men grunted and pressed into the lower half of her body, seemingly a million miles away.

Tonight, this last night in her cramped two-room flat, is not such a night. Gillian stands at the cracked panes of Sargasso-green glass, letting the cool metal tang of night air rush through her lungs. Outside and below, hooves clop and ring on the cobblestones, round a corner and fade; while distant trains rumble on tracks in and out of the city center, loaded with anything and everything that can be ripped from the lands and towering mountain range—Cordillera del Tenebroso—that makes up the narrow edge of the southern continent. Even a hundred miles away, nestled in the folds of the smaller mountains, she hears the sound—there are that many tracks, that many trains. Twenty-four hours of every day, there is always the stormless thundering of steam engines.

"Someone will see you." Emanuel lies on the bed, barely visible in the squares of warped light seeping through the glass. His arm is raised, holding out her worn robe.

"I don't care, it's too hot. No one can see inside, anyway." Nonetheless, she slips it over her naked skin. Emanuel is by nature a jealous man, but he is often prudent, cautious—something she is often not, despite her seemingly calm, detached demeanor. If there is a door open, or a window cracked, he wishes it shut, always. She wants it opened wider, to see what is beyond, where she might go—a nature forged by a childhood spent in the mines, where an open tunnel ahead meant "come inside." And she always did. Time and time again, Gillian found fat anthracite seams that the company men, with all their sophisticated instruments, could not. She found them because she did what they would not do. She went further. She went deeper.

"Is Jasper still here?" Emanuel squints as Gillian points to the sagging cot on the other side of the room, empty save for a faded mattress and Gillian's and Emanuel's matching portmanteaus, packed for the journey. Beside them lie matching envelopes from the Ministry—Emanuel received his after her meeting with Shattuck had ended. "Too much wine for dinner. I didn't even hear him leave."

Gillian glowers at the warped wooden door leading to the second room. Jasper had spent the evening packing, showing his displeasure at her leaving him behind by banging the chairs and dresser drawers until the neighbors com-

plained. "He doesn't want to live in the tailor's basement with all the other apprentices, but he doesn't have a choice. He's not making money, so he can't keep these rooms. His anger finally wore him out. It usually does." She walks to the bed and curls down beside Emanuel's bare legs. "He's like you that way."

Emanuel smiles. "You mean, he's like you that way."

"Oh, thank you, sir."

"He is. I saw the way you brooded after you left Shattuck's office today. Don't say you didn't want to put your fist through a wall. Which I still don't understand. You're going to Hellynbreuke. Why do you always see something bad in all the good?"

Gillian pulls the robe from her shoulders, and slips under the sheet next to Emanuel. "I wasn't angry," she says. Her hand slides over his chest, and his heartbeat pulses through her palm. "It's about going to Wormskill. I don't want to travel all the way out into the country to drag some broken bit of statuary back into the city. It's ridiculous."

"I've been to Feldspar before. It's not quite 'country.' Far from it, in fact."

"What? You've been there, and you never told me?" Gillian doesn't try to hide her annoyance. "Why? What did you do there?

Emanuel sighs. Gillian's body rises and falls with his breath as he speaks. "I didn't say anything because it never came up. I mean, there was no reason to bring it up, I didn't do anything exciting. I was part of the team that was sent to disinter the bodies and pack up the markers and statuary for travel. It was almost twenty years ago, it was mindless grunt work, that's all. Like digging ditches. I did some quick restoration, some patching up of stonework, they paid me well, and that was that. I haven't thought about it since then. It was largely forgettable."

"How long were you there?"

"A couple of—months."

Gillian hears the slight catch in his reply, the way his voice swerves around an almost-spoken word and hitches itself to "months". She is certain he was going to say *years*.

"Were there any bodies or tombs you had to leave behind?"

Emanuel shrugs. "I was positive we accounted for every grave and marker—we dismantled entire mausoleums, even. But it was a nightmare to find anything: overgrown weeds and bushes, thorns and brambles everywhere, some of the graves had shifted or sunk. Obviously we missed something. I'm surprised a single reliquary is the only thing we overlooked."

A thought surfaces in Gillian's mind, like a river eel thrashing through the polluted muck of Becher Canal. "If everyone left the cemetery after it was relocated, who was there who would have found the reliquary? Why didn't they take it to Hellynbreuke themselves?"

Now Emanuel's body stiffens ever so slightly. He's going to lie to her, and he doesn't even know it: but his flesh can't lie, to itself or to her. Gillian feels his subconscious fight to control it, as the tremor moves from his arms and chest down to his legs. For a moment, it's as if she's holding a department store mannequin, and the thought repulses her. She resists the impulse to push him away, knowing the moment will pass.

"We'll have a traveling companion—she has rather formidable psychic abilities, but she needs an escort. Long journeys are hard on her. She'll be staying behind to thoroughly excavate the site."

"A psychic," Gillian says. "So, this isn't just a pick-up. It's also a delivery."

"More or less. The object is the important thing, of course."

"What's her name?"

"I don't think she has one. Here, I have something for you." Emanuel sits up, shifting Gillian aside as he reaches over to the wooden crate that serves as her nightstand. "Hold out your hand." Gillian does so, and she feels his fingers press a square of marble onto her palm. She sighs, almost a groan, as if the weight of the stone is pushing her through all the floors of the tenement building into the pipe-riddled ground.

"Please. I want something in my pocket, for luck."

"No." Gillian tries to sit up, but Emanuel presses her back against the sheets.

"Just one more time, love," he says. "And I'll never ask again. I promise."

"You promise?"

Emanuel places his hand against his heart. "I swear to the Dreaming God."

Gillian holds the square up to the light. It's a chip of *Arihant Spider Green*, dark as the wild forests and jungles far beyond the northernmost edges of Obsidia, supposedly. Gillian's never seen any type of wilderness in person, never ventured beyond the crush of buildings into any part of the world where Obsidia is *not*—but she can imagine it. The whorls of her fingertips press down, catch against thin white veins caught within the green. She doesn't know what part of the world the chip is from, or if there are forests and trees where it once lay, but no matter. Her fingertips warm the smooth surface, and images unfurl in her mind, a combination of her own imagination and the antediluvian strands of memory embedded in the stone: ragged outcrops of mossy boulders, erupting from forest lands like bones tearing apart aging skin, pocked and smoothed by autumn rains. Her fingertips move, caress, and the marble replies, moves; and grows still.

"Done." Gillian places the chip back into Emanuel's hand. An exquisitely detailed leaf has appeared on the surface, crisscrossed in veins and ragged at the edges, as though it had been nipped by insects and animals. It looks chiseled—to the ordinary human eye, that is.

"Are you sure it's not alive?" As always, Emanuel has grown unsettled at watching her work. "How does the stone always know? How do you speak to each other?"

"I've told you before, I don't know. It's a different kind of speaking, a different way of being alive," Gillian says. "It's not something I can explain or write down. I just know."

"It's hard to believe you learned this in the mines. I can't imagine what you created down there, inside rock so large and old."

Gillian thinks of Jasper, of all the flesh and blood she left behind. "You don't create things in mines. You only destroy."

"Have you ever wanted to read me like that?"

She stares at her lover, so opposite her in every way, so warm and alive and she so pale and *Carrara*-cold. "Humans are a different kind of life. I can't read that kind of life the same way. I wouldn't want to."

"You wouldn't need to, love. There are better ways." Emanuel slips his arms around her, drawing her close. She feels the chip press into her back, leaving indentations amidst her mine-scarred flesh. Gillian's fingers surreptitiously touch the skin between her breasts before traveling down Emanuel's body, as she wonders if this time the flame will spark, and she'll feel something, anything, for the man she should love. But her heart beats no faster than before, and that beat is slow as geology, as rare as Antarctic rain.

"Will it at least be cooler in Feldspar, even if it's not really the country?" She breathes the words into his neck as he parts her legs, presses into her again. "Will it be peaceful?"

"As peaceful as the—"

Gillian kisses him hard, so he cannot finish the sentence. All she hears now is the crack of canary wings, plunging from the obelisk into a room without a sun.

PART TWO
I am the Stone the Builder Rejected

Highgate Station clings to the lowest slopes of the mountain that forms the southern edge of Marketplace—which is to say, it towers above anything else in this part of Obsidia, save the forest of factory chimneys. In the pitch of night, the gothic-spired building glows like the translucent skull of a dragon, jagged maw opened wide to disgorge twenty-odd trains to all points across the city: suburban enclaves, bustling business districts, and industrial sections—even through the miles of elevated train yards that divide the entire metropolis neatly in half, keeping the slums underneath festering in a perpetual twilight of iron and steel.

Gillian watches the trains from the large bay window of the quiet Club Room, an enclave reserved for the most powerful travelers of the city's rail systems. She's been allowed entrance this one time, so she doesn't waste an opportunity she knows will never come again. A glass of fresh-pressed juice in one hand, she carefully bites into the center of a *pain du chocolate* and stares in stark awe at dawn creeping onto the edges of the city below. This is a view she has never seen before. Always she's been in the middle of it, an insect blindly feeling its way through shifting rubble, too close to the mechanical monstrosities and marvels to truly comprehend their vast size. Now, she can barely comprehend the sprawling empire below. How is it that people can live inside all that steel and fire? How is it that any of them are alive?

"Incredible, isn't it." Emanuel sits in a chair to the side, reading the morning paper as he finishes his second café. Archduke Assassinated in Sarajevo, one headline declares. "It's almost six, dear. Earplugs."

"Yes, I have them." She bites into the *pain*, but doesn't chew.

From her feet to the horizon, Obsidia stretches out and up: deep valleys of smoking furnaces and factories to snow-capped peaks of the Tenebroso crowned with stacks a hundred stories high, jetting green fire against the red disk of the rising sun. Countless train tracks catch the morning rays as they shoot from the bowels of the city, filled with the riches of the earth—copper, coal, silver, potassium nitrate and iron ore—and disperse up the hemisphere to all corners of the world. And in between the dark edges of industry, hazy spherical glimpses of another city rise from Obsidia's midst, the strange geometries of their god's city made real as it's pulled from dark ocean waters thousands of miles away, and reassembled in their midst. In this moment, behind the thick glass: peace, or as much of it as the city can spare. She'll remember it later in the day, when traffic roars through every slender lane and cyclopean boulevard, and she rushes past it all in a train bound to a dying town.

In the back of the room, a clock begins chiming the night away. Gillian reaches for two small plugs of hard foam in her pocket, each carved in the cephalopodic shape of Obsidia's ubiquitous god. The sixth bell sounds; and outside the station, horns howl the shift change, cleaving the moment between night

and day with a single deep note that sets her bones trembling as hard as the window panes.

"They're going to come to us someday," she says, the non-sequitur erupting on her tongue like bile—a common occurrence amongst Obsidians whenever the factory whistles blow, as though the sonic dissonance dislodges some unseen truth from their pineal eyes. "We're going to arm the world with a guillotine for its own neck." No one hears her speak. All across the horizon, as far as eyes can see, clouds of inky smoke shoot upward from ten thousand shaking brick and metal stacks, rigid fingers pinching out the sun. Morning shift has begun, and those who work the daylight hours above ground must rise and earn their keep. This city and its gods demand no less.

Emanuel tosses the paper down and rises, motioning that it's time. Gillian pulls the foam from her ears. "You know, I used to hear the shift change underground, all the time. This was the first time I've ever seen it like this." She kisses him lightly on the cheek. "Thank you."

Emanuel holds up their tickets. "Thank your new employer. Come on. We have to meet the rest of the team. They're already on the train."

"There are others coming? I thought it was just the psychic."

"Yes. And a few others, to help with setting up and running the camp; and transportation of the reliquary, if we need it." Emanuel's face turns neutral as he speaks, and Gillian grows dismayed. How much more does he know that he hasn't said?

As they leave the room, a grey-feathered chingolo begins serenading the rays of sunlight sliding through the windows. Several children gather around the cage, slipping bits of bread through the bars, despite knowing it's no pet for their amusement, but there only to gauge the levels of toxic fumes in the room. Gillian doesn't feel sorry for it. There isn't a creature in Obsidia that doesn't know why it was born, and how it must die.

The lower levels of the station are all grey granite and sharp echoes, with occasional glimpses of smoking black steam engines resting on tracks, waiting to devour their passengers and race away. Names as terrible and magnificent as their quaking frames adorn onyx sides in letters of silver and gold: *Lord of the Seventh Kingdom, Fantasma Imperador, Fist of the Southern Star*. Gillian finds Track #16 at the far end of the wing, beyond a thick arch of rough-hewn stone. Under the low vaulting of the tunnel, *Empress of Devastation* awaits, her long black body throbbing with every pull and pound of the pistons and gears. Steam explodes from the stack and undercarriage, filling the space with python-sized coils of wet smoke. That *Devastation's* six-foot-high wheels float several feet above the tracks makes Gillian understand that this is a lucid dream, that her body is already somewhere within the real *Empress*, fast asleep as her mind sinks in the oubliette of images flickering through her brain.

"Ma'am, it's time to board."

A platform conductor points to the closest car with a look on his malformed face that indicates stern disapproval of stragglers; and only seconds after Gillian hoists herself from the top of the rickety stepladder into the compartment, he slams the carriage door behind her: they are moving. The raised roof of the station slides away, revealing a sunless morning sky, and now they slide down gleaming tracks, toward the fiery heart of the city. Outside the car, clogged streets, crumbling factories and tangled knots of building-sized machines sail past in an uneven landscape, obscured only by trestles and the long blur of trains rushing in the opposite direction. Obsidia passes around and below her in all its filthy glory.

You're like the lemon tree. You haven't been planted in ground where you can thrive.

Gillian looks away from the window. Shattuck stands at the top of the aisle. At his back, the entire front of the train has disappeared, and the car is open to a bank of grey fog washing through the city, obscuring the ends of the rails and the factories until only twinkling light and flame remain. They rush headlong into the bank, the engines beneath her feet pounding like metronomes, a sound that recedes as the dream rolls forward with the train. They are traveling to a place without sound, without light or air: images of another dream lick at the corners of her mind. The weed-choked rails, the empty city, the gaping mouth of the tunnel, opening wide....

A million miles away, her legs thrash helplessly.

Don't avoid remembering. Embrace it.

No. Gillian is numb. Her eyes are open, and they cannot blink. Shattuck leans in, touches her cheek. The air has grown cold around her, and shards of ice fleck off her skin, reforming as quickly as they melt.

Go back down.

Never.

Shattuck raises his hands in a gesture of helplessness. *Then, we must take you there.*

Obsidia has disappeared in the thick mist. She sees only the rails, the mouth gobbling up the ends.

Show me how you speak to the God.

There is no God. Outside the dream, in the world, she's pissing herself.

Shattuck grins, his teeth filed to points. *That's not what you told your mother.* Silence fills the car.

Tell me how you speak to the stone. How does it answer?

Gillian raises her hands. Shattuck sucks in his breath, but before he can move or speak, she's on him, one hand against his face, the other gripping his throat. Shattuck howls as her glacier-cold skin burns against the lids of his eyes. He stumbles back, sliding along the side of the carriage seats as she shoves him over to the stone walls of the car, pinning him like a bug. Before he thinks to push back, Gillian moves her hand from his face to his chest, pressing her palm flat against his rib cage. Her eyes close.

It answers like this.

Rows of headstones rising from a cold paved land, mountain landscapes covered in uncarved slabs of ancient schist, cold rain jetting from slate skies, washing away any hint or speck of life. Beneath her hands, Shattuck writhes, his body shuddering and twitching as his skin breaks apart like a rotting corpse. Water-smooth megaliths, glacial effluvia spreading across dying tundra—muscles split, spilling organs and bones not down but across the stone in stinking rivers of crimson and muddy brown. Cartilage snaps, bones clatter and split into shards, swirl across the smooth slabs in tightening spirals until they work their way inside, subsumed by the metamorphic and igneous slabs. His skull and ribs are the last to disappear, grinning teeth clattering as they grind down into chalky threads that sink slowly into the rocks, and vanish. Shattuck is gone. All that remains is the dead country, a vast expanse of rock and granite sky as far as her eye can see; and her hands flat against the wall, staring at an unmarked grave for a man rendered out of life and into Archean lands.

The surface of the marble ripples. A face forms, teeth dancing toward her fingers. She opens her mouth to scream. All that emerges is the low and mournful wail of a distant horn.

Gillian wakes up with a dry gasp. She's sitting upright, head against the upholstered side of a two-seat bench, her fingers tangled against her throat. Everything in the small private cabin vibrates with each turn of the wheels below. She can tell by the strange quality of the light seeping through the curtain that it's late in the day, but how late, she doesn't know. She feels unmoored from the world, adrift. *Go back down....* Gillian pulls one stiff hand away from her chin and reaches underneath her dress. Not surprisingly, the fabric is damp. Not even in the mines, when she was so young, so terrified, did she—no. She could sit here and wallow in shame, but keeping busy means she won't think about the dream, the places it leads her.

In the cramped cabin space, Gillian slips out of her clammy dress and undergarments and shoves them into the small porcelain basin in the lavatory, then pats the upholstered seat down with a towel. She contemplates throwing the dress away, but instead wrings it out and hides it with the towels—she didn't bring many clothes, and doesn't want to run the chance of a porter discovering it. The time on the clock by the door tells her she's slept most of the day away. No matter—she slipped several pieces of fruit and pastry from the Club Room into her pockets. Not that stealing is second nature to her; but survival is.

Two soft knocks at the door. Gillian looks around the cabin: wet dress hidden, new dress on self, blankets piled on seat—she smells her palms. Nothing but soap. She remembers the dream, what her hands did to Shattuck. She stares at all the scars and calluses, mesmerized. What's underneath that tortured skin that she doesn't yet know about? She turns her hands around, to inspect the ragged crescents of her nails. All of them, black with dried blood. It takes her a second of horror to remember they've always looked like that, stained like stray shards of coal.

Another knock, sharp and insistent. "Gillian?" It's Emanuel.

"Sorry—come in."

The door cracks open, and Emanuel's face appears. "You slept through lunch. I came by earlier, but you were out like a light."

"I know. We were up so early, and we didn't get much sleep last night."

"You changed."

"I fell asleep in the other dress. It was all wrinkled."

"Come on." Emanuel holds out his hand. "I want you to meet our third party."

"Let me put on my gloves first."

"What do you need gloves for?"

"My hands are a mess. I want to look proper for once."

From front to back, the train is largely empty. They were last to board, and Gillian had assumed all the other passengers were already seated, her only explanation for the empty platform beside the train. She was wrong. *Empress of Devastation* is not an ordinary train. There are few coach cars with general seating, most are made of compartments like hers, interspersed with bench-lined private rooms for four or six passengers. The rooms are as dark as the unlit hallways and appear equally empty, but as Gillian's eyesight adjusts, she spies movement behind the glass doors, or the flame of a small candle illuminating a body or two. Two of the cars they pass through have no seats at all, only odd-shaped, shallow depressions in their windowless carapaces. It profoundly disturbs her, this silence and lack of light cocooned inside each segment of the

rushing machine, this lack of humanized space. It reminds her too much of the mines.

Emanuel pulls a cloth mask up over his mouth and nose before opening the last door. She does the same—there's no need for their heavy ventilators on the train, but this last car doesn't have a covered connection. He opens the door, nodding for her to go ahead. The gritty, cinder-sparked air hits them like the bellows of a blast furnace. "She's expecting you," he shouts over the noise. "I've already seen her, so I'll wait right here!"

"You're not even going to introduce me?"

"She wants to see you alone!"

Gillian furrows her brow, but he offers no further explanation. The door across the platform offers no clues, its single window masked in curtaining. "Go on, you'll be fine," is all he says, and steps back, closing the door. She stands alone on the quaking metal platform between the cars. Beyond the grime-caked railings, the filth and sleaze of the Trestle District rushes below the tracks in a river of brick and gaslight, while freight trains roar overhead them all, sending smoke and ash raining down through the shaking layers of buildings like snow. She grips the rail and leans over. Ten stories down, the slums rush past at full throttle, a tangled mess of tightly-packed tenements and streets clogged with human and mechanical traffic. Despite the charcoal lining in her mask, whiffs of gasoline, manure and smoke seep into her lungs. An unidentified piece of trash bounces off her cheek—Gillian steps back, taking it as her cue to go inside before she loses an eye. She grabs at the large copper handle, barely able to keep a firm grip. On the third tug, the door slides open, and she stumbles through, tripping over the metal guard as the door slams shut behind her. The world now somewhat muted, Gillian pulls down her mask.

The first thing she notices is that the car is far narrower than any of the others, by almost half, giving it the effect of a slightly larger hallway rather than a true passenger car. The space is gutted, empty save for an iron box in the center, similar in shape and size to a child's coffin. Each corner of the lid has a hook and chain fastened to it: all four chains meet in a pyramid halfway to the ceiling, merging into one that continues, presumably, through and out the roof. In front of the box sits a large block of *Onyx Camello*. It is uncarved.

A pale hand at the far end of the car motions for her to come closer. Gillian barely makes out two figures, seated in chairs at the back. Green curtains are drawn across each of the long windows, giving the car the appearance of an aquarium, or those tanks at a *carnaval* she took Jasper to many years ago, with women floating in gallons of algae-choked scum, acting out underwater fantasies of mermaiden consorts bound and wed to the Great Dreamer. As with the *carnaval* tank, there are no lights in here, only the slow creep of light and shadow, the illusion of movement and life and a story where there is none. She tries to give the box a wide berth, but there's little room, and a faint, unfamiliar odor of chemicals hits her lungs as she sidles past it. Whatever is inside, it burns.

A curious, familiar squishing sound rises and falls, accompanied by the definite scent of ocean water. From the back of the car, a young, pale-skinned man in an ill-fitting suit emerges from the gloom, squeezing the spray bottle trigger every several seconds to let the saline mist float across the aisle onto the bulging, coelacanthic face of the other figure, the third member of their team: a woman, a chimera, a *grotesque*. Gillian stops, her mouth open in soft shock. She has heard of Obsidia's newer residents, half human and half something else, dredged up from the ocean along with the pieces of their reassembling city, but thought it might be only more fantastical rumors, so hard to tell apart from fantastical truth. This creature sitting before her and gaping with puffed, wet lips, is the truth.

"Emanuel sent me."

The chimera blinks. Eyes like cenotes, perfect circles in the jungle of her flesh, pure fathomless grey, like winter clouds. She's blind, Gillian realizes—or at the least, what the creature is capable of seeing lies beyond the sight of any human. Gillian imagines pushing her finger right through the jellied surface all the way to her last knuckle and never reach the curving wall of the skull, that those eyes only start in the surface of the chimera's face, but end someplace beyond the ends of time itself. Gillian grabs her twitching fingers in a tight vise, holding them close to her breast. The creature, perhaps, influencing her thoughts. Why else would she think such a thing?

"If you're waiting for her to say something, she doesn't speak." The young man puts down the spray bottle, and begins cracking the joints of his knobby fingers. "At least, very rarely. It's difficult enough for her to breath, let alone form words. Not unless—well, you know." He picks up the bottle again, and begins spraying the chimera's face.

Gillian steps forward. "Yes, I was told. My name is Gillian Jessamine."

The man looks up, a slight smirk on his face. "I know who you are. We know all about you. Emanuel told us."

Gillian feels the heat rising in her cheeks. "Really."

"You bring the body of God to life." He points to the woman's lap. Gillian leans forward, and her curiosity transforms: the chimera's crooked, elongated fingers hold the square of marble she carved for Emanuel last night, tracing the outline of the leaf in endless repetition. Repulsion washes through Gillian's frame. It's as if she's watching the chimera fondle a piece of her innermost self.

"I carve headstones and markers. I'm an artisan."

"So that's what you call it." He waits, as if expecting her to challenge his comment, then sets the bottle into a satchel at his feet. His hair is long, the color and consistency of dirty straw and tied in a tail at the back of his neck. Gillian notes the jagged half-moons of his nails, the permanent smudges in the creases of his face.

"What mine were you at?"

"What?" He rummages through the satchel, not looking back at her.

"I worked in Gwaunclawdd, then transferred to Anthracite Internacional. Didn't you used to work in the mines, too?"

"Sorry." He flashes her a stiff, tight smile. "Don't know what gave you that idea. I've never been anywhere underground, not even a basement."

"Ah. My mistake." Gillian studies him. His pallor isn't Welsh ancestry, it's lack of sun: he fairly glitters with anthracite embedded under his skin. He's never worn a suit before, she realizes. An underground animal, dressed up as a human being. Gillian knows exactly what that looks like. She saw it in mirrors and window panes for years. But she never lied about her origins. He's right, he's no miner. That only means he's something else.

"Here, put this on." The man holds out a respirator—a full face mask, with the goggles attached.

"There aren't any straps."

"It's a newer model. It doesn't need straps, you just place it against your face. Go on."

Gillian doesn't move. The man's eyes narrow, but instead of pressing the point, he stands and places it on the vacated seat. "Well, it's here if you want it. She'll speak to you when I leave."

"What about the water?" Gillian points to the satchel, now under his arm. "Do you need me to spray her face?"

"No, she can't use it while she's working. It impedes her abilities."

"Her psychic abilities? I didn't know water could—"

The man cuts her off. "She's not a psychic."

"Then what's her ability?"

"What's yours?"

Neither of them speak. Finally, he turns and walks down the car to the door. Gillian watches him leave, not sure if she should be relieved. When the door swings shut, she picks up the respirator and sits down. The chimera stares at her, mouth opening and closing with soft pops. Her breath sounds raspy and labored.

"Are you—is it difficult for you to breathe in this air? I'm sorry, he left with your squirting bottle—" Gillian points in the direction of the door. The chimera shrugs, and shakes her head. A short bark erupts from her chest—is she laughing? Gillian allows herself a sort of half-smile in return. "Yes, he seemed a bit absentminded, didn't he? Rather strange." Her words feel self-conscious; they drop out of her mouth like birds hitting the ground. Is this how women sound when they have conversations with each other? She's never had a woman friend, so it's difficult to know—although, this hardly seems such a moment of intimate female camaraderie, and the creature before her is no woman.

The chimera coughs again—she wasn't laughing. A thread of drool spools out of her mouth and hits her flat breasts. She's dressed in a plain belted smock that's almost transparent, and Gillian notices the mottled flesh, the strange configurations of bones straining against the bruised skin, as if ready to split it wide open. The rheumy fog of her eyes isn't just blindness, but malnutrition, dehydration, disease. She's dying, but Gillian can't stop staring into the creature's ink eyes.

"I disthgust you."

"No—no, not at all! I didn't mean to stare, I'm just concerned for you, that you're all right."

"Ith's all righdt." The chimera raises her hands, a gesture dripping with futility, and a touch of self-deprecation. "Honesthly, I disthgust myselph."

"No." Gillian is emphatic. "You do *not* disgust me at all. I'm—I just—I don't know how to help you—" The breath hitches out of Gillian's lungs, along with sentences spilling from her mouth in a rush of nerves. "I used to work in the mines, and sometimes they'd have me dress the wounds because I'm a girl, but even then I wasn't sure if I was doing it right, everyone screamed no matter what. I used a sewing needle, just a regular needle. It was horrible. Even when I was in accidents, and the mine fire, no one could help me, and I didn't know what to do." Gillian presses her hand against her forehead. Some strange emotion is building behind her eyes. "I'm sorry. I don't know how to help you. I don't know what you want me to do."

"S'all righd." A hand more like a fin slips onto Gillian's tight fist, resting on her shaking knee. The chimera pats her gently, smiling. She has few teeth. "S'all righd. You are doing fighn. You are fighn."

"I'm doing fine," Gillian echoes her. "Doing fine. I don't even know why I'm here."

"Whadth elsthe happendth in the mineths?"

Empress of Devastation roars down the tracks, pulling cars and rolling stock behind her like a widow's veil. Once again, Gillian feels her heart fall into sync

with the beat of the engines. Hot tears roll into her mouth, and the salt stirs primordial memories. The chimera's eyes open wider. Her breath is the ocean, and all the little secrets of Gillian's life are floating up, up from the benthic deep into the naked waves, cresting and tumbling.

"I was a year younger than my son Jasper is now when I got pregnant. A foreman led me into one of the dead tunnels of Anthracite Internacional, where I canaried for methane and carbon dioxide. He knocked me up hard and good. I was barely twelve, but I wanted it, I was able, I knew what I was doing. Pregnant women aren't allowed in the mines, and if I ever wanted out, it'd have to be with child, or in a burlap sack sewn shut like a sack of coal. I'd already been with some of the miners, boys my age or a little older, just fooling around. You know. But the foreman. I fixed on like a star. I can't—I can't describe him, I hardly remember his face, or if he even had one. He was an obscenity. But it was like fucking a mountain. Like fucking the world. He could read the rock as well as me, he always knew where to find the thickest seams. There was gossip that he had a touch of *grotesque* in him. Maybe that's what drew me to him, some bit of unreadable earth running through his veins. I never saw him after that, after that one time. I kept away from him. His mouth—I didn't want him to find out. I gave birth down there. I never told Jasper. I took my son and left everything else behind."

"Whathd elthe did you leaphe behinthd?"

It's like her old dream. Following the rails into the tunnel, into blissful, endless night.

"Blood. Placenta. Bits of flesh. She was already dead. There was nothing I could do."

"Dithd you giphe her a nambe?"

"Peridot, green for the leaves. Peridot Addiena. She came out first. I left her in the stones."

The box chains rattle, grow taut. The spell broken, Gillian sags over her lap, and lets out a ragged breath. Just a little ways further in, and she would have been there. But where?

"Don' be scarethd." The chimera releases her hand, and sits back in her seat. "Justh puth on thad—" she points to the respirator "—anthd sith there. I'll be fighn."

"Why should I be scared? What's going to happen?"

"You tolth me the truth of yourthelph. Ith's my thurn now."

"To tell the truth of yourself?"

To tell the truth of you.

The chains slide down, draping over the lid: and then rise in a screeching clatter, taking the slack and the lid to the ceiling. As the car turns red from the light of bright flames, the chimera leans forward, breathing in the fumes.

Gillian has no time to react: she places the respirator against her face. At once, she feels the edges seal against her skin, locking it in place with a prickling heat. Four sharp jabs make her cry out in pain, but the heavy filters mute the sound. She opens her eyes, blinking the tears away as she adjusts to the smoky glass of the goggles. The iron box appears as a blur, thin liquid bubbling and popping inside. Gasoline, perhaps, or a fine grade of oil, it's hard to tell. The heat, she can feel, and the air undulates in waves as fumes flood the room; but there's no trace of smoke. Gillian touches the two round appendages of the mask where the charcoal filters sit, and takes a deep breath. No trace of chemicals enters her lungs—not that it would harm her, if it did. Nonetheless, Gillian feels her breathing grow shallow. "I'm sorry," she says, unsure if she can be heard behind the weight of the respirator. She backs away from the chimera, slow and deliberate. "I can't stay here. I have to get out."

Stop, the chimera speaks in a marble-cold voice—*Haveli Selwara*, to be precise. The creature's pupils contract, and Gillian sees new colors form in her eyes, traces of gold *Alimoglu Travertine*.

You have abilities you have not yet mined.

Shapes form and move behind the green curtains, as though ghosts hover outside the car, surrounding it an unbroken chain.

You are the distinct line through P *that does not intersect* I.

Light spills into the car from all sides as the green curtains slither up into folds at the top of the ceiling. Outside, in the ash-colored evening air, the Trestle District rushes past, choking in electrical wires and steel girders, barely visible beyond the glare of electrical lights pouring through the glass. A car within a car, Gillian realizes—the smaller one surrounded by a brightly-lit walkway created between the two nesting carriages. Men and women line the walkway, observing her. She cannot see their faces. They appear only as masked silhouettes, sinister bodies without human mouths or eyes. Gillian wonders if Emanuel is among them, then stops herself. No, she does not wonder at all.

Planetesimal creation. Deflection, flight and fall. Metavolcanic cradle rocked by the subduction zone.

Nonsensical phrases spill from the chimera's mouth, all spoken with absolute precision. The creature isn't psychic. She's a Sibyl.

"Gillian."

Emanuel stands at the window closest to the connecting door, speaking into a small amplifying device. His voice floats through the car, tinny and distant.

"I need you to show the Sibyl what you can do with stone. Pick it up and carve it."

Gillian shakes her head no.

"Gillian, I cannot let you out until you carve the stone. This is imperative."

There are close to twenty strangers, in all, hands pressed against the glass, watching the chimera's body bend and twist over the bubbling crucible like soft taffy.

"You said you loved me. How can you do this to me?"

"I do love you. I've never not loved you. But you *must* carve the stone for the Sibyl. She needs to see what you do, to see if you are able to—do what we need you to do at Wormskill."

"Which is? What?"

Emanuel pauses, then: "Shattuck has kept very close tabs on Jasper, he cares for him as a grandfather. I love him like my own son. But you risk his life if you do not do what I ask."

Gillian pulls the respirator off her face, ignoring the pain as the small hooks disengage from her skin. Small lines of blood trickle down her forehead and cheeks, dotting her dress. She takes a deep breath. "Fuck your threats. My son can take care of himself."

She hears the smile in his voice. "I knew there had to be more to you," it whispers across the car. "Canary in a coal mine, a million of them every year carried out on stretchers, but not you. Never you. What other abilities do you have?"

"So, this is your idea of love."

"I also love my god, darling. His love comes first."

"Why are you making me do this?" Gillian shouts her question to the ceiling, ignoring Emanuel's figure behind the glass. "What is it you want me to do at Wormskill?"

"Just what Shattuck said—retrieve an object and deliver it to Hellynbreuke."

"Something you need me to carve?"

"Yes."

"You want me to bring something, some piece of stone, some boulder to life."

Emanuel's voice hesitates. "Yes."

Gillian understands now. She's seen this happen before, in the mines, among men and women isolated too many years below-ground. "You found a lump of stone, and you want me to turn it into some kind of magical being you can dance around naked—"

"Pick up the stone—"

"—smearing dirt into your faces like little children and chanting at the ground—"

"Pick up the fucking stone or your son dies."

He has no idea how much of a non-threat his words are. She doesn't fear for Jasper, he's smarter than she ever was, wiser and deadlier, and Shattuck's a drunken old slug—chances are, he's already dead, and her son slipped away into the city like so much dust. But Gillian lets the respirator drop to the floor. She's tired and hungry, and wants this over with. So they want to play secret pagan cult to an imaginary earth god? Fine. She'll carve this marble, then whisper sweet nothings to a lump of slag, probably leftover waste from some old steel mill, and take it to Hellynbreuke. It's nothing to her. She's never believed.

The block of *Onyx Camello* is warm to the touch. Gillian lifts and cradles it in her arms. It's perfectly cut and polished, with hundreds of layers of cream alternating with caramels and browns, like layers of baby blankets. Gillian cringes. Soft curves of flesh, and the marble lies against her breast, already just the right size—is this what they want her to do? She feels the block shift, the edges soften. "No," Gillian says, and bites down hard on her tongue. Saliva and blood fill her mouth, and she thinks of the furthest reaches of Obsidia, where industrial sprawl gives way to the ice and chill of the Southern Ocean. A hard and dangerous country, where humans do not live. Glaciers pour from mountains, stream together into a solid moving cliff of ice, rising hundreds of feet in the air; while overhead, seagulls mass and swell, rising and falling with the stiff Antarctic currents, weaving through thunderheads and lightning bolts, at one with both sea and sky.

She turns, and lifts out the block to the chimera, then lets it drop to her feet with a thump. "There. It's done." Her arms are slick with sweat, and her body feels like she's running a fever. Heat from the burning oil prickles the old scars with pain, from the nape of her neck all the way down to just above her knees.

"Nothing." Emanuel's voice drips with disappointment.

"No, there's carving—" Gillian gives the block a light touch with her toe. Gulls, entwined and tangled all over the surface of the stone, beaks and feet and wings morphing in a single mass, as if trying to collide themselves into something larger, more formidable.

"I'm sure there is. We needed to see something more, love. I think you can do more."

"I told you I don't know that kind of life." Gillian crouches, hands on knees as she fights the wave of weak nausea washing through her. "I only know stone."

Voices rise up behind Emanuel's, heated and urgent. She hears him replying, and then: "Gillian, I need you to stand up. Turn around and show the Sibyl your back. Show her your scars."

"I'm not undressing for you. I did what you wanted. Unlock the door. I need fresh air—I'm not completely immune. I'm not immortal."

"You don't need to undress, darling. Look at the windows—look at your reflection."

With a tortured sigh, Gillian rises and turns, letting the light from the windows illuminate her back. A faint image of herself looks back, a slender figure in a light-colored dress, printed with yellow roses. Underneath the dress, the old mine scars glow neon-red.

Heavy traces of a Widmanstätten pattern within her recrystallized structure. Result of a monumental impact-heating event at the time of the arrival of the parent.

Behind the glass, the men and women say nothing. She doesn't need to see to know what emotions warp their faces. They are looking at her scars, which are a single scar, a single radiating half-whorl of a fingerprint, embedded in her skin. *The God*, someone whispers. But they don't understand. The fingerprint is nothing. It's minuscule. What she encountered in those mine fires, what reached out through the roiling flames, could not truly perceive her existence anymore than she can see the individual fibers beneath her heels. And yet it was not a god, it was only a wounded creature, trying to escape. There are larger things, further down, that fathered them all.

Olivine bronzite chondrite descendent of 4 Vesta. The God cradle awaits her, in the deep. She will take the godhead to the Towers of Pain. She will deliver The God. The chimera takes one last breath from the fumes before collapsing in her seat, head rolled back and eyes closed.

"That's what we needed to know. Thank you, Gillian. You're free to go now." Emanuel's voice sounds relaxed, relieved as he turns off the intercom. All around her, glassine and shadow figures talk and gesture in bright animation. As the door opens and several men walk into the car, a portion of the roof slides away, and fresh air whips the fumes up into the night. The men pass her without comment, offering only guarded stares, tinged with a bit of fear. Perhaps they are thinking, this is the creature who will bring their God to life. Perhaps they want to worship her as well. Or perhaps, they wish to kill her. Gillian will find out, soon enough.

Along the walkway, several women begin feeding the chain back up into the roof. The men guide the lowering lid back onto the iron box, their hands protected by thick, fireproofed gloves. Gillian hears the little squirt bottle wheezing away, as the young man tends to his chimeric ward. Everything back to normal, of a sort.

"Gillian." Emanuel stands before her, handsome as ever, a look of concern on his face. "Will you ever forgive me?"

"How long have you been planning this?"

Pain crosses his face, or what he believes to be pain. Now she sees it for what it is, more of a constipation of the truth. And to think she'd ever felt concern for his feelings, and guilt at the lack of her own.

"Please, don't bother trying to lie. You never do it very well, I could always tell."

"Really?" Emanuel appears genuinely offended. "How disappointing. I thought I lied very well."

"You were in Wormskill far longer than a few months."

"Yes." He leads her out of the car, and through a hidden side door onto the narrow walkway, now empty and dark. They stand alone between the walls, with the group rushing about inside, and the floating city outside. "I was there several years—we all were." He gestures to the men and women. "In the middle of disinterring the cemetery, we found something. Not a body or a monument—a stone, but not a stone. Something more. A woman with us, a chimera, would breath the fumes from the mine fires seeping up through the ground, and she began to interpret—it spoke to us through her. Broken bits of dreams, equations, images—visions of a future far beyond our comprehension." Emanuel takes Gillian's arms in his hands, squeezing them tight in his excitement. "We transported it out of the cemetery, took it someplace safe. We did everything, worked every kind of magic, every kind of science. Nothing. Our Sibyl only gave us bits and pieces, but nothing we could use. Most of the group remained. Shattuck and I and a few others came back to the city eventually, but only to find something that would work, so we could go back and free it. Free him. He is the son of a God, trapped in stone, and he needs someone who can read and carve away that prison to release him. The moment I met you, the moment I saw what you could do with stone, I knew."

"Whatever your Sibyl said, she was wrong. The fumes from those fires— they're toxic, Emanuel. You know that. They don't open the third eye, they shut everything down. She was poisoning herself, she was hallucinating, dying. You were probably all hallucinating."

"You said it yourself, it's a different kind of speaking, and the Sibyls understand it because of what they are. You also said, it's a different kind of being alive. And you can bring it to life, because of whatever you are."

Gillian shakes her head. "Stones are not alive. I've told you before. Earth, metal, rocks—it's not life. Not *that* kind of life. I can't help you."

Emanuel presses Gillian close to him. His breath smells warm, like the fumes of the burning oil. She feels herself grow small in his arms. She doesn't fight

him. Now is not the time. His lips brush her ears, and his voice pours into her lungs.

"You will read that stone, and you will bring it to life and convince it to reveal the true of name of his Father to us, as I know you can. You will free him, and together we will take him to Hellynbreuke. And then you and he will free our one true God who is imprisoned there, you will free everything there, everything that slumbers and waits and dreams, and bring down all the false temples, destroy all the false prophets and faiths. No more waiting for Obsidia. No more searching the ocean depths for a god from another time and space who can't be bothered to do more than dream eternity away, a being that doesn't even exist. Our God is here, and His time is now."

Gillian raises her lips to meet his. "And what if it's not the son of a god?"

"Ridiculous. How could he be anything else? What else could he be?"

"Something worse? Worse than a god, even?"

"What could be worse than a god?"

Gillian closes her eyes.

In the still heart of the night, when even the stars appear to fall asleep and slip from the sky, Gillian creeps through the train again, tracing her path from earlier in the evening. *Empress* moves in inches down this portion of the track, more rocking cradle than racehorse, and what little light and movement she'd seen before in the compartments has vanished. Either all the passengers are asleep, or they are elsewhere. Or perhaps, they watch her secret progress in the dark, lidless eyes dilated and shining like stagnant puddles of oil. Her heart beats in sharp, painful thumps against her ribs, and she holds her breath, letting it out only when she's between cars, afraid even those exhalations will be detected, and she'll be sent back to her cabin.

When she finds the first windowless car with the hollowed-out contours in its floor, she stops, and lies down in the depression, settling in against the thick carpet lining the strange curves. With her back against the floor, Gillian stares up into the nothingness of the car. The moorings of her mind loosen, as they did long ago, when she first taught herself this false escape from the mines, when the thought of all that rock pressing around and onto her threatened to send her screaming into madness. In the compleat dark, there would be no tunnel. There would be no machine-carved ceilings and walls. Overcome by the vertigo of losing all sense of up or down, the rock at her back unfurled into bituminous wings, and she would thrust forward and travel through the darkness of space, falling until she flew, endlessly plummeting and soaring, free of the constraints of physical space and time.

But this is a train, not a tunnel, and she is surrounded not by the earth but by a shuddering, moving machine. A carpeted floor is no substitute for wings of stone, and she cannot escape the relentless pounding of the *Empress*, her unstoppable pistons and wheels. Feldspar rushes toward them, closer with every second, and everything else in her life fades to grey. She knew it from the moment Shattuck spoke the name. Wormskill will be the end of her. Yes, she whispers to the night. All Obsidians know how they will die. This was always meant to be.

The train's horn sounds out, three piercing sobs. Gillian jolts out of her vision and sits up, noting that she can see the formation of shapes and shadows, both inside the train and out. A large mass of light throbs and glows in the far distance to the left, as though the entire car had turned to glass. *Empress* moves toward it in slow, rhythmic bursts of the engines. Gillian sits in the hollow, knees up to her chin, watching the light take shape. It's phosphorescent, a luminous bile green that with each pulse casts the shadows away, illuminating everything with a sickly glow. They are traveling through a part of Obsidia Gillian knows nothing about, high on a trestle, passing a forest of needle-thin towers and twisting spires; and some colossal being that glows like the aurora australis, that moves like a thunderstorm, resides in their midst. She feels like she's the only human left in the world, the only thing left alive. The train continues its slow pace, blasting the horns with military precision, as if pleading with the light to let it pass unscathed. Gillian slides around and down into the hollow, curling up until she's nothing more than a hard ball of flesh and bone, eyes pressed tight against the curves of her knees. And still she sees it, feels the light trickle into her veins like fire ants swarming into the ground. *Empress of Devastation* slides past the light, and Gillian senses the luminous creature turning upon the train one single, unblinking, cyclopean eye: it sees her.

The eye closes, and the light fades, and the train moves on. Gillian is left alone in the dark.

Because, it knows, and she knows.

She belongs to something else.

PART THREE
Ride easy, lover:
Surrender to the land
Your heart of anger.

Early in the morning, five mornings since *Empress of Devastation* departed from Highgate and traversed over half the length of the city, through the choked inner core of factories and train yards and far past the northernmost suburbs and warehouse districts, the train slides into the skeleton of Feldspar's long-abandoned commuter station, wheels squealing to full stop in explosions of wet clouds. Gillian only fully wakes up when the engines quit their shivering beneath her seat: it's the utter absence of noise that shocks the sleep fully away. Sunlight sifts through the dust-coated windows, strong and bright: outside, she sees the rib cage of the rooftop soaring in parallel arcs overhead, broken glass and iron fretwork binding each beam like patchwork sails. Gillian pulls her sleeping mask down, and unlatches the window, pressing her nose against the narrow crack. The air is clean and crisp—it smells *wide*, a quality she never thought air could contain. *I can hear myself breathe.* Wonder steals over her, so heady that it takes a second look at the small crowd milling on the platform to realize that everyone else has disembarked. They're waiting for her. The wonder burns away. She pushes her fingers out the window, letting the sun and cool air play over her skin. "The last morning," she whispers. "The last day."

She joins Emanuel on the platform, placing her portmanteau next to his before walking over to the far edge, beyond the train's caboose. The rails lead back through low ruins to a bridge crossing a narrow gorge: it is after the gorge that Obsidia proper begins.

"They dug the gorge to stop the fires. It goes down for almost a mile." The young man walks up behind her—following her, no doubt, to make sure she doesn't run away. He no longer wears the ill-fitting jacket, only the slacks and shirt, untucked and flapping at his waist. "I think they were going to fill it, but—you know. Public funding, red tape, et cetera. It will be centuries before it's finished, if ever."

"It wouldn't have worked, anyway," Gillian says. "There's not enough fly ash in the world to fill that gorge."

"As long as people keep being born, there's enough ash."

Beyond the gorge, Obsidia fans across the distant horizon, a rusting blight on the land. From this vantage point, it's the length of the city that impresses, not its width; and here she can also see for the first time how high the Cordillera del Tenebroso truly is, as though the earth punched a hole through its own skin, thrusting the mountains up to bat away the sun, the sky, the stars.

"Look." The young man points to a cluster of megaliths rising thousands of feet in the air, notable not as much for their somber weight and height as much as for the fact that they stand untouched by the presence of factories and machines clinging against their steep bodies. In a sea of pollution and fire, they alone are naked and clean. "El Torres del Pain."

Gillian shivers in the stifling air. The Towers of Pain, a circular ridge of megaliths in whose twisting foothills mysterious Hellynbreuke lies. Where Emanuel's god lies imprisoned, supposedly. "I didn't realize how large they are. It looks like a giant necropolis."

"El Patagones, eh?" the young man jokes. "A cemetery for a lost race of giants?"

"I believe that as much as I believe in *Ciudad de los Césares* and *El Dorado*. I only meant that it's large. It doesn't seem real."

"Well, you'll find out how real it is, soon enough. We all will."

Gillian slips on a pair of dark-tinted glasses, and studies the man closely as they make their way back up the platform, stopping before the remains of the station. "What's your name, if you don't mind my asking?"

"Joaquin."

"How old are you, Joaquin?"

He seems taken aback. "Why do you want to know?"

"Were you born here? You're younger than me."

"I'm not that young." Joaquin turns and slips past the broken doors into the tiled waiting room. Gillian follows. In the middle of the room, surrounded by worn stone and wood benches, a tree stands, a fat sprawling oak whose roots erupt from the once-perfect mosaic of floor tiles. The placement is perfect, it couldn't be coincidence. Someone must have planted it, years ago. Gillian walks up to it and caresses one of the leaves. Green, pliant, strong.

"But you're not that old. Call it a hunch, but I doubt you're much older than my son, and he's not yet fourteen. So, either you were born here with the team, or…." Her voice echoes through the broken space of the room, and a small flock of birds bursts off the exposed beams and wheels away at the unexpected sound.

"My older sister was the first Sibyl, before she died." Joaquin looks away, back out the door to the group. More birds flutter up from the branches through the holes in the ceiling, into the cloudless blue sky. All crows. No canaries. "There are a number of families still living here. Not everyone evacuated. Some of us

hid. We don't want trouble, but we don't want to leave, and we shouldn't have to. This is our home."

"Is your home underground? In the tunnels?"

Joaquin frowns.

"I don't care if it is—I lived underground half my life. I recognize the look, that's all."

"My grandparents and parents—when the town was first evacuated, looters came through, criminals, rapists. Everyone wanted to pick the bones. Sometimes other things came, from out of Obsidia. So we stayed in the basements, and then—" He shrugs. "—we went deeper. Not all the land under Feldspar is on fire, yet. It's still safe, for now."

"Do you believe that that object I'm supposed to bring to life is the offspring of some forgotten god? A god from under the ground?"

"With all my heart." Joaquin nods his head, emphatic in his conviction. "He's of this land, our land, not some alien god from half the world away. This is the god Obsidia deserves, one that will honor us, lift us up and make our city and people whole, not tear us apart with disease and destruction and ruin. You should be honored that you have such a gift, the gift to free Him."

Gillian touches his shoulder. "If you really think I have such a gift, you should go home and get your family, and run as far away from Feldspar as you can."

Joaquin starts to smile, but Gillian grabs his arm.

"I'm not joking. You took something out of the earth that belongs in the earth, and now you want me to bring it to life. Do you think it's going to thank you?." She lets go, and steps through the doorway into the sun. "You should run."

The group walks into Feldspar from the station. The rails run further into the heart of the town, but the conductor refuses—there's no way to know what shape the rails and land under them are in, he insists, and he's not about to find out the hard way. And there are other, unseen passengers, those with the lidless eyes of black fuel who never left their cabins, who the conductor insists must not remain outside the limits of Obsidia for very long. So they leave him and the crew behind to ready *Empress* for departure. No one speaks except in occasional low tones—their respirators prevent most conversation. Gillian's respirator was left behind on the train, and no one asks her if she needs it, or insists she put one on. Still the canary, after all. They follow the rails toward the city limits, past ghost neighborhoods clustered around the cracked remains of forgotten crossroads. Buildings list and sag, victims of subsidence—cave-ins— from the mines beneath their foundations. Vent pipes stick up in distant fields, their open mouths spewing out clouds of white steam and fumes from the fires below. From so far away, they look like city fountains, elegant and regal.

Up ahead, Feldspar looms, a graveyard of iron and steel.

The younger men and women take turns wheeling the chimera in a light, hand-pulled sedan with a roof to block the sun. She now wears a mask that completely envelops her head and neck, presumably to guard her weak lungs from the dry air. They sign to her with their hands, stopping at intervals so that Joaquin can remove the mask, speaking to her in sibilant whispers as he replenishes her water. Their hushed voices and shuffling footfalls sound naked and small, unnatural in a landscape where nothing stirs, not even the air. Gillian walks to the center of the tracks during those rest stops. She stares at the dulled, pitted lines of steel, noting how they plummet like arrows straight into the empty town. So many buildings and factories, and they are the only humans she sees. It's everything the rest of Obsidia was not meant to be: empty, still. She can't tell if it's beautiful or perverse. In the distance, thick black mountains bake in the sun—culms, the unusable remains of coal and other mined materials. Even so far away those are some of the largest heaps she's ever seen. They remind her of graves.

A touch at her arm draws her away. "Miss Jessamine." It's Joaquin. "We're heading this way now." He points toward the crossroads, to a dirt road leading away from the town center.

"Aren't we going into the town? I thought the cemetery was by the steel mills."

"We moved Him, remember? He's hidden outside the town limits, where no one will find Him, and where we can protect Him. Come on."

Gillian stares down the tracks again, resisting the urge to blink as the sun beats into her pupils till the horizon becomes a black fuzz. She touches the tip of one boot to a rail, and feels the immediate rush of metallic-tinged vertigo racing up her bones to her head. *It's that way*, she wants to say, the knowledge so thick, so bitter on her tongue. *Can't you feel it? It's in the center, underneath the fire, waiting. Just follow the rails. Follow them in, and down.*

"Gillian!"

They trudge down the road, watching the culms grow wider and higher, until their ragged summits nudge the heel of the noonday sun. Slowly, surely, workers' dormitories and tenement buildings give way as they head into the valley: processing plants and winding towers, coal bunkers and blast furnaces rise up and around them like bones jutting from the corpse of a beached whale—and then, just as gradually, industry fades away, revealing once again the broken countryside, dotted with the dead remains of the mines. A summit breaker sags into itself, rows of broken windows catching the afternoon sun and transmuting them into a waterfall of sequined light. Chimney stacks lie in spiraled

slices on the ground or rise in the air like empty flag poles. A flywheel as high as a house leans impossibly alongside a tree, the trunk grown around its curved, rusted base. They stop again, and everyone begins switching their shoes to hobnail boots, while Emanuel passes around walking sticks.

"Are we climbing?"

Emanuel points to the nearest culm, several hundred feet of black shale piled into a flat-topped mountain. "Up there. That's where he is. No one goes near the culms, and we can guard him better up there."

"Guard him against what?"

"Everything."

It takes another hour to reach the top, even with Emanuel moving back and forth, herding the slower climbers and stragglers along. Gillian offers to help carry the chimera, but the creature's handler's seem so repulsed at the suggestion that she quickens her pace, joining the front of the group so she won't be near them. As they ascend to the flat top of the culm, Gillian studies the layout of the town with an expert eye—she sees how Feldspar exploded in growth, so haphazardly and quickly that the workers' houses and dormitories butt against the factories, where noxious fumes probably sent them in droves to the doctors and the graves long before the fires ever did. The culm isn't the highest one lining the edges of Feldspar, but it's high enough that as they reach the top, for the first time in her life, Gillian see lands beyond Obsidia, a place where Obsidia *isn't*: green forests to the north, and tundra-like steppes and desert to the east. It won't last, that wilderness. Obsidia will gobble it up someday, until no one remembers a time or place when Obsidia wasn't the name of the world.

"Over here." Emanuel heads toward the center of the culm, where a massive depression has been dug. Gillian understands now why they chose this spot to hide their stone deity. The culm is barren waste product and nothing more, difficult to climb, and free of predators. And it's hidden in plain sight—only travelers in a plane or dirigible would be able to spot the hole. The rest of the group, save for the chimera and the young man, drift to the edge of the pit, listening.

"You did this yourselves? All of you?" Several people nod.

Emanuel takes off his mask, running his hand over his red, sweating face. "After we disinterred the cemetery, we brought the equipment up here," he explains, "steam shovels, trucks to haul away the excess rock. When it was finished, we erased all traces of the road back down as best we could."

"I have to admit, you did an excellent job. I'm impressed." Gillian isn't lying. Before her sits a depression approximately one hundred meters in diameter and twice as deep, with graded spirals of paths that wind down to a flat, circular center. They essentially created a strip mine, similar in shape to the huge copper mines outside the limits of Obsidia, further north. Here, the effect is of a pitch-black amphitheatre. No: an impact crater. A cradle of birth.

You don't need to know your father's name, Morwyn had said, melting into the fading lights like a glacier. *You couldn't pronounce it.*

"Are you all right?" Emanuel slips a hand against her waist. After all he's done to her, she knows any ordinary woman would push him away in anger, but she doesn't move away.

"Yes. It's been a long day, that's all."

"We'll get some food in you, and you'll be fine."

"And that?" Gillian points to the figure at the center, a story-high mass covered in mud-colored cloth, obscured by long shadows from the high pit walls. "Is that the child of your God?" Behind her, someone gasps. Emanuel grabs her hand and pins it down to her side, the mask of pleasant demeanor gone.

"Never point," he whispers. "*Never.* Would I go to your temple and point at the statues and altars like some gawking, unbelieving fool? This is not a game, no matter what you think. Show respect, and act accordingly."

"Of course." Gillian draws her hand out of his grip, gently. This man that she thought was so grounded and real, is so lost. It would sadden her, if she could care. "I apologize."

"We need to prepare. Go keep the chimera company. We'll come for you when we're ready." Emanuel walks away, and the others follow. Gillian stands there for a moment, unsure of what to do. An impulse to rush upon him, push him over the edge of the pit and watch him tumble down the ledges until he cracks his head open onto his god comes and goes too quickly for her to savor. She's never been violent, anyway. Life provides violence enough, without provocation. And she wants to see this through to the end, because she knows it will not end how Emanuel thinks. She wants to see his face at that moment, to see that transformational moment of understanding. It will be as if she's giving birth, all over again.

Under the canopy of the small passenger sedan, the chimera lies on several filthy pillows, staring at the distant town through a scrim of gauze. Gillian sits next to her, her body wedged into the tight space so that their knees press against each other. Sweat trickles under her arms and breasts, staining the faded fabric of her second-best dress. Both hold flasks of water, the chimera taking hers through a glass straw. A touch of whiskey flavors Gillian's water, courtesy of Joaquin. Beyond the scrim, beyond Feldspar and the thin gorge, far-off plumes of factory lights flare and fade.

The chimera leans forward until her scaly face is inches from Gillian's. She smells of brine and dying flesh and softening bone.

"Thiths is notht going to end well, is ith?" she whispers in Gillian's ear.

Gillian smiles. "Well, no," she says, "it's not quite that. It's simply going to end however it ends. There's no good or bad about it. The mines burn and the town dies. It's not malice or judgment. It is what it is."

The chimera coughs out a small laugh.

"All right," Gillian admits. "Probably not."

"Then why dithd you come?"

Gillian opens her mouth, to talk about fate and birth and death, and the great wheel of Obsidia upon which all citizens helplessly spin like pinned insects: the chimera slides a webbed hand over hers, clasping it tight. "Don'th lie. I'm really am thycic, too."

"I thought so."

The chimera reaches into the bag at her feet, and rummages around, pulling out a small ampoule filled with yellow smoke. She pops the cap and sticks the end into the O of her mouth, sucking hard. Gillian says nothing, shocked. The chimera's eyes roll up, and she shudders, then after a long minute, lets out a soft, languorous sigh. Gillian sniffs the air, but detects no odor of any kind. Whatever the creature inhaled, she completely absorbed it.

The chimera drops the empty ampoule into the bag, and smiles. "I'm also a drug addict." Her voice is succinct and clear, though her lips hardly move. It's as if she's speaking from within Gillian's forehead. "Certain abilities and gifts require augmentation to fully work. It's the price I've paid for moving from one world into another."

"Aren't you part human, though? It shouldn't be this bad for you, breathing air."

"I'm human on my mother's side. Evidently, she wasn't human enough. Now, let's try this again. Relax. Tell me why you're here."

Gillian lets herself slide inside the calm, round pools of ink and shadow. "A dream I had," she begins, "when I was a child. Before the mines. I dreamed of Feldspar, or a place like it. Empty, abandoned. I dreamed I was in an empty city, looking for something."

"For what?"

"Something—below. I don't know."

"Your daughter?"

Gillian squirms. "I didn't—I wasn't expecting twins, not that it would have mattered. She was stillborn, which was a blessing. She was—wrong. Deformed, horribly—I buried her in the mines, and took Jasper. I'm not sorry I left her body down there, and I'm not sorry I left. She was already gone. I gave her a name and a grave. That's more than most of us get who actually live."

The chimera draws back, but keeps her hand pressed against Gillian's. It feels as if they are welded at the joints, sharing the same bones and blood. A smoky taste steals over Gillian's tongue, and the sun grows brighter, coats the culm in a platinum veneer.

"Not your daughter, then. Not your son. Do you look for your creator in your dreams?"

"I don't believe in god, or gods."

"Did I ask you about the gods?"

"You asked me about my creator. I don't believe in him, in it."

"It believes in you. Its endless thought is upon you, pressing against your back like crushed wings. It is a hook in your soul, and the chain is yours to grasp, the way to him clear. It has always shown you the way. It's as easy to see as—"

"—train tracks, running through the desert into a nova sun—"

"—it is the metronome at the earth's core, marking time until the continents align—"

Gillian swallows hard, fighting the drug, fighting the cenote eyes.

"—no, it's stars, it's supposed to be the stars. What we're taught, when we're young."

"Is it? Does a being with an iron core heart care about the stars? What do we care most about? What do you care most about in the world?"

"My son. I was never the best parent, I'll admit, but yes, I care about my son."

The chimera smiles. "A parent always cares about their child. More than life itself. More than the world itself. And why is that, I wonder?"

"—when you create a child, you're creating yourself, again—"

"—creating a new world—"

"—world within a world—" Gillian stares. She sees the tracks.

"—what's in the tunnel with you?"

Blackness rushes across Gillian's vision. An answer is in there, somewhere in the dark: the answer is all around her. But her throat constricts, and she chokes on the words as she tries to speak. They words aren't enough. The chimera breaks the spell, pulling away her hands. Nausea rushes over Gillian in a tidal wave: she leans over the side of the sedan and vomits onto the ground. "I'm sorry," she croaks through strands of drool and bile. "I'm so embarrassed."

"A hazard of my habit. The apologies should be from me. Here." The chimera hands Gillian her handkerchief, then reaches into the bag again, and pulls out the leaf-carved chip of *Arihant Spider Green*. "For luck, was it?"

"I thought it was lost."

The chimera presses it into Gillian's palm. "It was wasted on Emanuel. Not that he didn't try. He really does love you as best he can, you know, but—you should give it to someone who understands what it means, who can read that kind of life. Who can read you."

Gillian puts down the rag, and examines the marble as if she's never seen it before. In a way, she hasn't. This is a relic, a tombstone of another life, a life now dead and gone. After a moment of consideration, she presses it back into the chimera's hand. "Please. Take it as a gift from me—I insist. You've been very kind."

"Really? Well, if you love something—you know the saying." The chimera's scales shift in the sunlight, sliding from pearly grey into petal pink. She holds it tight for a minute, then puts it into her pocket. "I'll find a way to thank you."

"Well, there isn't anyone else who can read me like you can. You've been the only one I've found. Not that I was looking." Gillian stares back out at the city.

"You were born, weren't you?"

"Of course."

The chimera smiles, and pops open a second ampoule. "Then there are two others who can read you. At the least, there is one."

In the northernmost corner of the great metropolis known as Obsidia, nestled in the outskirts of a dead and forgotten town, twenty or so odd figures wend their way into the earth, away from the light of a weary afternoon sun. From the highest point of a mound of slate and slag, they wind in an inverted spiral around the sides of the central pit toward the dark figure squatting in the flat center. Gillian looks up as she descends, noting how the sky becomes a single disk of blue, with a yellow iris floating toward the edge. Soon the iris will slide off the disk altogether, and the great eye of night will be revealed, its unending sight firmly fixed on her—even now she feels it, the great colorless void beyond the day. No matter the time or the place, she is always watched. The gaze is upon her, relentless and everlasting.

What Emanuel and the others did to prepare the site, she cannot see. There are no lights in the pit, she doesn't smell incense or scented wax, she never heard chanting or prayers. Although the heavy respirators are still clamped to their heads, none of the men and women traded their garments for ceremonial robes, as they would have in the neighborhood churches and temples of Marketside. Perhaps they are saving ceremony for Hellynbreuke. They wear no clothing of any kind, though. Gillian dug in her heels and refused—it's not nudity that bothers her, but what it represents, that they are nothing. After a few tense minutes of negotiation, she relinquished her undergarments and boots, but keeps her second-best dress. Razor-sharp metal and coal shards rip through the soles of her feet, but she's felt worse pain, and it feels so distant, anyway, as if it's happening to someone else. Against the barren coal walls, even the darkest-skinned of the group appear as white, wriggling grubs, with the expressionless faces of flies. The group stripped the chimera bare, too—including her mask—but she alone wears her nudity with perfect grace. Her crooked body glides down the sloping paths as though she's floating through invisible tides.

Gillian was first to enter the pit, trailing humans behind her like a chained bridal veil, and now she is first to place her feet on the flat floor. Some of the group hang back along the sides of the bowl, standing along the ramps while the rest fan out around the object. Gravel rattles down the slopes, as the wind picks up speed, and the edges of the cloth roll up, revealing a dark mass that Gillian can't identify. As Emanuel removes his mask, she catches his glance and points to her feet: surrounding the pit in an unbroken circle is a small trough formed from the shale itself, filled with a viscous oil.

Expressionless, Emanuel gives his respirator to a young girl, then steps onto the floor, followed by a woman built like a prizefighter. In unison, they each walk to a front corner of the cloth, and remove a large railroad spike pinning the fabric in place. The spikes set aside, the woman nods her head, and two more people walk up with lengths of copper piping, each piece close to ten feet tall. No one says a word as Emanuel and the woman work the pieces of piping into a seam at the edge of the cloth, until both pipes meet in the middle. Gillian sees what they're doing—it's clever, she must admit. The pipes inserted, Emanuel and the woman, with the help of two others, lift the now stiff corners of the cloth, holding the pipe ends and using them as curtain rods. The pipes are lifted until they form an inverted V: Emanuel and the woman walk back, pulling the heavy cloth away as they uncover the bound stone son of their god.

"Oh." Gillian steps forward. "It's beautiful."

It's not slag, as she imagined it might be—not compacted industrial waste or the discarded inner workings of some oversized machine. It is a single, massive piece of rock, albeit one so curved and dappled that it resembles piles of fecund limbs topped by a somewhat flat, lopsided head. Gillian knows what this is. It's a glacial erratic, a boulder pushed around the earth for tens of thousands of years by rivers of ice, then left behind as the glaciers receded, to sink into the earth or be rafted by floods to new lands. Gillian raises her hands.

"Stop!" someone calls out, and several people rush forward.

"No, let her." Emanuel says. "Let her do what she's here to do." Frozen, Gillian glances at the woman, who steps back only after Emanuel gestures her away.

"I'm sorry," Gillian says. "I should have asked. Did you need to pray first?"

Emanuel doesn't take her bait. "Do what you need to do." His brow furrows as he speaks. It's not quite anger—remorse, perhaps? Gillian doesn't know anymore—his face is strange to her, as if those four years together were a dream. Funny how she thought she knew him, thought she could read him, despite all her protestations that she couldn't understand that kind of life. She was right, after all. She should have taken her own words to heart, instead of trying to impress them on a man who had never listened.

Her hands make soft patting sounds as they move across the mottled surface of the boulder. Limestone. She's carved a cemetery's worth of headstones and markers out of this material. At the very least, if she tries, she can make something out of this, draw the story of its life out of its ancient body and onto the surface. Not real life—her touch, her flesh tells her that there's no sentience in the stone. Maybe, though, if she carves something truly spectacular, they'll forgive her. Before they kill her, that is.

"It's very old," Gillian says. "And very large. I've never carved—worked with a single block of stone as large as this before. It may take a while—days, perhaps."

"No, it won't." Emanuel smiles. "You underestimate your talent. And besides, you're going to have help. Everyone, back on the ramps." He motions to the woman, who begins to light a torch.

Gillian feels her stomach drop. How stupid of her. Of course that oil was placed there to be lit. This was their preparation. "Emanuel, don't do this. If you start a fire up here, it'll spread to the other culms, it'll never go out. All of these mountains, burning. There are—" she drops her voice to a whisper "—there are people still living in Feldspar. Don't do this to them."

"I know. But we need the fumes."

The chimera steps forward, led by Joaquin.

"How is she going to help me?"

The chimera places a hand at Gillian's throat. "Trustht me. I will."

"How are you going to help?"

The chimera moves behind her, placing one hand on each shoulder blade as she whispers in her ear. "Justht a puthsh or thwo, from the sthone to your minthd. The fumeths will help. Althso, this." The chimera's head rests on her neck as Gillian hears the familiar popping of an ampoule cap. She must have kept the glass tube hidden in her elongated hands—or maybe Joaquin knew, and let her do it anyway.

Familiar odors hit her nose, slick and oily sweet. Joaquin has taken his place on the ramps above the floor, and the flames from the circle of fluids illuminate his thin body. Emanuel walks toward her, seemingly out of the flames, the respirator once more masking his handsome face. A certain solidity fills his muscular body up, as though being in the place grounds and defines him in a way no other place, no other person, ever could. It suits him. Desire flares up in her, brief and hot. "Hands back on the god," he shouts through the heavy filtering. Gillian turns back to the boulder, bowing her forehead against the stone as her forearms slide up to frame her face. From behind, the chimera gives her a gentle push forward, until Gillian's entire body presses against the boulder.

"How do we do this? I've always done this alone."

"Have you?"

Gillian doesn't answer.

"I'll be on the other side," the chimera whispers. "Think of me on the other side of the rock. I'll find you. I'll come to you, and you bring me through." Gillian feels the creature's hands slip away. The crackling of flame fills the air, and smoke settles into her nostrils. The weight of the group's stare settles over her, pressing down. Ignore it, she whispers, closing her eyes. Only you, only me, only the land. Calm, cleansing dark flows through her mind. Time falls away.

Grey, rising up from the dark.

More smoke, the hiss of dark clouds fuming over the bulging curves of malleable limestone, like the clatter of waves over an empty pebbled shore. Roiling clouds of hot magma pump from a soft mud floor into waters the color of a coelacanth's scales. This is not the boulder she is reading. Gillian tries to break contact, but her body is gone, the boulder is gone, and she floats, staring down at a watery world. Far from the coast of Obsidia, under the steel-grey waves of the Southern Ocean, a vast indefinable shape is thrashing its way to the surface. *I'll be on the other side.* Blood runs from Gillian's nose, and the droplets fall like a chain of rubies into the swallowing waves. No. Her lips form the word, but it rushes from her body like the blood, too quick for her to hear. There's too much power in whatever is rocketing from the ocean depths, too much anger and pain. Gillian forms the word in her mind, imagines sending it out through every pore of her body, blanketing the surface of the ocean. NO. At her back, she imagines anthracite wings and all the weight of her subterranean life cracking apart, raining down like pyroclastic ash. The skies vomit fire onto the churning waters. Waves rush up only to collapse into themselves, their movements becoming sluggish. Beneath the slow-forming crust, the creature's movements harden and still; the ocean follows suit. Gillian hangs over the dead country, the Archean lands. Shattuck lies there now, and so does the chimera, or whatever

hideous new creation she would have been, if Gillian had allowed her to transmute back through the ancient stone.

Gillian falls onto the floor of the pit. Above her, the afternoon sky devours smoke from the burning fuel. Before her, the boulder stands, not a single carving or new mark on its worn skin.

"Again." Emanuel grabs her hand, pulling her up before she can protest. "Try it again." She pushes him away.

"Get off me, get away from me." Joaquin is in the pit—she grabs at him as he passes. "Don't touch that stone!"

"Where's the chimera?" He whips her away and circles the boulder. Gillian and Emanuel follow. Several more people step onto the floor, pulling off their respirators. "Where is she?"

Gillian follows him to the opposite side of the boulder. From this angle, the mass looks like an angry fertility god, all breasts and stomach and head. A current of wind whips through the pit, whining as it collides with the stone. "She's here," Gillian says, goosebumps racing up her arms. "She's right in front of us."

"What did you do to her? Where is she?" Joaquin pounds at the boulder with his fists, and Gillian flinches hard.

"Gillian?" Emanuel touches her waist. She runs her fingers over his, squeezing. It's the last vestige of feeling she has to give him.

"Please, Emanuel. Go back to the ramp."

"Until this is finished, I'll stay where I am," Emanuel says. "So will you."

Cold despair washes over her. "I know." The boulder squats before her, swathed in black vapors. A long crack on the top fold looks like a crooked, toothless smile: it wasn't there a second ago. Her hands tremble as she touches it once again. *Are you inside?*

I am the inside.

The words burst into Gillian like hammer strokes: she staggers back, clutching her head. But before she can howl out her pain, the boulder shifts, raising a fold of itself up like a large paw. Somewhere, someone screams. Gillian doesn't see the strike: she slams into the ground, head first. For a moment, she feels only distant surprise, and the sense that her body has disappeared. Then pain floods her, sudden and sharp. She cut her head open, she feels blood pouring into the shale, and every muscle and bone throbs. "Come on." She forces the words past her broken teeth. "Finish it. Let them run. Come to me." Her plea bleeds out into the air.

Emanuel is first. The chimera picks him up in a shifting fist of limestone, and squeezes tight. His life jets out between the stone digits like waterfalls of steel sparks, and when he's dry, the chimera pounds her hand repeatedly against the shale until his head comes away. When she opens her fingers at last, she scrapes them against the sides of the pit. Rubble cascades like water. Gillian lies on her stomach, head bleeding into the rock. Her broken arm is flung out from her side as if reaching, compelling all the pieces of her lover to rise and come together, become whole again. After the second body hits the ground, she closes her eyes. Vibrations bounce the slag against her cheek as the chimera thunders past. She doesn't try to move. She doesn't have to. It won't touch her.

Time passes behind her eyelids in a perpetual river of bright flashes and drawn-out screams. Dust settles onto her legs, prickling her skin like ants. Gillian presses her nose into her shoulder, but the smell of hot organs and excrement seeps into her lungs anyway, a mephitic vapor that disturbs the forgotten recesses of memory. Time hemorrhages inside her, and her childhood seeps out in carnelian memories: cartilage, cracking as it's pulled from her face, and the volcanic touch of stone as it pours into her cavities, turning her broken remains into a cauldron, a cradle in which she will be reborn. Gillian is now and she is then, she is all the times she has been dead and alive, pregnant with life and pregnant with iron, broken with fire and marble-cold whole. She sees the falsehood of herself, and the truth. Everything about her life has been a lie, except for one small thing. Bile dribbles from her mouth.

A touch at her arm. Gillian's body jolts, and she opens one eye. Joaquin lies beside her on his back, tears running down his filthy face. Gillian has never seen such fear before. It makes him look younger than her son.

"You're alive," he whispers. "I thought—I saw you breathe, but I wasn't sure."

"How long—" Her voice cracks.

"I don't know. Forever. Why is she doing this?"

"I don't know."

"We did it wrong. We never should have...."

"Well. I told you to run."

More screams, floating like sparrows along the wind, followed by silence. Seconds later, a heavy object hits the nearby ground. Joaquin squeezes his eyes shut.

"If we just lie here, if we pretend we're dead, it'll go away."

"No. She won't. She'll find you."

"She'll come for you, too."

"Forget me. I was born dead. You have to get out of here." Ignoring the pain, Gillian raises her head. Nausea rolls through her, and blood washes down the right side of her face.

"No no no don't move don't move," Joaquin pleads.

"Shut up." Gillian rises, rolling her body so that she's partially sitting up. The edges of the pit are black against the early evening sky, lavender and rose with tinges of orange, like a garden in riotous bloom. "She's not here. She's outside the pit."

"If it knows we're alive, it'll come back for us. I'm begging you, just lie down."

"I can't do that." Gillian grabs Joaquin by the hair and pulls him up. Almost instantly, he freezes in her arms, too frightened to even fight her. Gillian holds him as she scans the rim. "Look up at the edges of the pit," she whispers. "Wait for it."

A quiet minute passes. They breathe in unison. Joaquin's hair brushes against her mouth, leaving more blood. The sun lowers further, and the colors staining the sky deepen into a collar of jewels. Then: a head, sailing over the curve of the pit and onto the ramps, bouncing its way to the floor.

"Forgive me, Great Dreamer," Joaquin whispers.

"The opposite way: go. Run." Gillian pushes at him. He stares at her, and she pushes her face into his, baring her broken teeth. "Run now or die."

Joaquin runs. Gillian watches him scramble back and forth up the paths to the top of the culm, into the setting sun. She watches his figure grow black and small against the deep purples and pinks of sunset; and she watches how, at the last, another, larger figure appears from the side and from behind, almost from out of nowhere, and overtakes him in quick, decisive strides. Even in her bulky rock form, the chimera still moves with such grace. Gillian watches how they dance like shadow puppets against the aniline-bright hues, black figures outlined in a dazzling corona, merging in and out of each other until they are one. And Joaquin comes apart, inevitably, pieces scattering skyward, a human asteroid. She watches how the chimera stands still after the last of him parts her stony hands, watching the crimson disk sink in an ocean of colors. All the reds of the bleeding world, slipping off the earth with a young man's soul. It is a spectacular sunset, after all: on that, she will agree with the creature. She shouldn't miss it. It's going to be her last.

Shale crunches under her bare feet as she makes her way to the top, and blood stains her gravel-studded soles. There isn't a clean way up. Everywhere she looks, broken bones poke up through shining masses of veins and organs, still warm, still pumping blood. Some of the bodies are ground so thoroughly into the slag, they can no longer be called human. She doesn't see Emanuel: then again, she doesn't look for him. Gillian averts her eyes, staring at her hands as she guides her feet around the dead. What would it take for her to lay her hands on each one, let the memories of the stone rush into her body and mind, gather up each glistening particle and bind them together? Would they come alive again? Would they walk and talk, make their way back into the world, grateful to be half-human yet half-stone, damaged yet alive? She touches the fine line of a scar, just under her jaw. A woman stares up at her with one surprised eye, her head half beaten into the rock. Limbs fractured, torso cracked and spilling onto the ground. Ribs like striped fingers, rising from her flesh to touch tips as if in prayer. Gillian licks her lips. She's seen this face before, this terrified surprise commingled with wet red sorrow.

The chimera sits at the edge of the culm, her faceless bulk looming over the lightless hole of Feldspar. Beyond the gorge, Obsidia shimmers across the horizon, consuming the sun. Gillian curls her broken flesh into a sitting position. The chimera does not acknowledge her. Blood dribbles down her surface, drying in brown lines. She smells like freshly-forged steel. Together they watch the light fade from the sky. Gillian sits under the lights of the galaxy, watching cyclopean tentacles comprised of infinite suns whorl overhead and past the horizon. They came from those bright spiraling arms, these horrible, enigmatic gods of Obsidia, their dark bodies plummeting into the earth and the oceans. But something was already here. They are not the oldest Gods. No, not even elder. Not at all.

The air is hot and still. Gillian loses track of time. All around and above them, indigo night stretches past, an infinite, eternal train. By the time streaks of grey light appear at the eastern curve of the land, the chimera's smoking stone frame brushes against Gillian's *Carrara*-cold skin. Neither of them breathe, as if neither wishes to break open this peaceful spell, and reveal the end. Gillian knows it's coming. She can feel the chimera in her mind, rising up from the cacophony of her life like the impassive Torres del Pain. Unstoppable. Undeniable. Clean.

What was in the tunnel with you? What waits for you?

Gillian opens her mouth, and the black night rushes into. Her mother, slipping away in the dying light, leaving the failed creation she called daughter behind in the subterranean night. There was no tunnel. His mouth. There were never any mines—Morwyn's childhood memories, all of them. Gillian never had a childhood. She only had the dark, and the obscenity she called father and lover, building her up from scratch once more, fusing bones and blood, silicates and nickel-iron, time and time again. It never stopped, all those thousand permutations, all those thousands of selves, brought to life and ground back into red mist and dust. It had to stop. But it was like fucking a mountain. Like fucking a world. She never knew his name. She couldn't have pronounced it, anyway.

Tell me the truth of yourself, Gillian. The deepest truth.

"Peridot. My daughter. Down in the dark, in the abyss. I didn't want her to be like me. Damaged. Abandoned. Forgotten. And I knew I would do the same terrible things to her that my mother did to me. I knew I would destroy her and leave the bits behind, like she did with me. Because I'm like Morwyn. I can't feel a thing. There's nothing inside. There's only stone. And that's what I do. I mine things. I bring things out of the deep."

Deeper.

"I did them to her anyway. Bashed her head in with a rock. There wasn't any light. I had to feel the bits of skull to make sure she was dead. Her brains and blood, all over my hands. Under my nails. I could never get it out, no matter how hard I sucked them clean."

Deeper.

"I knew it was the thing I *must* do, but I couldn't leave her behind. It would have found them, like it found me. And then…. I had to hide her. From him. From myself. So I dug her up—and—put her back. Inside."

Deeper.

"I still feel her bones on my teeth, taste her on my tongue, every time I say her name."

Silence. The sky squeezes its velvet fist. Stars blur, prickling Gillian's eyes with tears as they fall to the ground. The chimera places a malformed hand on Gillian's chest.

Surrender your sorrow, and rejoice. You feel her because—

All across the valley of Feldspar, all across the broken land and burnished sky, everything stills as the morning sun crests the horizon, fire and light of the world birthed in a single thought, detonating in their minds like the midnight sun.

She is still alive, in the deep.

"I am the deep."

PART FOUR
I ride the wings of the morning sun, and dwell in the uttermost arms of the deep

When the sky is deep morning grey, casting a muted silver sheen over all the land as if in the iron grip of a storm, Gillian rises. Her chthonic creation remains seated, bulging eyes open and unblinking. She touches a limestone fold: it crumbles to the ground like crushed pumice. The rest of the hulking mass follows. It sounds like the rustling of feathers. When it ends, Gillian reaches down, plucks out a small, blood-stained square of *Arihant Spider Green*, a delicate leaf carved on its smooth face. She holds it, hard, until her nails pierce her filthy palm, until she opens her hand and finds the stone gone, only the impression of the leaf remaining, a faint outline of glowing green. Pale green, like peridot. Someday the stone will appear again, whole and unstained, resting in the iron-bone palm of her daughter's hand, rising from the earth into a clean morning sun.

Now, she will go down.

It isn't necessary for her to wander, searching for the way. She only has to lean out, drop from the edge of the culm, let the invisible tentacle of perception hook into her heart, drag her below the surface into the endless, dreamless deep. Gillian floats through the ruins like the terrible train of her dreams, and Feldspar flows around her, mute with age and the tired defeat of time: buildings of dust and ash and memories, bricks forged of blood and pain, and the voracious kiss of underground fire, consuming until there is nothing left to eat save itself. There, in the center of the town, surrounded by buildings stacked like broken jaws, the avenues unfurl to reveal an underground train yard. Gillian hovers at the overpass, a black lightning-shot *Dark Emperiador* chryon floating in steel-flecked air, looking down into a pit of rails and rotting ties. So many fingers of iron and steel, all of them pointing into the low wide mouth of a tunnel. It is as if she is staring into her soul.

It waits down there. It stares up through all the layers and strata of rock and time, and it sees her. She knows, because the gaze has never left her, not since her mother squeezed and coaxed her squalling body from some profane crucible within the world's core, not since the Welsh witch Morwyn split her apart and ran, leaving the spurting wreckage to the geologic being that fathered her. It is the gaze of her true self, a self not of this world, this space, this time—the self that never left the darkness, that always knew what she would have to sacrifice, how far she would have to travel within to save her daughter. And she will descend until she finds that geologic womb where the silence is three billion years long, and she will break herself apart. Gillian will rend her *Carrara*-cold tombstone of a body, draw Peridot up and out of every sliver of metal, blood and bone, and forge her daughter back into life.

And there is nothing now. No birds, no crackling of broken glass, no keening of wind. Her heart beats once, twice: and stops. The overpass slides away as she pushes off, and like the old dream, Gillian soars, slow and serene, down through the carapaces of the factories, over the rusting bones of the rails. The city rolls back and fades away and she is diving into the maw of the tunnel, and

there is nothing else except the long fall and the anthracite void, the billion-year smell of the earth, and something older, someplace further than she has ever gone before.

And then there is the crack of wings, distant and sharp, darting through the opening of a sunless door, plummeting past the black and into—

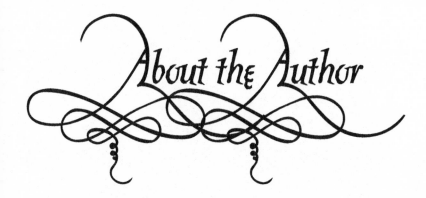

About the Author

LIVIA LLEWELLYN was born in Anchorage, Alaska, and grew up in Tacoma, Washington. In 1994 she moved to Manhattan, working various odd jobs in coffee shops, bookstores, theatres and movie sets until finding her calling as secretary-by-day in the oldest publishing company in America, and writer-by-night of erotica and dark fiction. She's currently at work on her second collection of stories, and a novel. You can find her online at liviallewellyn.com.

CPSIA information can be obtained at www.ICGtesting.com
Printed in the USA
BVOW08s0655240715

410093BV00003B/108/P